DARKNESS CHOSEN, BOOK 3

INTO THE SHADOW

CHRISTINA DODD

THORNDIKE PRESS

A part of Gale, Cengage Learning

GALE
CENGAGE Learning

Detroit • New York • San Francisco • New Haven, Conn • Waterville, Maine • London

GALE
CENGAGE Learning

Thorndike Press® Large Print Core.
The text of this Large Print edition is unabridged.
Other aspects of the book may vary from the original edition.
Set in 16 pt. Plantin.
Printed on permanent paper.

LIBRARY OF CONGRESS CATALOGING-IN-PUBLICATION DATA

Dodd, Christina.
    Into the shadow / by Christina Dodd.
        p. cm. — (Thorndike Press large print core) (Darkness chosen ; 3)
        ISBN-13: 978-1-4104-1121-1 (alk. paper)
        ISBN-10: 1-4104-1121-4 (alk. paper)
        1. Large type books. I. Title.
    PS3554.O3175I68 2008
    813'.54—dc22   2008033290

Published in 2008 by arrangement with NAL Signet, a member of Penguin Group (USA) Inc.

Printed in the United States of America
1 2 3 4 5 6 7 12 11 10 09 08

For Susan Sizemore —
You let me borrow
your amazing brain for plotting,
You bless me with your wit and humor,
Most of all, you've given me years
(and years and years) of true friendship.
That's the best gift of all.

ACKNOWLEDGMENTS

Writing a book like *Into the Shadow* is, as always, a joy and a challenge. Thank you to my editor, Kara Cesare, for her questions, comments, and enthusiasm. Thanks to Lindsay Nouis for all she does for me. Thank you to Kara Welsh and Claire Zion for their support for the *Darkness Chosen* series. Finally, a profound thank-you to Anthony Ramondo and his team in the art department for the fabulous original cover.

DARKNESS CHOSEN
FAMILY TREE

THE VARINSKIS

**1000 AD—In the Ukraine
Konstantine Varinski
makes a deal with the devil.**

**A Thousand +
Years Later**

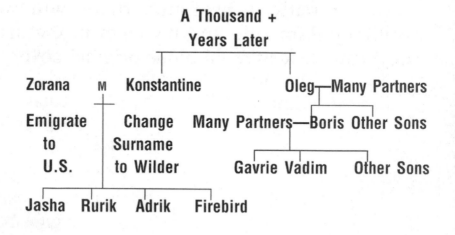

Zorana ᴍ Konstantine   Oleg⎯Many Partners

Emigrate   Change   Many Partners⎯Boris Other Sons
to   Surname
U.S.   to Wilder   Gavrie Vadim   Other Sons

Jasha   Rurik   Adrik   Firebird

PROLOGUE

On the border between Tibet and Nepal

"Ye're not normal."

"You know, Magnus, when you get drunk, that brogue of yours gets so thick I can barely understand you." Warlord's voice was as soft and smooth — and as deadly — as the single-malt Scotch they'd stolen.

"Ye understand me verra well." Magnus knew he would never have had the guts to make comments about Warlord, no matter how true, if it weren't bloody damned dark out here in the middle of the Himalayas in the middle of nowhere, and if he hadn't imbibed a wee bit o' that fine whisky — that is to say, most of a bottle all to himself. And if he weren't second in command of the mercenary troop, with a responsibility to point out the trouble abrewing. "Ye're not normal, and the men here, they know it. They whisper that ye're a werewolf."

"Don't be ridiculous." Warlord sat high

above the camp, silhouetted against the night sky, his arm crooked around his knee, his rifle in his hand.

"That's what I said, too. Because I'm a Scotsman. I know better. There's no such thing as werewolves." Magnus nodded wisely, and broke the seal on the second bottle. "There's things much worse than that. Do ye know why I know?"

Warlord said nothing.

He never said a word more than necessary. He was never kind. He was never friendly. He kept his secrets, and he was the meanest son of a bitch in a fight Magnus had ever seen. Yet while the lads were celebrating their latest plunder, he took the watch on the highest spot overlooking their hideout. For a man who excelled at stealing from rich tourists and government officials, and never caviled at killing when the occasion called for it, he was bloody decent.

Magnus continued, "I grew up on the bleakest of the Outer Hebrides islands, far to the north, where the bloody wind blows all the time, not a plant dares grow, and the old tales are repeated and repeated through the long winter nights."

"Sounds like a good place to be *from*." Warlord took the bottle from Magnus's fist and tipped it down his throat.

10

"Aye, that it is." Magnus watched his leader. "Ye dunna usually drink."

"If we're going to reminisce, I could use something to blunt the pain." Warlord was a dark blot against the stars — an unnaturally dark blot.

In the morning, Magnus knew, he'd be sorry for nattering on like this. Like every man up here, he'd been scarred by cruelty and betrayal, the only damned thing he excelled at was fighting, and if he was ever caught by any government in the world, he'd be hanged — or worse.

But whisky made Magnus gregarious, and he trusted Warlord — Warlord made the rules, and he was ruthless in enforcing them, but he was goddamned bloody fair.

"Do ye miss yer home, then?" he asked.

"I don't think about it."

"Ye're right. What's the point? We canna go back. They'll not want us. Not with so much blood on our hands."

"No."

"But today we washed some of the blood away."

Warlord lifted his hand and looked at it. "Bloodstains last forever."

"How do ye know that?"

"My father made that quite clear. Once you take a deliberate step into evil, you're

11

marked for life and destined for hell."

"Aye, my father said the same stuff, right before he took off his belt and whaled on me." Magnus drooped, then perked up again. "Today those Buddhist monks were grateful, though. They showered us with blessings. That's gotta help. Isn't that why you freed them?"

"No. I freed them because I hate bullies, and those Chinese soldiers are assholes who think it's funny to use holy men for target practice." Warlord's voice vibrated with rage.

"You do have a thing about that. But this time we got paid in more than blessings." For the raid had been profitable, bagging them firearms, ammunition, and a Chinese general who had surrendered his liquor and his gold to keep the photographs of his liaison with the local Communist chairman's young son secret.

Magnus grinned up and toward the east, where a glow on the horizon marked the rising moon. "You and me — we've whored together. We've fought together. And I still dunna understand how ye always seem to know where the money is hidden and the liquor is stored and the scandals are richest."

"It's a gift."

Magnus shook his finger at him. "Dunna

distract me with yer blather! How did ye come to be such a creature?"

"The same way you did. I killed a man, ran away, and ended up here." Warlord lifted the bottle and toasted the snowcapped peaks that dominated their lives. "Here, where the only law is what I make, and I don't have to beg forgiveness from anybody."

"That's not what I mean, and ye know it. Ye've got a bad way about ye. The shadow ye cast is too black. When ye're angry, you sort of" — Magnus made a wiggling motion with his fingers — "shimmer around the edges. Ye have a way of appearing out of nowhere, without a sound, and ye know things ye've got no business knowing, like that the Chinese general was buggering that lad. The men swear ye're not human."

"Why would they say that?"

"Because of yer eyes . . ." Magnus shivered.

"What's wrong with my eyes?" Warlord had that smooth, deadly tone in his voice again.

"Have ye looked in the mirror lately? Bloody spooky, they are. That's why the men have followed ye. But now there's grumblings." Magnus braced himself for a wee bit of unpleasantness.

"Why would there be grumblings?" Warlord asked with deceptive smoothness.

"The men say ye're not paying attention to business, that ye're distracted by yer woman."

"By my woman." Warlord's obsidian eyes gleamed in the dark.

"Did ye think no one would notice that ye disappear nights? They see you go, and they gossip." Magnus tried to lighten the atmosphere. "Bunch of old women, our mercenaries."

Warlord was not amused. "Are they not happy with the results of this raid?"

"Aye, but there's more to business than merely having a good fight and stealing a glorious amount of money." Magnus got down to business. "Our boys are worried about their safety. There's rumors that the military on both sides of the border are tired of us thumbing our noses at them, and they're bringing in enforcers."

"What kind of enforcers?"

"Canna get that answered, exactly. They're being bloody secretive, they are. But they're equal parts gleeful and, well . . ."

Warlord leaned forward. "Gleeful and . . . ?"

"I'd say they're scared, too. Like maybe they started something they can't stop. I'll be frank with ye, Warlord. I don't like any of this. We need ye to stop fooking the girl and find out what's going on." There. Magnus had passed on the message, and Warlord hadn't ripped his head off. Yet.

Magnus settled his back against the rock. The granite was cold. Of course. Except for the brief summer, these mountains were always cold. And in this valley, bound as it was on three sides by cliffs and on the long side by a gorge that dropped straight into a raging river, the constant wind whipped through his thinning hair and cut deep into his bones. "I hate this fooking place," he muttered. "Nothin' good ever came out of Asia except spices and gunpowder."

Warlord laughed, and it almost sounded as if he were amused. "You're right about that. My family's from Asia."

"Pull the other one, man. Ye're not a Chinaman."

"A Cossack from the steppes, from what is now the Ukraine."

Magnus knew his geography; he'd worked that area of the world as a con man and a soldier. "The Ukraine — that's close to Europe."

"Close only counts in horseshoes and hand grenades." Warlord looked up at the stars. He sipped the whisky. "Have you ever heard of the Varinskis?"

Magnus went from mellow to murderous in a few seconds. "Those bastards."

"You *have* heard of them."

"Eight years ago I was working the North Sea, doing a little pirating, picking up a few things, and three Varinskis caught up with me. Informed me it was their territory, said they were taking everything." Magnus stuck his finger against the indentation in his cheek where he was missing that molar. "I told them not to be greedy, I had enough for everybody. And listen, I'm no stranger to beatings — my father took the belt to me every day of his life — but those guys . . . They're why my nose is crooked. They're why I'm missing three toes and both little fingers. They about killed me, then tossed me into the ocean to drown. Doctors said that was why I didn't bleed to death. Hypothermia. *Varinskis.*" He spit their name like venom. "Do you know the reputation those monsters have?"

"Yes."

"I hate those sons a' bitches."

"They're my family."

Cold fear trickled down Magnus's spine. "The rumors about them are —"

"All true."

"They canna be." Magnus clutched at his

16

rapidly evaporating liquor-induced bliss.

"You said the men claim I'm not human."

Magnus dismissed that with as much bombast as he could summon. "The men are a bunch of ignorant savages."

"But I *am* human. A human with special gifts . . . the most marvelous, pleasurable, enticing gifts." Warlord's voice wove a spell around them.

"No need to tell me. I'm all for a man keeping his secrets." Magnus struggled to stand.

Warlord's hand clamped around his arm and jerked him down with a thump. "Don't leave, Magnus. You wanted to know."

"Dinna want to know that bad," Magnus muttered.

"You wanted reassurance. I'm giving it to you." Warlord handed Magnus the bottle. Handed it to him as if he would need it. "A thousand years ago my ancestor, Konstantine Varinski, made a deal with the devil."

"Fook." Magnus had always hated stories like this. Hated them because he believed them.

He wished that the moon could wipe out the shadows, but it was barely half, and the bleak white light poked at the shadows but could not vanish them. He wished for some more of the men to keep him company, but

17

the fools were in the valley, gambling, drinking, playing their stupid video games, and puking. Nobody knew he sat up here, unearthing secrets better left buried, and now in fear of his life.

"Konstantine had a reputation on the steppes. He delighted in killing, in torture, in extortion, and it was whispered that his cruelty rivaled the devil's." Warlord's voice warmed with humor. "Satan didn't like those stories — I'd guess he's a little vain — and he sought out Konstantine with the intention of removing him from the competition."

"Dunna tell me Konstantine defeated the evil one," Magnus said incredulously.

"No, he offered himself as Satan's best servant. In return for the ability to hunt down his enemies and kill them, Konstantine promised his soul, and the souls of all his descendants, to the devil."

Magnus peered at Warlord, trying to see him, but as always the shadows around his leader were thick, dense, impenetrable. "You're his descendant?"

"One of many. A son of the current Konstantine." Warlord's strange eyes gleamed in the dark.

"I told ye. Long winter nights, and all the old tales told to frighten the children."

"The children should be frightened." Warlord lowered his voice to a whisper. "They should shiver in their beds to know creatures such as me are abroad in this world."

Magnus knew what evil was. His father had preached to him every day while he tried to beat the rebellion out of him. That was why, now . . . Magnus could almost feel the flames of hell scorch his flesh. "That's a fantastic tale." He cleared his throat. "In a thousand years, I imagine it's gathered some frills. Some storyteller spiced it up to make it more exciting in the telling . . . don't ye suppose?"

A low growl rumbled out of Warlord's hidden form. "Why else do you think men seek me out when they want their enemies tracked down? Why do you think they hire me? I can find anyone, anywhere. Do you want to know how?"

Magnus shook his head. He did *not* want to know.

But it was too late.

"To Konstantine Varinski and to each Varinski since, the devil bequeathed the ability to change at will into a hunting animal."

"Change . . ." The light of the moon had reached them now, and Magnus stared at

Warlord. Stared because he was afraid to take his gaze away. "So ye *are* a werewolf?"

"No, we Varinskis are not stupid beasts ruled by the phases of the moon. We are ruled by nothing but our own wills. We change when we wish, when we need to change. We live long lives, breed only sons, and nothing less than another demon can kill us. We leave a trail of blood, fire, and death wherever we go." Warlord laughed, a throaty purr. "We are the Darkness."

"Aye, that you are." Magnus saw the darkness every time he looked into Warlord's eyes. Still he argued, because he didn't want it to be true. "But ye're not Russian. Ye're from the US."

"My parents ran away, got married, moved to Washington state, changed their last name to something that sounds good, solid, and all-American, and raised my two brothers and my sister and me. They don't approve, especially not my dad, of that Varinski blood-fire-and-death thing. He said we had to control ourselves." Warlord's bitterness was thick and angry. "I suck at control. I like the blood, fire, and death. I can't fight my real nature."

Try. For the love of God, try. "Can the pact be broken?"

Warlord shrugged. "It's held for a thousand years. I imagine it'll hold for another thousand."

Magnus's head whirled, and the rice and lamb he'd eaten for dinner now warred with the Scotch. "But ye're not like the other Varinskis I met. Are ye *sure* ye're a Varinski?"

"I want you to reassure the men that they don't have to worry. I can keep them safe from any enforcers the military has hired." Warlord placed his rifle on the ground. He removed his boots, tossed aside his coat and shirt. He unbuckled his belt, dropped his jeans, stood up, and let the feeble moonlight bathe him.

On those long winter nights when the whores visited the camp, Magnus had seen Warlord naked and in action. He was just a man, a guy who made his living fighting.

But now, all around the edges, his form grew less . . . defined.

Magnus lifted the bottle to his mouth. His hand shook, and the glass rim clicked against his teeth.

"I'm going to hunt . . . and kill." Warlord's bones melted and re-formed. His dark hair spread, sprouting on his neck, his back and belly, down his legs. His face changed, grew cruelly feline. His spine shifted; he dropped onto all fours. His ears . . . and his nose . . .

21

his hands . . . and his feet . . .

Magnus blinked again.

A great, sleek ebony panther stood before him with white, sharp claws and teeth, and fur as black as a shadow. And his eyes . . .

Magnus found himself backing away, screaming and screaming, while the great hunting cat stalked toward him, his paws never making a sound, his familiar black Warlord eyes fixed on his prey . . . on Magnus.

CHAPTER ONE

It started as it always did, with a gust of cold Himalayan air striking Karen Sonnet's face. She woke with a start. Her eyes popped open.

The darkness in her tent pressed on her eyeballs.

Impossible. Tonight she'd left a tiny LED burning.

Yet it *was* dark.

Somehow he'd obliterated the light.

The constant wind blew through this narrow mountain valley, buffeting the ripstop nylon canopy that protected her — barely — from annihilation, and ringing the holy bells hung across the tent flap. Her interpreter had left behind the scent of tobacco, spices, and wool. The menacing cold slipped its cold fingers into the tent. . . .

Karen strained to hear his footfall.

Nothing.

Still, she knew he was here. She could

sense him moving across the floor toward her, and as she waited each nerve tightened, stretching. . . .

His cool hand touched her cheek, making her gasp and jump.

He chuckled, a low, deep sound of amusement. "You knew I would come."

"Yes," she whispered.

As he knelt beside her cot, she breathed in his scent: leather, cold water, fresh air, and something else — the smell of wildness. He kissed her, his cool lips firm, his breath warm in her mouth.

She hung suspended in time, in place, in an ocean of pleasure. As his kiss lingered her body stirred, her breasts swelling, the familiar longing growing deep inside.

The night she'd arrived here, she'd come awake to the touch of a man's kiss. Just a kiss, tender, curious, almost . . . reverent. In the morning she'd thought she had dreamed it. But the next night he'd been back, and the next night, and every night he'd taken her further into passion. And now . . . how many nights had he visited her? Two months? More? Sometimes he didn't come for one night, two, three, and on those nights she slept deeply, worn out by hard work and the high, thin air. Then he'd return, his need greater, and he touched

24

her, loved her, with an edge of violence sharp as a knife. Yet always she sensed his desperation, and welcomed him into her mind . . . and her body.

This time he had been gone almost a week.

He slid down the zipper on her sleeping bag, each tooth making a rasping noise, each noise making Karen's heartbeat escalate another notch. He started at her throat, cupping it, pressing on the pulse that raced there. He pushed the bag aside, exposing her to the cold night air. "You wait for me . . . naked." He pressed his palm between her breasts, feeling her heart beat. "You're so alive. You make me remember. . . ."

"Remember what?" He sounded American, without a hint of accent, and she wondered where he was from and what he was doing here.

But he didn't want her to think. Not now. Greedily he caressed her slight breasts, one in each palm. His hands were long, rough, calloused, and he used them to massage her while with his thumbs he circled her nipples.

She made a raw sound in her throat.

"You're in need." His voice deepened. "It's been a long time. . . ."

"I've been waiting."

"And that was my torment, that I could

not be here with you."

It was the first time he'd ever suggested he needed this as much as she did. She smiled, and somehow, in this pitch dark, he must have seen her.

"You like that. But if you've tormented me, I must torment you in return." His head dipped. He took one pebbled nipple in his mouth and suckled, softly at first, then, as she whimpered, with strength and skill.

He made her go crazy.

Yet any woman who welcomed a midnight lover was already halfway to insanity.

She grabbed a handful of his hair and discovered how very long it was . . . and soft, and silky. She tugged at him, pulling his head back.

"What do you want?" His voice was a husky whisper.

"Hurry." She was chilled. She was desperate. "I want you to hurry."

"But if I hurry, I won't get to do this." He pushed the sheet down farther, caressing her belly and thighs. Lifting her knees, he spread her legs, exposing her to the cold, shocking her, making her suck in a startled breath.

"Let me see." He tilted her hips up. "Are you really ready?"

His fingers glided from her knees along

the tender skin on her inner thighs to the dampness there. With a delicate touch, he opened the lips and dabbed a touch on her clitoris. "I love your scent, so rich and female. The first time, it was your scent that called me to you."

Horrified, she tried to draw her legs together. "I bathe every night."

"I didn't say you smelled. I said you have a scent that calls to me." His nails skated up and down her thighs, pushing them apart again . . . and they were sharp, almost like claws. Almost a threat. "Not to any other man. Only to me."

"*Are* you a man?" The question slipped out, and she regretted it. Regretted injecting reality into this delicate, lovely dream of passion.

"I thought I had conclusively proved my manhood to you. Shall I do it again?" The hint of warning was gone; he sounded warmly amused, and the finger he pushed inside her was long, strong . . . and clawless.

The impact made her fling her head back, and when he pushed a second finger inside, her hips moved convulsively. "Please. Lover, I need you."

"Do you?" Slowly he pulled his fingers back, pressed them back in, pulled them out . . . and as he pressed them in, he pinched her clit between his thumb and forefinger.

She screamed. She came. Orgasm blasted her away from this cold, bleak mountainside and into a fire pit. Her thighs clamped around his hand. Red swam beneath her closed eyelids. Heat radiated from her skin.

He laughed, one compelling stroke following another, feeding her madness until she collapsed, shivering and gasping, too weak to move.

He covered her with himself.

"I can't," she whispered, and her voice shook. "Not again."

"Yes, you will."

"No. Please." She tried to struggle, but he stretched out on top of her. Her head was buried in his shoulder; obviously he was tall. His body, heavy with muscle, pressed her into the cot. His flesh was cool and firm. His shoulders, chest, and stomach rippled with vigor, and his heart thrummed in his chest.

Power hummed through him, and he easily held her as he probed again . . . but not with his fingers.

She was swollen with need, and his organ was big, bigger than both his fingers. As he worked himself inside her she whimpered, her body gradually adjusting to the width, the breadth, and all the while the aftermath of climax made her inner muscles spasm.

He held her wrapped in his arms, clutching her as if she were his salvation.

And she embraced him, her arms gripping him against her chest, her legs clasped around his hips, giving him herself, absorbing . . . absorbing all his ardor, all his need, knowing this was a dream and wanting nothing more.

When the tip of his penis touched the innermost core of her, they both froze.

Darkness held them in a cocoon of heat and sex and emotions stretched too tight for comfort.

Then their passion flashed bright enough to light the night.

He pulled out and pushed back in, thrusting fast and hard, dragging her with him on his quest for satisfaction.

She held on, rapture flowing through her with the heat and intensity of lava.

The tempo built and built until, above her, his breathing stopped. He gathered himself, rising high above her, holding her knees behind him . . . then plunged one last time.

Ecstasy exploded her into tiny fragments of being. She came, convulsing with pleasure, until she was no longer an austere, lonely workaholic, but a creature of joy and light.

Unhurriedly, he dropped back on top of her, bringing the silk sheets and sleeping bag up to cover them. Reaching down to the floor, he pulled a large blanket over them . . . but no. She touched it with her hand and discovered fur, thick and soft. A skin of some kind, then.

Had he taken her on a trip back in time, back to a century where a man brought the woman he desired proof of his hunting prowess? Wasn't that a better explanation than madness?

As the perspiration cooled on their bodies, as their breath and heartbeats returned to normal, she slid easily into sleep.

She stood on the edge of the cliff, the blue sky surrounding her. The wind blew hard, tumbling her hair around her face, and in its voice she heard the wails of mourning women, the hoarse sobs of lonely men, and a child's anguished wail. She tried to back up, to get away, but her feet were too heavy. She fell. . . .

Just before she hit, she started violently.

She woke to find him leaping to his feet. She heard the click of a gun's safety.

"What's wrong?" he asked. "What did you hear?"

"Nothing. A nightmare." A phantasm of

30

her mind, one that had threatened her since she was a child.

Since the day her mother had fallen from that cliff.

Slowly her lover placed something beneath the bed — a firearm of some kind, she now realized — and slid back between the covers. "You weren't completely asleep."

"That's when I . . . That's when it always comes."

"A monster?" He pushed the short, straight strands of dark brown hair away from her face.

"Death." Shivering, she wrapped herself around him.

She reclined on her narrow cot in her tent at the foot of Mount Anaya. The darkness pressed down on her; the sense of wrongness in this place oppressed her. She hated everything about it.

And tomorrow she would rise. He would be gone. And she would go to work, another day spent in hell.

So she wept.

He caressed her face with his fingertips, found her tears, said, "No. Don't do that."

The tears only flowed more quickly.

He kissed her. Kissed the dampness from her cheeks, her lips, her throat . . . He kissed as if they hadn't made love only ten minutes

31

before. He kissed her with passion. He kissed her with intent. Finally she forgot to cry, and remembered nothing but desire.

Afterward, as she slid off to sleep, she thought she heard him say in a slow, hoarse voice, "You make me real again."

CHAPTER TWO

In the morning Karen woke to the chime of bells, the slap of frigid mountain air on her face, and Mingma Sherpa's traditional greeting.

"*Namaste,* Miss Sonnet."

"*Namaste.*" Eyes closed, Karen waited tensely, but Mingma didn't exclaim about a man in the tent, or comment on the new animal skin.

Karen opened her eyes and scrutinized the tent that had been her home for almost three months, and would be for another two, if the mountain was generous and didn't chase her off with an early blizzard. The tent was five by seven, with enough room for her cot, a travel desk with her computer, and a trunk with her personal belongings. As usual, Karen's secret lover had swept away all signs of his presence.

He was her secret, and he intended to stay that way.

"Warm water." Mingma, her cook, maid, and translator, held a steaming basin and bowed, then placed it on the small table below the mirror.

"Thank you." But although Karen knew the water would cool quickly, she couldn't bring herself to leave her warm nest and leap naked into the cold.

Then Mingma said the magic words. "Phil is not here yet."

Karen flew out of bed. "What?"

"The men are here. Phil is not."

"That worthless . . ." Digging down in the bottom of her sleeping bag, Karen found the long underwear she stashed there every night and dragged it on.

This whole project had been nothing but bad luck and trouble, requiring every bit of Karen's concentration and every bit of Mingma's diplomatic skills to keep the men at work. She'd never thought her assistant project manager, Philippos Chronies, would be the main delay. "Where is he?"

"He left the village last night. Was gone for hours. Returned, and now his tent billows with his snores."

Karen's father never assigned his best men to her, but Phil was a new low. He knew the business, but made his contempt for the native workers clear. He tried to take imaginary Greek Orthodox holidays off, and when she pointed out that she had a satellite Internet connection, and research had turned up no holidays on that date, he sulked.

Karen did a quick PTA — pussy, tits, and armpits — and shrugged into her clothes: khakis built for warmth and constructed to stand up in the toughest conditions, a camouflage parka and wide-brimmed hat, and sturdy hiking boots. "All right. I'm going down."

She stepped outside. The bells chimed softly.

Mingma followed. The bells chimed again.

When Karen had first come to this place, she'd taken down the bells at her door. But Mingma had been so distressed, and so insistent that the bells kept the evil one away, Karen put them back. Because she didn't mind indulging Mingma in her superstition. And because as time went on, anything that kept the evil one away was all right with her.

The day was calm. Still. Silent.

Karen had learned how little that meant up here.

"The men are not happy," Mingma said.

"Neither am I." Karen sighed. "What's wrong?"

"They grow closer to the heart of evil."

Karen didn't scoff.

Her father would have.

Her father owned Jackson Sonnet Hotels, a chain that specialized in adventure vacations. The resorts were in prime locations, and offered classes in flying, rock climbing, skiing, camping, river rafting, mountain biking — whatever an adventure enthusiast wished to learn, Jackson Sonnet Hotels could teach him. Whatever adventure a tourist imagined for himself, Jackson Sonnet Hotels offered a way to enjoy it.

Jackson Sonnet was a genius at knowing what the armchair adventurer craved, for he prided himself on being a man who could do it all, and he had made damned good and sure his daughter, Karen, had learned everything, regardless of her fears — or else. Because, by God, he wasn't going to put up with a daughter who was a coward.

Climbers and trekkers looking for the ultimate challenge flocked to the Himalayas, to the world's highest mountain range. They wanted rough and tough, and here they got it. The altitude was high, the air thin, and with the unexpected storms and the persistent rumor of international thugs, even the most traveled paths required stamina and courage.

So Mount Anaya, set high on the dry side of the Himalayas on the border between Nepal and Tibet, seemed to be the ideal site to build a boutique hotel — at least on paper.

Mount Anaya had a reputation for being unclimbable. That was its attraction.

All the eight thousanders — fourteen peaks over eight thousand meters above sea level — were tough, so tough there were charts showing the death rates per ascent.

Mount Anaya was different. Sherpa guides went up unwillingly, or not at all. Mountaineers spoke of the mountain in hushed tones as if it were a living being, using words like "malicious" and "malevolent." The unlucky came down in body bags. Altogether, only fifteen expert climbers had managed to reach the top. Of those, six lost toes or fingers — one a foot — to frostbite. One had had his arm crushed by a rockfall, and amputated it himself. Two died within a month of their triumph. One went quite insane after reaching the peak. Among the climbers who attempted the mountain, legends were whispered of a siren's voice calling a man to his doom, or an inexplicable fire in the storm, or a demonic face shining in the snow.

Every climber looked forward to the challenge. No one ever believed the stories . . . until they got here.

She certainly hadn't. At twenty-eight, she had already supervised the building of hotels in the outback of Australia, on the African veldt, and in Patagonia in Argentina. Each one had offered its own challenges.

None had been like this.

"While you comfort the men, I will fix your breakfast." Mingma had simply appeared one day, installing herself as Karen's assistant. Karen thought Mingma was anywhere between forty and a hundred, a sharp-eyed widow who had buried two husbands and now supported herself. Her teeth were stained with tobacco, her expression was serene, and her English was good.

"I'll do more than comfort them." Karen strode across the high, flat area where she'd set her tent and down the path to the construction site. Gravel rolled out from under her boots and tumbled onto the site.

The stone roots of Mount Anaya grew around the spot where the hotel would be built. Once the foundation was properly installed, the hotel would be secure against earthquakes, or so said the architects and structural engineers.

She'd been here since spring, the start of the construction season, and immediately she'd realized that the architects and structural engineers hadn't taken into account the mountain itself. Granite tumbled like giant building blocks throughout the long valley, legacies of rockfalls so massive they had obliterated the landscape. Here and there tiny green plants struggled to poke their heads up, but they were damned. The thin soil quickly loosened, slipped, and carried them away. Nothing was allowed to live here, for over it all the mountain loomed, massive, bleak, cruel.

Karen tried never to look at Mount Anaya, but as always the peak drew her gaze — up the side of the hill, up the sheer stone slopes, up the glaciers and snowfields, to the top of Mount Anaya. There the pinnacle stabbed the blue sky with a point of white and gray.

Mountains, all mountains, formed the stuff of her nightmares, but Mount Anaya . . . In Sanskrit, it meant "evil course."

The natives believed the mountain was cursed.

After two months of living in its shadow, Karen believed it, too.

The mountain ruined her days, and the midnight lover haunted her sleep. She was trapped here by her father's expectations and her own sense of duty — and by Phil Chronies.

A dozen men lolled around, leaned against the two ancient and exorbitantly priced backhoes they'd hired from Tibet, petted their yaks, and chatted.

As she walked up, she smiled.

Their interpreter, Lhakpa, came forward and bowed.

She leaned forward and spoke to him only. "Thank you for taking command of my men until Mr. Chronies can arrive."

"Yes. Of course. I command the men." Lhakpa bowed again.

"Last night, when Mr. Chronies reported to me, he told me there would be blasting today."

"Yes. He tells us where to place the dynamite." Lhakpa beamed happily.

"I tell *him* where to place the dynamite."

As she walked toward the locker containing the dynamite, Lhakpa's eyes grew big. "Mr. Chronies will be unhappy if you —"

She swung around and faced him. "Have you not seen Mr. Chronies report to me morning and night?"

"Yes, Miss Sonnet."

"Have you not seen me direct Mr. Chronies every day, all day long?"

"Yes, Miss Sonnet."

"Mr. Chronies obeys me in all things." She smiled with toothy good humor.

It was true enough; Phil obeyed her grudgingly, but he obeyed her. She had a system, and she'd be damned if she would allow Phil and his laziness to put them farther behind; that would erode her already precarious position as a woman in a man's occupation.

Besides, she'd learned her job from the bottom up. She knew how to do every task on the site. And performing the task of setting the dynamite, she knew, would gain her the men's respect, because, like all men, these were very impressed by loud explosions that blew large boulders into small pebbles.

If she could only feel sure the mountain would be as impressed, and let her construct this cursed hotel.

He lay flat on his stomach on a boulder above the construction site, watching Karen Sonnet while resentment and lust roiled in his belly.

Why was she here? Why couldn't it have been someone else? A man, preferably, some guy like all the rest, who knew hotel construction, who drank and smoked, who was amenable to a little graft and corruption.

Instead, he had little Miss Sweetness-and-Light.

The first time he'd seen her, he'd been waiting at the train station in Kathmandu. She caught his eye; pretty women did that, and she was pretty enough. Short, probably five-three, with a slender figure that looked good in khakis. Brown hair and perfectly tanned skin, the sort of skin they made commercials about. But he didn't think much about her, figured she was just one of the thousands of trekkers who descended on Nepal every year to hike through the Himalayas. He did grin derisively as she directed the porters to load her huge stash of camping equipment. He amused himself by wondering how many porters she would have to hire to carry it up and down the mountain trails, if she had an industrial-size hair dryer in that mess, and where she thought she was going to plug the hair dryer in.

Just when he was transferring his attention to the next female, Karen did something extraordinary.

She looked right at him, and smiled.

She had the most extraordinary blue-green eyes he'd ever seen, with a fringe of long, dark lashes, and that smile . . . She tapped into some inner joy, and everything he'd thought about her changed.

She was beautiful.

He was stricken with need.

Her smile faded. As if his staring made her nervous, she glanced away. She spoke to the porters; she was patient with their stilted English, and she knew a few words of Nepalese.

He didn't move, but called one of the pick-pockets who hung around the platform. Flipping him a coin, he said, "Find out who she is and where she's going." Not that it mattered; he had a job to do. He didn't have time to obsess about a woman with aquamarine eyes.

Then, when he got his answer, he cursed a blue streak.

She was going to be right there at the base of Mount Anaya, within arm's length, for months and months, building Jackson Sonnet's hotel.

He had comforted himself with the knowledge that she'd never be up for the challenge.

Instead she bossed everyone around, and if they balked, she smiled at them. Look at Lhakpa, hovering close while she set the charges. Look at the other guys, all grinning and flirty while they got ready for the blast.

She was changing everything, and if he

didn't watch it, she'd change him, too.
He had to get her out of his life.

CHAPTER THREE

Karen made sure the men were at a safe distance, donned her ear protection, sounded the alarm that meant they were about to blast . . . and pushed the plunger. The ground shook beneath her feet. The solid rock lifted, shifted, and re-formed into a rubble of boulders, perfectly placed for removal.

She hadn't lost her touch.

She removed her ear protection and waited, tense, for the roar that meant she'd disturbed the mountain, and it was taking its revenge in a rockfall to obliterate all her work — and her men, and her. After a full minute of silence, she gave the guys a thumbs-up.

They cheered weakly. Lhakpa and Dawa walked for their backhoes. The ancient engines rumbled to life. Ngi'ma rounded up his team of men and yaks and headed in.

She climbed up the path to grab a quick breakfast before going back down to the site for a hands-on demonstration of why she was in charge. She was near the top when that feeling caught her, that prickly sense of being watched. She'd had it frequently of late, and she turned and scanned the heights· — and there was Philippos Chronies coming down the path from the south, his bald head shining in the sun.

Phil was Greek-Canadian, short, wide at the middle, with a body that tapered up to a broad face and down to tiny feet. She hadn't worked with him before, but it hadn't taken more than a day for her to judge his character.

They'd met at the airport in Kathmandu, caught the train toward the work site, and within the first hour he'd hit on her. When she'd pointed out his wedding band, he'd shrugged and said his wife knew her place.

Karen announced that she did not, and interrogated him about his work experience.

Things had gone downhill from there.

Now she planted her boots on the rocky ground and waited. When he spotted her, she gestured him to come up and report. Turning her back, she finished her hike to the flat where she'd pitched her tent.

A tiny fire of dried yak dung burned in a

fire pit dug into the ground. The spiral of smoke rose straight toward the bright blue sky.

Mingma handed her a cup of hot, milky, sweet tea.

"Thank you." Karen wrapped her hands around the cup and sipped, trying to warm the coldness in her belly.

"Eat." Mingma indicated the small, clean bowl of potatoes, meat, and vegetables mixed with spices and colored green by . . . something.

Karen didn't care what the *something* was. During the course of her work, she had eaten spoiled meat, rancid cheese, and artfully prepared insects. She was thin, she was muscled, she knew how to survive under the roughest conditions. She could take care of herself, but she didn't have to — she had Mingma.

Sitting on the camp stool, she ate with a spoon made of yak horn. She'd packed her own equipment, but the night she'd arrived a freak storm blew through, taking one entire box of necessities down into a gorge and scattering them into crevasses and into the raging torrent that formed in an instant and disappeared by the next afternoon. Since then, Karen had discovered that freak storms were the norm here. Freak rain-

47

storms, freak snowstorms, freak wind-storms, freak storms that formed on the mountain and reached down to flick her away like a gnat off its massive flank.

She wouldn't be flicked. She couldn't.

She paid no attention when Phil presented himself. While he fidgeted, she finished eating, and only when she put down her spoon did she say, "Phil, give me one good reason I shouldn't fire you right now."

"Haven't got one. I was just ill last night, but I should have come to work anyway —"

"Last night? You were ill?" She stared him right in the eyes. "That's why you were out visiting your girlfriend?"

He cast a resentful glance at Mingma. "Yeah, I didn't . . . I mean, I was looking for someone to help me get better so I could work today." He used a damp whitish handkerchief to dab at the sweat that dripped off his broad forehead.

"One more chance, Phil. One chance, or you'll be kicking shit down the road." Karen jerked her head toward the site. "Now go to work."

She didn't watch him leave, but she could hear him shrieking orders as he descended the slope.

Standing, she walked over the edge and looked down on the site. The workers swarmed like ants, moving the boulders loosened by the blast. The backhoes moved the largest stones, while huge black-and-white yaks lumbered after their trainers, dragging rubble into a pile.

When she had been a little girl in her bedroom in Montana, dreaming of princesses and happily-ever-afters, this was not the life she had envisioned.

Mingma joined her on the edge, and the two women stood in silence.

Finally Karen asked, "How is Sonam?" One of her workers had been moving a boulder with his yak when a huge rock had tumbled down the slope, hit his shoulder, then bounced up and struck his yak. Sonam's collarbone was broken, his yak was dead, and he was terrified.

"His bones are mending." Mingma puffed on her cigar, and smoke eased from between her lips. "But he will not come back to work. You seek to build on the heart of evil."

Karen had heard that so many times since coming here. *The heart of evil.* Everyone seemed to know what it meant. Everyone except her, and she didn't want to know. By remaining ignorant, she hoped to beat Mount Anaya.

Now, driven by the same defiant impulse that made her meet every challenge life and her father flung at her, she lifted her arms to the mountain. "You can't chase me away so easily!"

Mingma threw the cigar to the ground. "Don't, miss! Don't anger Anaya. We are already in mortal peril."

A cold wind blasted down the slopes.

Karen staggered backward, chilled by the ominous reply. "What makes this place evil? It's more than just Mount Anaya. It's the whole place, Nepal on one side, Tibet on the other —"

"That is truth, miss." Mingma lit another one of the slender cigars she smoked. "And Warlord is mighty."

"Warlords don't exist anymore. Not in the civilized world. But maybe here . . ." Drugs flowed through this area. Slaves, too — male slaves to work deep in the Siberian mines, female slaves to serve their masters. Although the governments protected the trekkers, sometimes a raid occurred on a particularly rich party. And from across the border in Tibet, rumors floated through the air of battles between the Chinese troops that controlled the area and insurgents.

"We all want money." Mingma looked up at the mountain and blew an appeasing puff of smoke in its direction.

"Not you." Karen smiled at her.

Mingma stared solemnly and repeated, "Money is evil, but we *all* want it. Because it is Mount Anaya which pulls like a magnet all the bad people of the world."

"Why? It doesn't make sense."

"But, yes, miss, it does. A thousand years ago a village abided below the mountain." Mingma gestured toward the valley. "They dwelled in the sunshine, growing the crops, herding their yaks." Her powerful voice dropped to a whisper. "Then the Evil One came."

"*The* Evil One?"

"The Evil Which Walks as a Man. One by one he corrupted the villagers, promising power and glory if they would guard his treasure. They sought to obtain all he promised, and more, and so they agreed to sacrifice their heart."

"Their . . . heart? They had only one?" Karen wasn't mocking.

But Mingma frowned, her tanned skin wrinkled by long exposure to the sun. "It is a legend."

"Yes, but somehow it must be true." Karen's gaze swept the site. Here even the sunlight was tinged with gray.

"Then listen." Mingma pressed her hand to her chest. "They made their cruel sacrifice, and when their heart had ceased beat-

51

ing, then they realized how the Evil One had tricked them, for they had all the power they sought, but without a heart they were no longer living beings. They became one with the mountain, tainting the sky it pierces, the flesh of the earth around it, the stones that are its bones. Since that day the mountain has been cruel, destroying all who strive to live in its shadow, all who try to tame its heights. The mountain holds the heart and the Evil One's treasure, burying them deep, protecting them from all who seek it. The people of the village are forever alone, cold and cruel, and that is their punishment."

"Heartless." Inevitably, Karen thought of her father. "Yes, I understand how being heartless can take your humanity, but I don't know if a village can become one with the mountain."

"At night do not you hear the sobs of the mothers who have lost their children? Do not you hear the husbands mourn their wives?" Mingma's voice lowered to a whisper once more. "Do you not hear the wails of the lost babies, forever damned?"

If only Karen could be amused about Mingma's quaint superstition, but in the night she had heard it all — and then in her dream she fell. She always fell into nothingness. "I wish I had never come here." She paced away.

Mingma joined her, making one round between the viewing point and the fire before squatting beside the pit. "You had no choice. Your destiny was set the day the creator first thought your name. There is no escaping it."

"My destiny? I have a destiny?"

"As do we all." Mingma's slanted brown eyes watched and weighed Karen's impatient movements.

"Yeah, but right now mine sucks." Karen paced back, picked up her cup, and poured herself some tea. "So I take it we're digging close to the place where the villagers buried their heart?"

"The heart of evil. The mountain will protect it against the machines, the men — and you."

Karen had trained herself not to be sensitive. With a father like hers, to be sensitive was to ask to be hurt. But right now, as the problems multiplied and she lost her apparently feeble hold on sanity, this felt very personal. She lifted her resentful gaze to the mountain and rose to her feet. "We're almost finished with the site prep, damn you, and I swear —"

Mingma leaped to her feet. "Don't, miss,

don't swear, don't provoke the —"

An inhuman scream pierced the air.

The two women raced to the edge overlooking the job site.

The men were running, scattering like rodents away from a trap. One man fell getting out of his excavator. He crawled a few yards, looked behind him in obvious terror, scrambled to his feet, and fled.

Phil was yelling at them, gesturing wildly, trying to herd them back to work.

They paid him no heed.

As Mingma watched the panic, her face was still, carved from stone. "So. It has begun."

CHAPTER FOUR

"Stay here." Karen started down the rough path.

Mingma caught her arm and swung her back around. "Don't, miss. Don't go down there!"

But duty called, and Karen always answered. "I have to."

"Run with me. If you come now, I can save you!" Desperation filled Mingma's eyes.

"It's all right. I'll be fast." Karen shook her off.

Mingma unlooped the string of bells and wound them around her own wrist. "Miss, I must leave. Please come with me!"

"Go on, then. It's okay. I'll catch up with you!" Karen scrambled down the rugged path as quickly as she could, hearing the chime of the holy bells as Mingma fled in the opposite direction.

As she reached the first pile of rubble, Phil

met her. "For shit's sake, it's just an old burial. A mummy, it looks like."

"An archeological find?" Karen's heart sank.

An archeological find was the bane of commercial construction. It meant work had to stop while they called in the authorities to determine its importance and excavate the remains.

"If we don't tell anybody, we can dispose of the body and keep building —"

She gave Phil a withering look. "Like nobody's going to hear those men screaming their heads off."

"I can shut 'em up," he said sulkily.

"But can you make them return to work?" She walked toward the still-running backhoe and turned it off. The situation was obvious now. The operator had lifted one of the huge boulders out of the way, and there, nestled in a hollow, was a cloth-wrapped bundle.

The skull was clearly visible, and that must have set off the panic. "Turn off the rest of the machines," she told Phil. "We can't waste the gas. It's too hard to find and way too expensive."

As Phil obeyed, she went and knelt beside the body.

It was the body of a child, maybe five years

old, curled up and resting on its side in a hollow in the stone, with its hand tucked under its cheek as if asleep. The high, dry, cold air had dried its skin, stretching it across the bones, giving the body personality.

It had been a pretty child. Its fine woven clothing was still intact, with only a few holes and frayed edges, and Karen could see faded colors that decorated its robe. A hammered gold necklace hung around its neck, gold earrings pierced its ears, and a bracelet wrapped its . . . *her* narrow wrist. Another cloth lay under the body and protected her from the cold stone.

A beloved child. An important child. A child interred with love and care — and brutally sacrificed.

For among the wisps of pale brown hair that still clung to her head, a hole cleanly pierced the child's skull.

"Ah." Karen's eyes filled with tears. "You poor thing." She knew she shouldn't touch it — when the archeologists arrived, they would scold her mightily. But something about the girl called to her. Something about that long-ago murder broke her heart.

Reaching out a trembling hand, she laid it gently on the child's head — and the child opened her eyes.

They were aquamarine, like Karen's — *like Karen's* — and the girl *looked* at her. Karen clearly saw the wealth of sorrow that filled those eyes before they closed again — and the body crumbled to dust beneath her touch.

Karen knelt, frozen, disbelieving, knowing what she'd seen and knowing it was impossible.

She glanced wildly around her, wanting someone close, another living human, but there was only Phil, sitting in the seat of the excavator, cursing the engine as it sputtered and moaned.

She looked again at the shrunken clothes, the gold glistening in the dust of the body.

And in the place where the head had rested, where the bones of the child's head had held it, was a square white tile a few inches across. Carefully Karen lifted it from among the remains. With a gentle hand she brushed it clean, and gazed at it.

It was an icon, a stylized painting of the Virgin Mary of the type that had hung in Russian homes for over a thousand years. Her cherry red robe and glittering halo made the icon a precious work, yet it was Mary's large, dark, sad eyes, looking at right at Karen, and the single silver tear that traced her cheek that brought answering tears to Karen's eyes. This was the Mary of sacrifice, the mother who had given her son to save the world.

Karen's gaze shifted to the dust of the child slaughtered in obedience to the devil's command.

Had *her* mother cried as they drove the pick through her skull?

The village had sacrificed their heart . . .

High above her, the mountain groaned, and again Karen would have sworn someone — or perhaps some*thing* — watched her.

She looked up Anaya.

The peak lifted itself toward the sky, and it seemed to have grown, swelling from the inside, the fires of the underworld pressing it upward.

She looked around — and saw him.

A strange man, dressed all in black, poised on the cliff's edge overlooking the building site. He stood perfectly still, a living statue betrayed only by the wind that blew his long black hair and beard.

He stared.

She stared.

Neither moved.

Who was this man who watched her with such ferocity?

Then Phil's voice, directly behind her, made her jump. "Hey, what's that?"

His hand reached over her shoulder.

She jerked the icon back to her bosom.

But he plucked the gold necklace out of the dust of an ancient tragedy. "Son of a bitch, what do you think this is worth?"

"Don't!" She wrapped her hand around his wrist.

"Why not?"

"The archeologists will be furious that you touched —"

"It's not like *you* were waiting." His fat finger flicked the icon she held.

"It wasn't like that!"

"Yeah, right." He grinned into her face, all white teeth in a round, pink face. "You grabbed what you wanted fast enough."

He was completely, utterly obnoxious, a greedy worm of a man . . . the kind of guy the evil mountain drew to itself.

Maybe he was at home here, but she was not. She'd seen that child's eyes open. She knew now that the old legends were true. And for all that she had trained herself to be tough and strong, she knew better than to challenge the devil. "I'm getting out of here," she whispered.

The earth trembled, rattling like old, cold bones beneath her knees and feet.

Slowly she rose.

Earthquake?

No, but high above them she heard the mountain give a deep-throated rumble.

"Phil, did you hear that?"

"Yeah. So? It does that all the time." He planted his knees in the dust of sacrifice. "What happened to the body? Did the air make it disintegrate? I wonder what's hidden in the clothes?"

Sacrilege. Sacrilege!

"Phil, don't!" Another rumble shook the air, and a huge *crack* sounded as the mountain's bones broke. "Phil, come on. It's dangerous here."

"In a minute."

The urge to stop him warred with the need to escape. She was poised on her toes, ready to run. "The mountain's coming down!"

"Look at the gold they buried with this kid!" He dug through the remains.

She tugged on his shoulder. "We've got to run!"

He turned on her, his lips drawn back, his teeth glistening with spit. "Run, then. This is mine!"

Shocked by the demon of greed that peered from his red-rimmed eyes, she jumped back. Glanced up. Saw the dust of the massive rockfall shuddering toward her. Heard the sound of tons of stone descending the mountain. Realized that Mount Anaya had at last decided to crush them and their presumption.

She ran. Ran as hard and as fast as she could away from this place. From the heart of evil.

The ground shuddered. The noise rose, a cacophony of shattering stone and a roar that sounded like . . . like a motor.

A big, black motorcycle cut in front of her. Stopped. The stranger, the man who'd watched her from above, sat on the seat, his eyes ablaze with urgency. He snatched her around the waist, pulled her on behind him.

She grasped him.

He hit the accelerator.

They tore across the site, the bike hitting holes and rocks. The front tire danced to a crazy beat. He couldn't control the machine. He was going to kill them.

But he stood on the pedals. He skidded, leaned, avoided.

She wanted to scream in fear. And maybe she did. Then a glance behind them made her lean forward, urging him faster.

For the rockfall chased them, fueled by gravity and the mountain's spite. Boulders as big as buildings slammed behind them like a stone giant's footsteps, each one coming closer . . . closer. Anaya groaned with exertion. Dust rose, obscuring the sky, the site . . . Phil.

Phil had disappeared, crushed somewhere within the massive pile of rock.

Mount Anaya had once again protected the heart of evil.

Turning her head away, she pressed her face into the leather jacket.

He smelled of cold water, fresh air, and wildness.

She started.

She knew that scent. She'd dreamed about it every night.

This was her lover — not a dream, as she hoped; not madness, as she feared; but a man of daring and courage.

Of course. Who else would defy death to rescue her?

Desperately, she clung to him as Mount Anaya threw its final efforts into their destruction, bouncing boulders like huge rubber balls. The stones collided with one another, smashing into massive shards, sharp and evil. Slivers of rock battered her. Millions of tons of granite obliterated the old paths, the embattled plants, all evidence of the past.

The motorcycle reached the far side of the valley.

The dust cloud enveloped them.

The ground rose.

Each collision of boulder against earth rattled the bike and broke the ground.

Mount Anaya had won. Death had them in its grasp when the motorcycle broke over the top of the promontory and flew through the air — into nothingness.

CHAPTER FIVE

Karen screamed in earnest.

Her lover roared in defiance.

The bike landed hard in a pile of rubble. The back wheel skidded. He corrected. Accelerated. And they drove away from the mountain, leaving it behind to mutter and rumble in murderous frustration.

The rough path took them away from Mount Anaya. They descended in fits and starts, dodging through crooked passes and splashing through tiny streams. Although the altitude was still high and the air thin, the terrain changed. First tiny flowers and tufts of grass softened the stony austerity. Then the occasional tree grew, digging its roots into the thin soil. The hope so conspicuously missing from Mount Anaya existed and intensified with every mile they drove. Finally Karen's lover turned the bike straight up a hill, slammed down on the accelerator, and drove like a demon to the top, around a curve . . . and stopped in a narrow, hidden meadow bounded by mountains.

He turned off the motor.

The sudden silence was shocking.

Karen's ears still rang from the din that accompanied the landslide, from the roar of the bike, and now she could hear a stream babbling, a bird singing . . . sounds so normal and sweet, she wanted to weep with joy.

The mountain hadn't killed them. It had done its best, but she was alive. *They* were alive.

She slid off the seat. Her butt still vibrated from their wild ride. Her knees wobbled alarmingly.

She'd almost died.

She sank to the ground. The scent of crushed grass filled her head, and for a brief moment she leaned over and kissed the ground. Smiling, she glanced up at him. "Thank you," she said. "Thank you."

He didn't look at her. He sat absolutely still, almost as if they had never met.

And in truth, they hadn't. The nights of desperate, needy sex could hardly count as an introduction.

Yet not even the sight of his stiff figure could stop the slow rise of her exuberance.

One thought possessed her.

She was alive.

She got to her feet, took three steps away, and spun in a circle like a demented Julie Andrews. If she could carry a tune — which she couldn't — she would have burst into a rousing chorus of "The Sound of Music."

She felt as if she'd found Shangri-la. Here in the meadow, the sunlight was clear and pure. She ran toward the tiny stream. It cascaded off a ledge into a pool lined with smooth pebbles, then spilled down the creek bed. The water sparkled as it crossed the stones, and she knelt beside it. When she splashed water over her face, it was so cold it made her teeth clench. She was making a fool of herself, but she didn't care.

They were alive.

She laughed as she realized the dust sifting down from the sky really came from her hair — the dirt from the rockfall had coated her with grit. She stripped off her coat, shook it, and tossed it aside. With both hands she scrubbed at her head, and winced at a stab of pain. Carefully she explored; something, one of the rock chips, had sliced a small cut into her scalp behind her ear. The place felt sticky, and when she pulled her hand away her fingers were carmine with drying blood.

Yet such a small price to pay for being alive.

She closed her eyes, bowed her head, and thanked God, then stood, prepared to deal with what would happen next.

When she turned, he was there.

She shouldn't have been surprised. He always moved with deliberate stealth.

But this time she jumped in horror.

He was six-foot, broad at the shoulder and narrow at the hip. The same dust that coated her had settled on him, on his dark, sleek, long hair, on his wild black beard and mustache. Beneath the dirt that streaked his face his skin was toasted by the sun. Although his bone structure was vaguely exotic, maybe Eastern European, this man was Caucasian.

And his eyes . . . his eyes were black. Not midnight blue, not sable brown, not charcoal gray. *Black.* So black it looked as if the pupil had swallowed the iris. Black, opaque, and shiny, like obsidian, the black glass formed in the fires of a volcano.

She tried to stumble backward.

He caught the front of her T-shirt in his fists and yanked her close.

Drugs? Yes. Only drugs could cause his eyes to look like . . . that.

Drugs . . . or she'd really died in the

rockfall, and this was hell, and he was the devil.

Yet everything here seemed so real. *He* seemed real. They were close, almost touching. He leaned toward her, his breath touching her face. And as she stared into those eyes, she fell into a soul so dark and tormented nothing could ease his pain. Except maybe . . . her.

"What did you think you were doing?" The voice of her midnight lover, yes, but low, furious, intent. "Standing down there while the mountain got ready to kill? Don't you know Anaya's reputation? Didn't Mingma tell you the mountain would destroy you for trying to conquer it? No person has ever climbed it, built on it, or studied it and returned whole and unchanged. Don't you know the scent of evil when it fills your lungs?"

I smell it now. But she was too terrified — too smart — to say that. "You should have left me."

"Yes, I should have. But I couldn't watch you die." He breathed hard, his chest rising and falling like that of a man in agony. "Not you. Never you."

He might look like the devil, but he sounded as if he *cared.* And he kissed her with all the desperation of a caged animal, loosing his passion like an avalanche on her.

Yes. This was her lover. She recognized his taste.

But they'd never kissed like this. He dragged her into his embrace, held her fiercely. What had previously passed between them might have been a passionate game compared to his current need. He consumed her, swallowing her breath, her will. He burned her with his fever, and behind her closed eyes she saw eruptions of crimson and gold, flares of exploding heartbreak. Off balance, she clutched at him, the babbling stream behind her, his madness beckoning her on . . . and she kissed him back.

Because they were alive. She'd never *been* so alive. This man, who had shown her delight above all else, had saved her from death, brought her here to this perfect place, and now he wanted her. Wanted her.

Welcome to hell.

CHAPTER SIX

Karen forgot about her lover's strange, dark, shiny eyes and remembered only his skill. Lifting herself onto her toes, she slid a leg around his hip.

He grasped her bottom, whirled around, and, without moving a step, placed her in the grass. His hands went to her fly, lowering the zipper, pulling her pants and panties down to her knees. He growled in frustration when her boots brought him to an abrupt halt. He removed one easily, but on the second the laces were knotted, and in the depths of his black eyes she saw a flash of red. Red like fire. Red like the flames of hell.

With a jolt, reality returned.

She tried to sit up.

"No!" In one efficient movement, he stripped her pants off her bare foot.

The ground, lush with grass, was shockingly cool.

He spread her legs — and stopped. And stared. Stared as if he'd never seen a woman before.

Certainly she had never so boldly revealed herself. She tried to use her hands as protection, but he caught her. "No," he said again. He transferred both her wrists to one hand and used the other to open her to the light and the air. His fingers trailed down the center of her, a swift, light caress that brought every female nerve to high alert.

"I've never seen anything so beautiful," he whispered. He swirled the tip of one finger inside her. "Pale and pink, swelling as I touch you . . ."

Involuntarily she tightened, holding him there.

He closed his eyes, his face a study in the agony of desire.

Then he came alive with urgency. He unzipped and stripped his jeans down to his knees.

Briefly she saw his erection, sturdy, wide, demanding.

He opened her, lay on her, thrust inside.

"No!" She tried to sit up.

Why, she didn't know — she needed him as badly as he needed her — but this . . . this was too much, too sudden, not glorious lovemaking, but a frenzied affirmation of life.

She wanted to stop.

She needed to come.

He scooped up her thighs, used the crooks of his arms to spread them wider, higher, and thrust again.

"Damn you!" She was helpless against his strength, helpless to stop the blaze that entered her bloodstream and slid through her veins. She grabbed at his arms, digging her nails into his leather jacket, and used that leverage to lift herself over and over, small movements that collided with his need and fed her own.

As if she had spoken, he said, "All right!" and rolled over, bringing her to the top.

His black hair spread out on the green grass. His face beneath the beard was harsh, and his eyes were narrow slits of demand.

He loosened his grip. "Ride, then!"

He was a big-boned man. She couldn't straddle him and have her knees touch the ground. So, with her hands on his bare belly, she pushed herself up, put her feet under her, and rode.

It was decadent.

It was luscious.

She serviced him.

She serviced herself.

She listened for his groans and made him suffer. She probed for her own pleasures and repeated the movements that worked for her.

The sun beat down on her shoulders. The breeze caressed her nipples.

Beneath her he writhed. Inside he stretched her to the limit.

He was a beautiful animal, with long, wiry muscles and strength in his big hands.

And something about him slipped under her skin, into her blood, while at the same time he breathed deep, as if her essence fed his heart, his soul.

Her thighs burned with exertion as she rose and fell, rose and fell. She panted harshly, fighting to draw in enough of the thin, cool air to sustain this race to the finish. She moved faster and faster, dragging them toward completion.

Orgasm took control of her, a brief, glorious, pulse-pounding climax that expanded her senses to include the whole world, and shrank her focus to him — and her. She thought he was beautiful as he bucked beneath her, fierce, undisciplined, wild with passion.

They finished too soon. Throwing her arms out in an excess of jubilation, she laughed out loud. She'd never been so alive, so happy. She had escaped Mount Anaya. They had escaped death.

She wilted down on him, panting, exultant.

He wrapped his arms around her back and rolled once more.

She was under him, the heat of his body between her legs, the cool earth below her, and around her head tiny white flowers blossomed.

He stared at her as if she bewildered him.

She stared back, smiling, recovering from her folly. Slowly his dark gaze recalled her to normalcy, then to wariness.

She had had sex with this man, held him in her arms while he slept beside her, trusted him to save her life. Yet she knew nothing about him, and his eyes . . . his eyes chilled her with the same sense of impending disaster she'd experienced on the slopes of Mount Anaya.

With the fingers of one hand he pushed her hair away from her face. "You shouldn't have done that."

"What? What do you mean? I shouldn't have had sex with you?" In a tart tone she said, "I didn't know I had a choice."

"You shouldn't have done me. You shouldn't have loved it. Most of all you shouldn't have laughed."

She stared at him.

He looked so stern, like a revivalist minister preaching the Old Testament.

She struggled to divine his meaning. "I wasn't laughing at you, if that's what you mean. I was laughing —"

"— for joy. I understand."

He observed her so closely, she felt as if his gaze scoured her face, revealing more than she wanted him to know, and he made her aware of his weight pressing her into the grass, her widespread legs, her risky vulnerability. She shifted uncomfortably.

He stroked her hair again. "Someday I would like to hear you laugh again."

"I don't laugh like that very often." She didn't do any of this very often.

"Nevertheless." With every sign of reluctance he pulled away from her. He stood and stripped, a swift, efficient elimination of clothing and boots.

He tossed everything on the ground, then stood over her, looking down at her, his fists clenching and unclenching.

To suspect him of lifting weights was absurd; he led a life on the edge of civilization, doing God knew what for a living, yet he was long and lean, a sleek predator with coiled strength in the bunching muscles of his arms, in the bulk of his shoulders, the ripped power of his belly. His cock and balls hung between his legs, and although he was limp, she knew only too well the size and power he wielded there.

Charcoal black smudges etched jagged lines down his chest and arm. The marks seemed to form thunderbolts, but they were shrunken, pulling at the edges of his skin, eating into his flesh. She couldn't ignore them, and compassion made her ask, "What happened?"

Leaning down, he grasped her wrists and brought her to her feet. "It's nothing."

"Nothing?" She touched one lightly. "It looks like a burn, but there's a form . . . isn't there?"

"It's a birthmark."

"Is it painful?"

"No." He pulled away from her.

Whatever those marks were, he was sensitive about them. And the way he looked at her, like a man who had reached a decision, made her *think*.

She didn't want to think.

But she was, above all, a woman of good sense, a woman made tough by necessity, a workaholic who spent her life completing one job and going to another. Until this man had visited her tent, she hadn't bothered to take a lover for years. A lover was too much trouble. A lover always required attention, and she didn't have the time to waste.

Now she felt as if she'd been reborn to this world; too open, too raw, too new. She was like a child experiencing a swarm of new emotions — or were they old emotions set free? She didn't know.

But she did know her lack of discipline would have consequences.

Her pants hung around one leg. Her T-shirt was twisted around her waist. She stood lopsided in one boot. She'd just had unprotected sex — oh, God, what had she been thinking? — and his come wet her thighs.

She had never done anything so outrageous in her life.

The sunshine streamed down on them now. She could see him all too clearly, and questions hummed through her mind.

What now?

What if I'm pregnant?

Who is he?

And, *This man is savage.*

She knew it in her bones. That had been, after all, why she welcomed him to her bed at night.

Clutching the waistband of her pants, she tugged it up over her thighs in what she hoped looked like a casual attempt to dress. "I know you've already done so much, but can you take me down to the nearest phone? I've got to call my father, tell him what happened. Have him notify Phil's next of kin. Make arrangements to pay for the rental equipment we lost." Worries and responsibilities returned to crowd her mind. "Do you think Mingma escaped? My cook and interpreter? She said she was going to run. She did escape, didn't she?"

"Mingma is fine," he said without expression in his face or voice.

"Really?" She winced at her own chipper tone. "How do you know?"

"Mingma is smart enough to recognize danger when she sees it. Which is apparently more than you can do." He knelt before Karen, untied her boot, and tugged at it and her pants.

Karen didn't know whether he was referring to the danger of Mount Anaya or the danger he represented.

She tugged back. "Look, I don't know what you think you're doing. . . ." Actually, she was pretty sure what he thought he was doing, but caution had reared its ugly head.

"We're going to take a shower." He jerked his head toward the clear, cold waterfall.

"No. Way. I washed my face in that water.

Not to mention I was raised in Montana in the Rockies up by Glacier National Park. When I was a kid I stood knee-deep in a creek just like that, building a dam out of rocks. So I know what I'm talking about when I say I am not using that stream for a bath." She backed away.

He used her momentum to strip away her pants.

"How else do you propose to get clean?" He sounded prosaic, not dangerous, like some guy she'd met in college. "If the water's that cold, you can hardly accuse me of dire intentions."

Mount Anaya had destroyed her last three months' work. She'd lost a man on the site. She'd finally glimpsed her lover and realized she wasn't mad — but perhaps *he* was. She didn't think she had an ounce of humor left. But now she found her mouth crooking. "Well. That's true." She looked around. They were on the edge of a lawless borderland, with the most meager glimmer of civilization at least a day's drive away. There was no one to see them and, more important, no easy way to get cleaned up.

She looked down at herself. Her T-shirt was grubby. Her legs were bare. Now that he mentioned it, she felt sort of grainy.

One more hour would make no difference

to the outside world.

A crisp breeze eased through the pristine mountain valley.

With a yell that echoed up the walls of the valley, she grasped the hem of her T-shirt, stripped it off over her head, and ran toward the waterfall.

Behind her she heard a similar shout. He ran past her, his bare feet lifted high, and he hit the stream seconds ahead of her. Icy droplets sprayed in the air. He skidded to a stop, and she plowed into him. He wrapped her in his arms and thrust her under the icy cascade.

She screamed in subzero agony, and laughed and splashed as he used his hands to scrub her entire body. She rubbed him back, feeling silly, horny, free for one more foolish second.

They didn't linger; it was too cold.

But they got clean, and she knew why he always smelled so fresh and wild when he came to her bed.

First he came here to the waterfall.

He pulled her from the water and spanned her waist with his hands.

She looked up at him and laughed.

His face changed subtly, from shared amusement to a starkness, a bleakness that broke her heart.

Then he said them, the words that moved her from sorrow to rage. "I will never let you go."

CHAPTER SEVEN

Karen stepped back from this man she didn't know . . . this man she knew so intimately. "What do you mean, you won't ever let me go?"

Relaxed, confident in his decision, he scrutinized her, his black eyes impenetrable.

"Look. You saved me. I'm grateful. But that doesn't mean I want to stay here. I've got a job to do, and I intend to do it." Deliberately she turned her back on him and walked to first one piece of her clothing, then another, picking them up and flicking the dust off them. She was wet and cold and she shivered, but she didn't lie to herself. She shivered because she was afraid.

What had she gotten herself into?

She jumped when he strolled past her, silent as a cat, then watched to see what he would do next. And, because she couldn't help herself, she observed the way the long, lean muscles of his back and butt and thighs coiled and stretched beneath the golden skin.

He opened the saddlebags of his motor-cycle. He pulled out jeans and donned them, Comanche-style, and pulled a T-shirt over his head. Reaching back inside, he dug around and pulled out another T-shirt and tossed it in her direction. "It's clean. Put it on." He threw out another pair of jeans. "You can roll up the legs."

She stood still, trying to decide, for while his blunt commands offended her, her own clothes were dusty and sweaty.

Picking up his boots, he pulled them on, then reached back into his saddlebags. He turned to face her, a semiautomatic Glock steady in his hand. "Put my clothes on."

Her heart stopped — then raced. He *didn't* mean it. "You won't shoot me."

"Because we had sex? I wouldn't count on that." Those strange black eyes watched her, and she hadn't a clue what was behind them. "I've had a lot of women, and I don't give a crap about any of them."

That she believed. Oh, God. She really believed him.

Should she fight? She held a black belt in jujitsu; in her line of work, in the places in the world that she visited, self-defense made sense. But her master was Vietnamese, a veteran of the war with the Americans, and he had taught her to assess a situation. This looked grim.

This looked impossible.

"What are you going to do? Run naked through the meadow while I chase you down with my motorcycle?" Her lover straddled the seat and placed his free hand on the starter. "Climb the rocks while I use you for target practice?"

A recent memory blazed through her fear-frozen mind.

The child sacrificed to evil and buried beneath a rockfall with gold jewelry and a holy icon.

Karen looked down at her hands. She held her coat clutched tightly in her fists, and she groped for the pocket. She felt the hard, small square . . . the child had passed the icon on to her for safekeeping.

"I don't want you to use me for target practice." Karen had to live to keep that icon safe. So she would have to wait for a propitious moment and surprise this monster with a kick that would knock him out or, better yet, kill him.

"Then put on the clothes." The gun remained steady on her. "And your coat and boots. Leave the rest of that stuff here. You won't need it again."

She did as she was told, dressing in silence, knowing she'd had no choice but to let him rescue her, yet cursing herself for being such a fool and giving herself to him.

The jeans were loose around her rear, and she rolled up the hems four times so she could walk. As she shrugged into her coat, she slipped her hand into the pocket and smoothed her fingers along the icon's edge. The memory of the Madonna's gentle face gave her the courage to ask, "Who *are* you?"

"Warlord. I'm Warlord."

"You're a warlord?" One of the ruthless murderers who preyed on the locals and the tourists?

Could her situation get any worse?

It could. He looked straight at her, his obsidian eyes empty of emotion. "Not a warlord. I *am* Warlord."

As the sun set, the man who called himself Warlord drove his motorcycle up the steep, narrow path and straight toward a sheer rock face. Karen wanted to hide her eyes, but at the last second the path swerved, Warlord followed, and the motorcycle roared into a camp protected on three sides by cliffs and on the fourth by a dropoff that tumbled away into space.

The smoke of a dozen campfires twisted

into the clear air. A hundred men, dressed like Warlord, with hair and beards as wild and knotted, squatted in groups around the flames, cooking, chatting, playing video games on their handhelds, drinking, and reading.

Every head turned in their direction. Silence fell. The men observed them — observed her — with acute interest. Then they turned back to their meals, their conversations.

It was as if the couple on the motorcycle were invisible. As if . . . *she* were invisible.

Warlord slowly drove the bike through the camp, twisting and turning among the men. They drove past a huge central fire pit, now cold and blackened with charcoal.

Karen clutched Warlord's leather jacket with sweaty palms. She heard snatches of English spoken with every accent, of French, of German, of Asian languages, and of languages she could not identify. In a low voice she asked, "What is this place?"

"Our base."

"For what?"

"Our raids."

Warlord. He said he was Warlord.

"You can't be the only warlord," she said.

"I'm successful. I'm brutal. I've vanquished all my rivals. I'm the only Warlord who matters in this part of the world."

Like a dumb animal, she'd blindly run with him, trusted him to keep her safe, and she'd stumbled into this trap.

"They've all seen you now," Warlord said. "They know what you look like. They know that if you run, they'll get to stop you. I would suggest that you not run. They would enjoy it too much."

He made her sick with his threat, but she answered steadily enough. "When I run, I won't let them catch me."

For a second he let go of the handlebars, caught her hands, and jerked her forward until she rested against his back, cheek to groin. "Then I'll catch you — and I promise you won't like that."

"Are you under the quaint impression that I'm having a good time right now?" she snapped. "Put your hands on the bars, you fool."

He laughed, a rumble deep in his body, and took control of the motorcycle again.

She squinted through the deepening dusk, trying to guess which tent would be hers. Hers . . . and Warlord's. Until she could escape.

Because no matter what he said, what threat he made, she would escape. She was smart, in good health. The winter she was sixteen her father had sent her out into the Montana mountain wilderness with only minimum gear, and she had survived a brutal week alone. And Warlord couldn't watch her every minute of the day.

Yet the farther they went into camp, the more her hopes sank.

Perhaps Warlord couldn't watch her, but unless the camp emptied when the troop went on raids, she would be watched.

As they approached the end of the valley, he stopped the bike and pointed. "That's where I live."

Her gaze traveled up and up.

A wooden platform was built twenty feet above the valley floor, and into the cliff. Atop the platform was a tent larger than any she had ever seen, and she'd seen plenty.

"It's custom-made, warm in the winter, cool in the summer. I live there — and now you do, too," he said. "You'll be comfortable."

"No, I won't."

"Then you'll be uncomfortable. Your choice." He drove the motorcycle into a cleft in the rock and got off, then steadied her as she stood.

Her legs were shaky — from hunger, from fear, from the long trip to this place. Leaning against the stone, she realized how truly trapped she was. While they rode she should have twisted off his ears or gouged his eyes. Yes, they would have wrecked, but she would have had a chance of leaping free. . . .

"Come on." He took her hand and tugged her after him.

She dug in her heels.

Without looking back he said, "Do you want me to carry you? That would provide the men with entertainment." With his free hand he gestured up the rickety stairway that led to the tent. "And if we fall, it's a long way to the ground."

She stumbled forward under the pressure of his grip.

He pushed her the first few steps up the stairway.

It was steep, almost a ladder, and to steady herself she bent to clutch the wooden treads above her.

"Don't step on the third step. It will break under your weight." When she hesitated, he pushed her again. "Go on. I'm not interested in you now. Exhausted women have no life in them. I'll wait until tomorrow, when you've eaten and slept and you're able to fight."

He was such a bastard. Such a completely right bastard.

She was hungry, thirsty, and tired. The

pants he'd given her were drooping, the cuffs she'd made unfolding. She used one hand to keep the waistband up, and kept the other on the ladder, and her eyes resolutely lifted to the platform and the tent.

If he did as he promised and left her alone tonight, tomorrow she would have the energy and intelligence to find a way out of this.

It would probably include a ransom.

Eerily, he echoed her thoughts. "I imagine your father would pay well to get you back."

"What do you know about my father?" she lashed.

"I know he owns the company you work for."

At last she understood his motivation for taking her.

Ransom. Of course.

Nothing else made sense.

"You ought to do a little more research on your intended victims, because my father wouldn't pay a dime to get me back." There. She'd given him the unvarnished truth.

"Are you asking me to believe he doesn't care about his only child?"

"I don't give a damn what you believe." She wished the steps had a handrail, anything to give the illusion of protection from a hard fall.

He laughed, a low sound of amusement that licked along her spine. "If your father is truly indifferent to you, that's good to know. I won't have to worry about him sending help."

"No," she said bitterly. "You don't have to worry about that."

"Don't step on the fourth from the top."

She wavered, counting, then took a long step up. "If you'll get me a hammer and some nails, I'll fix that for you," she said sarcastically.

"In case of attack from a mercenary group with aspirations to my valley and my territory, those steps will give me the extra seconds I need to slaughter a few more of them."

"Oh." She used her elbows to inch her way up on the platform. The two-by-eight boards were springy, the nail heads were rusty, and when she looked down she could see the ground through the gaps in the boards.

He grinned as he watched her get as close as possible to the tent and stand, half stooped over, ready to drop in case the platform — or the world — tried to send her tumbling over the edge.

She looked out. "Is that likely? An attack? And slaughter?"

"Slaughter is a time-honored tradition on the border." Lightly he sprang up to stand beside her, observing every minuscule movement down in the valley and up in the mountains. "But don't worry. The valley is almost impenetrable. Attackers have to climb the mountain that surrounds it before they can rappel down the cliffs, and while they do, we'll pick them off like ducks in a shooting gallery."

"What if they use helicopters?"

"No mercenaries here are so well funded." Catching her wrist, he pulled her along the narrow ledge toward the entrance.

For one alarming moment she looked over the edge and all the way down. Just as in her nightmares, the ground rushed up to meet her. She took an unwary step back, stumbled on a tent peg, and almost went over onto her rear. As her arms windmilled, she swallowed a scream.

Warlord dragged her forward, into his arms, and steadied her. "You're afraid of heights."

"No, I'm not." At least, she shouldn't be. Not when there was so much more immediate to be afraid of.

"That's the nightmare that wakes you from sleep."

She denied it automatically. "No, it's not."

"These are the highest mountains in the world. The most dangerous. If you're afraid, why did you take this job?"

"I'm not afraid," she said, her teeth gritted.

The sun was gone. The stars' light barely glistened. The campfires flickered far below, and she couldn't really see his face. But by the tilt of his head she knew he studied her, and just as it had been on those nights when he visited her tent, she thought he saw clearly in the dark.

She didn't want him to see her afraid. Fear always unleashed that awful mockery, so she tilted her chin up and smiled tightly. "I have a question. Will you share me with your men?" She shouldn't have suggested it, but she had to know.

There were too many men out there, and she'd take that nosedive off the mountain if it came to a choice between that and them.

Catching the front of her shirt in his fist, he leaned close to her face, and when he spoke, his breath caressed her face. "I do not share what is mine. And you are mine; make no mistake about that. Mine forever."

"Forever is a very, very long time."

"An eternity." Unseen and unanticipated, he swept her into his arms, and in a symbolism that wasn't lost on Karen, he strode to and through the opening in the tent.

CHAPTER EIGHT

Warlord's arms tightened around Karen.

"Welcome home, my bride."

Yes. He'd laid his claim to her, and treated her like a bride, but a bride from the days when men captured their women and held them by force until they trained them to be docile.

He would have a hell of a wait. "You might want to keep an eye on your bride, or she'll stick a knife between your ribs."

"Every relationship has its small difficulties to work out." He let her slip down and onto her feet.

"Wow." In all her years of roughing it, Karen had never seen anything like this. Two LED camp lanterns hung on hooks up by the ceiling and shed a white light on the tent's spacious interior. The outer shell would attract no notice at all in any American camp-ground, but inside . . . a sumptuous hand-crafted wool carpet covered the floor, and huge tapestries hung along the walls. To insulate against the cold, Karen supposed, but also to lend the richness of their beauty to a wanderer's abode.

Yet a man — a raider — had seized what he liked. When she faced one direction a graceful tree of life grew on a green background. Another direction and a medieval knight pranced across a field. One wall was a modern rendering of a blue lake at twilight, and the other a graceful arch with pink roses spilling onto a path. The carpet was a glorious Kashmiri rug in cream, burgundy, and black.

"I guess the term 'feng shui' means nothing to you, huh?"

"I'm not into Chinese food."

Was he being funny? She couldn't tell, and she sure as hell wasn't going to laugh.

The rest of the furniture was as much of a hodgepodge as the tapestries — there were two chests, a French provincial desk, an ergonomic desk chair, a coffee table with cushions tossed around it for casual seating, or maybe for dining, Karen didn't know which. She didn't care. For there was also the bed. . . .

Ah, the bed.

It was nothing more than a queen-sized mattress set on the floor on a bed frame without legs, with a brass headboard and footboard and a canopy of mosquito netting. The posts shone as if someone polished it daily, a narrow leather holster was strapped to one upright bedpost, pillows billowed flirtatiously, and the whole glorious contraption should have whispered of *sin and seduction.*

Instead it shouted *rest and relaxation.* "What kind of mattress is that?" she asked.

"A Sealy."

She groaned with pleasure quite unlike the pleasure she'd experienced in his arms. "My God, how did you get it up here?"

"What do you care?" He took the collar of her coat and tried to lift it away.

She wrapped her arms more tightly around herself and glared.

He tugged. "Take off your coat before you lie down."

"No."

In an elaborate gesture he removed his hands. "I was playing the gentleman."

"That ship has sailed."

For a moment she thought he was going to laugh. "You remind me of . . ."

"Of what?"

"Home." He gave her a push on the shoulder. "Go to sleep. I have to find out what's happened with that shipment that's coming through today."

She stumbled to the bed, flopped sideways across the mattress, and promptly slid into sleep. . . .

She stood on the edge of the cliff, the blue sky surrounding her. The wind blew hard, tumbling her hair around her face. She tried to back up, to get away, but her feet were too heavy. Then the ground shook. The stones rumbled. The edge gave way. She hurtled toward the ground. . . .

Her own scream brought her back to a wavering consciousness.

Heart pounding, she opened her eyes — and stared into his. Into Warlord's.

He crouched on the bed, holding her. "Was it your nightmare? Did you fall?"

"Yes." She shuddered, and woke completely. "Yes."

His arms felt like safety, but that was a deception. For he watched her without expression, and now, without a doubt, he knew her weakness.

He would exploit her weakness.

"Do you want me to stay?" he asked.

"No." She pushed away, out of his embrace, and closed her eyes, rejecting him.

He could not seduce her with gentle words and comfort. She would not be his compliant bride.

She listened, heard nothing. Furious that he lingered so near, she snapped, "Get out, damn it!"

No one answered.

She opened her eyes.

She was alone.

CHAPTER NINE

Karen woke knowing exactly where she was. She knew why she was here. She remembered every last horrific moment of the day before, and most of all, she remembered Warlord.

She heard footsteps. He was in the tent. As he moved closer she carefully freed herself from the blankets and prepared to leap.

And she heard Mingma's soft voice say, "*Namaste,* Miss Sonnet."

Karen's eyes sprang open. She came out of the bed in a rush. "Mingma? You're here? He captured you, too?"

"Miss?" Mingma's brow knit as she stared in puzzlement. "What do you mean, capture? He bring me for you."

Karen thought she must be more disoriented than she'd realized, because that didn't make sense. "Where's the warlord?"

"Warlord is gone."

"Gone from camp?" Karen grinned with savage pleasure. "What time is it?"

"The sun will rise soon."

"We can get away."

"No, miss."

"Don't worry. I'll make the plans." Karen pushed her hair out of her face. She was good at planning, good at taking advantage of opportunity, and she needed to escape now, first thing, while this warlord guy was out drinking with his buddies and celebrating his new concubine.

Mingma *tsk*ed and shook her head as Karen tugged at the pair of men's jeans that sagged around her hips — Warlord's jeans. "That is not attractive. Warlord requested I find you new clothes to wear." With a smile, she gestured at a blue-green georgette skirt and midriff-baring shirt intricately worked in gold-threaded hand embroidery. "He says bring only the finest and most beautiful, and I do."

"That's a pretty fancy sweat suit."

"Sweat suit?" Mingma cocked her head at Karen's sarcasm. "I don't understand 'sweat suit,' but the color is like your eyes."

"Great. Just what I always wanted."

"Will you wash your hands and face before you eat?" Mingma gestured toward the hammered-copper pitcher and bowl.

"God, yes. Thank you." Karen splashed the cold water on her face, vanquished the last of the cobwebs, and felt a rise of confidence.

"Will you change before you eat?" Mingma stepped close and tried to tug at Karen's shirt.

"No! I'm not wearing *that*."

"You don't like it?" Mingma actually looked hurt.

"It would be hard to hike in. Are all the men gone?" Karen didn't wait for an answer, but opened the tent flap and looked.

The thin, gray premorning light spilled into the long valley, and from up here she could see it all — the cliff on one side, the gorge on the other, and the narrow bottleneck of an entrance on the far end. On the flat valley floor a dozen men slept in bags and tents, and two sat hunched over, cleaning their rifles. One of them glanced up at her, then glanced up toward the other end of the valley. Following his gaze she saw a guard sitting high on a rock, rifle in hand. Looking more closely, she saw other guards stationed strategically at lookout points, dressed in camouflage and holding an impressive array of firearms.

"This isn't going to be easy." Karen stepped out and scanned the mountains around them. "We can't fight our way out, so we're going to have to be crafty. I wonder if these guys are open to bribes."

Mingma stepped out beside her. "You want to leave?"

"Of course I want to leave!"

"Why do you want to leave Warlord?"

Mingma didn't understand. Obviously. So, in a voice gravelly with fury, Karen said, "Because the bastard brought me here against my will, that's why. To use me like . . . like a whore."

"Not like a whore. Like a wife. It is an honor."

"An honor? To be forced to have sex with an ignorant, brutal raider?"

"But is he not your secret lover?"

"What?" Stiff with shock, Karen swung on Mingma.

"Is he not the lover who heard your tears, who slipped into your tent at night to make you forget your sorrow?"

"You knew?" Karen stood, her hands slack at her sides.

Mingma *knew.*

"It is not good for a young woman to sleep alone."

Karen covered her hot cheeks with her hands. "Did *everyone* know?"

"No, miss. The men you could hire were

not good. Only the laziest would work in that evil place. Warlord keeps the best for himself." Mingma turned her solemn brown eyes on Karen. "I am the best, so he hire me to care for you."

Karen stared at Mingma, at the woman she thought she knew, and realized her jaw hung open. Snapping it shut, she then asked, "When? You mean today?"

"No. When you come to Mount Anaya. Warlord, he saw you in Kathmandu, and he know right away he would make you his."

"Did he now?" Warlord had been watching her on the train, and she hadn't noticed. She'd been too busy fending off a pass from Phil. At the time she'd thought Phil was the worst lecher she'd have to contend with in Nepal. What a fool she'd been — about everything.

"When he realized where you were going, he came to me. He said you would need someone to protect you. So I bring my lucky bells and hang them on your tent, and powerful soil from the god on Everest and spread it under your feet. Morning and night I say the prayers of defense from the Evil One, and at night I add sleep weed to your dinner so you not hear the cries from the mountain and go crazy and seek those who are lost." As if she expected praise,

Mingma smiled and bowed.

Karen did *not* smile. "So you worked for him. You *always* worked for him. You came because he's paying you."

"Yes, miss."

In less than twenty-four hours Karen had seen death, faced evil, embraced life, and discovered that her lover, her rescuer, was a warlord. *The* warlord. Yet this betrayal hurt her more than anything she'd seen or faced. "I trusted you," she whispered.

"Of course. As I trust you. We are sisters." Mingma seemed so calm, as if she didn't know she'd deceived Karen.

"No. Sisters don't hurt each other."

"I have not hurt you. I have cared for you and watched over you when your lover could not."

"For money!"

"Miss, I have a son, sixteen years old. Here, the schools are not good. So I send him to your United States, and pay for him to live with an American family and prepare for college. He is smart. He does well." Mingma glowed with pride. "So I pay."

"You pay for his life with mine."

"No, miss. Warlord is the best soldier here. He holds control." Mingma showed her clenched fist. "He will keep you safe."

"I don't want to be safe. I want to be gone!"

"He wants you here. Why should your desire be held higher than his?"

They were talking in circles.

Karen seethed with frustration. "Fine. You're his creature. So stay away from me."

"But, miss, I have your breakfast."

"Put it outside the door. I'll get it when I get my appetite back." Karen ducked back into the tent and stalked across the plush rug.

Mingma. Mingma had betrayed her.

She hadn't seen that one coming. And why not? She'd worked in construction as a project manager, where every con man and wastrel flocked to her jobs in the hopes of cheating the stupid little woman. She'd learned the hard way not to trust anyone.

Yet Mingma had slipped under her guard.

Thank God her father would never know. Thank God . . . yeah, because if she didn't break out of this prison, she'd end up being some wacko warlord's plaything until he tired of her, or until the end of her life, and those two events might coincide closely.

There had to be a way out of here. No self-respecting wacko would leave himself without an escape route.

He'd placed the tent high on a platform

against a cliff. Warlord was too canny to have done that by accident.

She lifted the heavy tapestry that covered the back wall, and examined the weather-resistant tent fabric.

There.

A seam snaked up from the floor to a spot about halfway up the wall. Karen knelt and ran her fingers along the length. The work was done as an afterthought, the seam basted together by clear, strong nylon thread. She tried to tear it — impossible. A knife, something sharp . . . She ran to the holster strapped to one of the uprights on the headboard.

Empty.

Glancing around, she grabbed a gold-plated serving tray off the table and used the edge to saw through the thread above the knot, then slipped the stitching free. She spread the material and looked out.

As she suspected, the platform jutted out a few inches beyond the tent, and just beyond in the cliff she saw the beginning of a path that wound into the mountains.

Yet . . . she looked down. The path was six feet from the platform, and the drop was twenty feet onto sharp rocks — a fall guaranteed to break her bones.

Warlord couldn't jump that. Could he?

He had to have some sort of temporary bridge. She knelt and groped under the platform, looking for something to span the distance.

Nothing.

She glanced inside the tent for a loose board that would hold her weight.

Nothing.

She didn't dare wait any longer.

Mingma would be back soon to try to convince Karen to dress in the harem clothes and play the coy maiden to Warlord's conquering warrior.

Bullshit.

Karen wouldn't do it.

Again she measured the span with her gaze. She stood on the edge — and almost jumped.

But like a sliver of glass, some sharp, bright thought cut her concentration.

The icon. She had to take the icon.

And her coat, of course. It was stupid to think of escaping into the Himalayas, even in the summer, without a coat.

Hurrying to the camouflage parka, she slipped her arms into the sleeves and belted it around her waist. Irresistibly she slid her hand into the pocket and pulled out the icon.

The Madonna stared solemnly at her.

"I'll save you," Karen vowed, and walked back to the hole in the tent. She slipped through and stood there, the breeze lifting her hair. She stared at the lip of the path six feet away.

She'd done a lot of climbing in her life. She'd jumped crevasses with raging streams below. She knew the length of her legs, and she knew her limits.

From a standing start . . . this jump was impossible.

She wrapped her arms around her waist and swallowed the bile that built in her throat.

She would fall.

She'd dreamed this a million times.

She would be horribly hurt, crippled, her bones shattered, her internal organs bleeding uncontrollably.

Her breath hitched, and her eyes filled with tears.

She was being dramatic. She was a coward.

But she was *afraid.*

On the other hand, if she stayed here, she'd be the plaything of a monster.

Jump.

So she jumped.

She stretched out like Superman, hands forward, trying in midair to propel herself onto the path.

She missed. She landed with a bone-crunching thump on her face and chest. Her legs dangled, wheeling madly. She slipped. Grabbed at the grass. Caught herself. The clump of grass broke. She slipped again. She was going down. . . .

Her foot found a rock lodged solidly beneath the overhang.

One hand caught the branch of a shrub.

She wanted to scramble up.

She forced herself to slow down, to balance herself, to concentrate. . . .

Gradually she inched her stomach onto the path. She flung her leg up onto the ledge. She rolled . . . and she was safe. Safe.

She took a long breath, the first one since she'd jumped.

Safe? No way. Somehow, some way, Warlord would come after her.

Magnus crawled forward along the rock at the edge of the cliff, his gaze fixed on the regiment below. He settled next to the man to whom he'd sworn his allegiance.

Warlord rested on his belly, watching the movement of troops through the valley. He liked to keep an eye on them as they marched around, officiously and ineptly patroling the long, narrow river valleys and murderous peaks where the mercenaries held reign.

Magnus wasn't afraid of him. Not anymore. No reason to be. The scratch along his cheek had healed, stitched by a skilled physician in Kathmandu. He seldom woke anymore from the nightmare of a big cat's weight on his chest and its hot breath on his face. He almost never thought of that night when he'd first realized the old, scary legends his poor mother had whispered in his ear were true, and monsters roamed the earth. Because, in the end, he knew he was already damned by his sins, and he'd rather die by Warlord's hand — or paw — than live like most men did, chained to a desk or a dock, and ground down by poverty.

Yet for all his loyalty to Warlord, he still kept a few careful inches' distance from his master. In a low voice he said, "The army's bloody casual about that payroll shipment."

"Why shouldn't they be?" Warlord smiled his expression of composed amusement. "They've transported two shipments through the mountains with no trouble at all. It's obvious the government crackdown has worked, and the rogue mercenaries are under control."

"Of course." Magnus slapped his forehead

in mocking dismay. "I should have known."

Warlord was coolly confident. "When I came here fifteen years ago, I was a seventeen-year-old driven from his home by fear and guilt, sure of his damnation. Today we're going to liberate the entire payroll for the Khalistan government officials."

"Ye've come up in the world."

"Yes. But have you seen the soldier who's using the binoculars? The one with the bolts in his ears?"

Magnus had. The guy was tall, burly, with a face that looked as if it had stopped a freight train. He wore earrings — earrings that looked not so much like jewelry, but like machinery.

"Aye. I wonder who he's looking for."

"He's looking for us."

"So he's one of the new mercenaries?"

"Good assumption." In a long, slow breath, Warlord pulled the air into his lungs. "I don't like the smell of him. He's . . . sour."

"Ye've got the nose for trouble." And now Magnus knew why. "Shall we take care of him?"

Warlord watched the big man. "No. That odor . . . it's barely a hint on the air. But it reminds me of something; I can't remember what . . . a danger to us." His black eyes grew unfocused. He seemed to be looking inward. "Something's coming . . . but it's not here yet . . ."

"Yer instincts are talking to ye, then?"

"Yes." The word was barely a whisper on Warlord's lips.

"It's good to see ye have yer concentration back," Magnus said.

Slowly Warlord turned his head and stared.

"You do have your concentration back, don't you?" Magnus asked anxiously. "Now that you have the woman in your tent?"

Warlord's voice was level. "Have the profits dropped?"

"No."

"Have the trades been untended?"

"No."

"Then what's your complaint?"

"Ye're still a wee bit distracted, and in our business that's asking for trouble." Magnus knew that with one swipe of a claw Warlord could cut out his heart. But he had a duty to the men, and to Warlord himself, and the words needed to be spoken. "Now that ye know she's safe, ye can put yer heart where it belongs — in the making of the money."

"Your savings are safe in Switzerland. And don't worry — my heart is just where it always was, cooking in hell." Warlord drew another breath deep into his lungs. His head snapped up. Without any care at all he stood. "Follow the plan. Lead the men. I've got to go."

"But . . . you . . . we . . ." Magnus could barely stammer his dismay.

Warlord leaned over, grabbed the front of Magnus's shirt, and lifted him to eye level. "*Don't* fail me."

In a single bound Warlord slid from man to panther.

CHAPTER TEN

Hurry. Hurry.

He would know. He would find her.

Hurry . . .

What was that?

Karen skidded to a halt. She turned.

The path stretched behind her, empty, rocky.

She looked around, yet saw nothing but the line of the Himalayas etched against the sky, jagged, pristine, indifferent. She listened, yet heard nothing but the ever-present wind, the thunder of a distant waterfall, the brief scream of a hawk overhead.

She'd been walking for a half hour, and she'd been nervous every minute.

But she was being ridiculous, granting Warlord powers no mere man could possess. He was gone from the camp. Unless he'd arrived back the very minute Karen left, she had a good chance of escaping.

She might not like the mountains, but she knew how to run, and she knew how to hide.

So she needed to *hurry.*

The path was no more than a slice of soft stone among the granite, but as long as it took her in the opposite direction from the warlord's camp, she would follow.

She turned back with renewed intent, walking briskly between giant stones and through a high mountain meadow. The path dipped . . . she heard the soft sound of a footfall . . . she swung around again.

Nothing was there.

She scanned the meadow.

Nothing.

A movement caught her eye. But when she looked at the place she saw only the shadow of a high and distant cloud.

Nevertheless . . . she would have sworn that some *thing* moved through the grass after her.

Impossible. It must be the wind that rippled through the flowers.

Yet the hair stood up on the back of her neck.

She would have sworn someone — or something — was watching her.

She turned back to her journey, walked around a corner, and skidded to a stop.

"Oh, help," she whispered.

The path skittered along a cliff above and a two-hundred-foot chasm below, and narrowed to only six inches of crumbling rock. Below, the raging river chewed at the stones, licking away at the support, and this crossing made the terrifying jump from the warlord's tent look simple.

When it came to heights, she was a coward. She knew it. Her father had taunted her often enough. And usually she handled her fear . . . but not today. Not when she was escaping a madman's clutches. Not when she was imagining a pursuit that wasn't there.

Taking a deep breath, she put her back against the cliff and inched forward, one foot after the other, eyes determinedly forward and staring across the chasm to the opposite cliff. She took deep, slow breaths, warding off hyper-ventilation. The cool breeze chilled the sheen of sweat on her face. She didn't want to faint. No, God, please, don't faint, because there was always a chance she'd live through the fall and suffer for days and nights of never-ending agony . . . like her mother. . . .

Worse, fear made her hallucinate.

She thought someone stood in front of her on the path. Someone who breathed hot breath on her neck.

With infinite care she turned her head to the side.

Warlord stood there, fierce and furious, staring into her eyes.

No. *Oh, no.* It wasn't possible. How did he find her so quickly?

"You would face *this* . . . rather than me?" he asked.

"What do you think?" Her insolence was instinctive — and misplaced.

For deep in his eyes that red flared, and he said, "I think you've made a terrible mistake." He grabbed her.

For a long, bitter moment she thought he was going to throw her into thin air, and she was going to die. Die as she had died every night in her nightmares.

Instead he twirled her around, shoved her back to the meadow, and manhandled her to the ground, face-first. Her cheek crushed the green grass, and her eyes filled with disappointed tears.

But not for long. She breathed deeply, got control.

Karen Sonnet did not cry. She did not complain. She did not whine.

She had failed to escape. She would take whatever punishment he handed out — and when she got the chance, she would run again.

He picked her up and moved her around as if she weighed nothing, pulling her arms behind her and snapping cold metal around her wrists.

Handcuffs.

Setting her on her feet, he shoved her up the path she'd so recently descended. Karen knew rebellion, fear . . . and a mortifying relief that she didn't have to continue down that narrow, dangerous, fracturing track.

What did that say about her? She would rather not know. "Listen," she said.

"When we get back." Warlord walked so closely behind her his heat and rage seared her skin. He held her arms, controlling her firmly.

"I don't want to get back."

"Too damned bad." He walked a little too quickly for her, bumping the backs of her legs with his, making her stumble.

"It's ridiculous to think you want me enough to commit a crime."

"I would never have thought you were a stupid woman."

She flung herself off the edge of the path and around to face him. "I am not stupid."

He spanned her waist with his hands, lifted her, and brought her close enough for their faces to touch. "What do *you* call a woman who doesn't recognize a man in rut when she sees him?"

She took a long, terrified breath as she fell into the flames in his dark eyes. "Men may be animals, but they do not rut."

"How many men have you slept with? One? Did you pick out the most anemic dweeb in your high school to perform the deed?"

"College!" she gasped, because she thought the dweeb was less dweeby if he was older.

Then Warlord laughed, a husky purr of lethal amusement, and she knew she'd made a mistake. "Of course," he said. "No glorious rush of adolescent hormones for you. You waited the proper amount of time, picked your man, and fucked him without an ounce of passion."

"That's not true!"

He wrapped one arm around her waist, brought her close against his chest, and slowly but surely let her slide down his body. "It's not true *now* . . . is it, Karen?"

Her mouth went dry with fear . . . and desire.

Damn him. She had told herself so many times that the soft emotions and strong passions no longer survived within her soul, and he made her feel them *all.*

He held her long enough for her to feel the heat of his erection. Then he turned her by the shoulders and marched her ahead of him again.

The walk back seemed to go too quickly, and each moment her tension increased.

Was he going to hurt her? Beat her? Kill her?

They reached his tent, and the narrow wooden bridge she'd searched for was now in place from the path to the tent. He shoved her across without a single care for her fear and hesitation, through the slit in the tent, and rolled her under the tapestry.

She heard Mingma's glad cry of, "Oh, miss!" as she hurried toward her.

Warlord held out his hand in a *stop* gesture.

Mingma skidded to a halt.

"Tomorrow, make sure you fix this seam in the tent." He motioned her out.

She backed toward the door, her gaze on him, her expression fearful. She stopped at the entrance, put her hands together prayerfully, and begged him with her eyes.

That, more than anything, sent a chill through Karen's veins.

"I won't kill her."

His harsh tone made Karen flinch.

As if that were the best she could hope

for, Mingma bowed her head and slipped from the tent, leaving Karen alone with a warlord.

Her handcuffed hands were an insurmountable handicap, but Karen struggled to her knees, unwilling to loll on the floor like a helpless slave.

But when she would have stood, he pressed his hand to the top of her head and held her in place. He pulled a long, shiny blade from his belt, stepped behind her . . .

She closed her eyes in the anticipation of pain . . . and suddenly her hands were free.

He pulled her arms from her coat and tossed it aside.

For a second the memory of the icon slipped through her mind.

The Madonna was safe.

Then she pulled her hands to the front and stared at them, then stared harder, trying to believe the proof before her own eyes.

The cold metal on her wrists wasn't steel, as she thought, but gold, not handcuffs, but wide and ornate gold bracelets. "What is this?"

He dangled before her eyes a cut rope, the rope that had connected the bracelets.

Still she gaped at the jewelry that wrapped her wrists so closely. The gleaming gold had been worked, decorated with tiny beads of gold that all together formed a panther on the prowl. In front of the great cat was the crescent moon, also created by a series of tiny gold beads. They were stunning, unique, barbaric — and she couldn't figure out how to remove them.

She tried to slip a finger between the metal and her wrist; the bracelets were tapered to fit close against her skin. She scratched at the seam, searching for a clasp; it was hidden by some clever device.

He watched, his mouth curled in a half smile. "They're beautiful, aren't they?"

"How do I get them *off?*"

"You don't."

"What?"

"Once they're locked, they can't be removed by anything but a jeweler with shears strong enough to cut them loose." He picked up one of her wrists and traced the panther. "See this? This is me. And see this?" He ran his finger over the moon. "That is you. This marks you as my possession, and if you run away again, everyone in this part of the world will bring you back to me."

She thought, then stammered, "B-but that makes them slave bracelets."

"Exactly."

Still she stared at the exquisite ornaments

on her wrists, trying to comprehend more than just the words. . . .

When she did, rage blasted through her.

Without a thought to the consequences, guided by instinct and blinding rage, she launched herself at him.

She caught him by surprise, too, punching him in the solar plexus, knocking the breath from his lungs while at the same time using one wrist ornament in a punch hard enough to drive the outline of the prowling panther into his cheek.

Blood splattered. He staggered backward.

"I am not a fucking decoration. I am not a thing you possess." She propelled herself up off the floor in a side kick that would have made her jujitsu master proud. A kick that should have hit Warlord's face and put him into a coma.

Yet it never landed.

Her first attack had caught him by surprise, but she wasn't the only one who knew self-defense.

He swerved down and to the side.

Her kick went over his head. She landed off balance.

He pushed her feet out from underneath her.

She hit the floor hard.

He flew through the air toward her.

Still moving, she rolled toward him.

And he missed.

Almost.

She tried to stand.

He caught one gold-covered wrist and jerked her back down.

With her last gasp she brought the other bracelet toward the back of his head.

He caught her arm, stopping her inches from her goal.

Just like that, he had her.

He used his weight and size ruthlessly, straddling her hips, pressing her wrists over her head. Leaning close to her face, he stared into her eyes. Blood dripped onto her cheek from the cuts she'd made with the bracelet. She didn't turn her head quickly enough, and a few drops splattered onto her lips.

His body weighed her down.

His blood colored her face.

She couldn't stand it. With a quick motion she wiped her cheek on the carpet, licked the blood from her lips.

Its coppery taste stung the tissues of her mouth. Then —

The first grenade flew from his hand in a beautiful arc through the bright blue Tibetan sky, right into the convoy, and landed in the lead Jeep. The little pissant of a driver screamed; then the explosion rocked the pass and blew the Chinese general into a million pieces of —

As abruptly as she'd left, she landed back on the floor of Warlord's tent. She sucked in a long gasp of air. Looked around wildly. Asked, "What was that?"

Warlord held her just as he had before she . . . before she what? Flew into a memory? His memory?

And he didn't know — because it hadn't happened. *What she'd seen was impossible.*

" 'What was that?' " he mocked. "My blood in your mouth, my body mastering yours — what do you think? You *are* a decoration. You *are* my possession. And it's time that I showed you what that means."

Still winded, she gasped harshly and managed, "At least I've marked you, too."

"I heal . . . quickly." He smiled, his teeth bright white and sharp, and the combination of his amusement and the drying smear of blood on his cheek made her rage cool, and made her realize just how untenable was her situation.

"You look at me with those big eyes that are the same color as the ocean in winter and wonder if I'm going to hurt you." He tried to kiss her, but she turned her head away, so he whispered in her ear, "I would never hurt you. But I promise that before I am done with you, every time you think of pleasure, you'll think of me."

CHAPTER ELEVEN

Karen stared into Warlord's black eyes.

Did he feel anything for her? About her? Besides murderous rage? Besides lust?

He turned her onto her stomach, lifted her, and dropped her onto the mattress. It was still bouncing as she flipped over to find him waiting for her, that ferocious smile in place. He swung the rope before her eyes like a hypnotist's dangling watch.

"No!" She grabbed the center, tried to jerk it away.

He clutched her wrist and wrapped the rope around the bracelet. Gently — he had no reason to be rough; her struggles were getting her nowhere — he pulled her arm up, slid the rope through the brass posts on the headboard, and grasped her other wrist.

They wrestled.

He won.

When he was finished, the rope wound around one wide bracelet, through the posts, and around the other bracelet. There was play in the rope; she could move her arms twelve inches in any direction, could use the ropes to leverage herself toward the headboard — but she was tied. "I hate you so much."

"You don't yet. But you will." He pulled out his knife.

A gush of fear struck deep into her core.

He was angry. So angry. The blade gleamed in the light of the lanterns. He pressed the tip of the knife to her throat right over her windpipe, and smiled into her face.

"Don't struggle," he whispered. "I'd hate to slip." He ran the point down her throat to the neckline of his T-shirt — and with one clean slice he cut it open down to her waist.

She shrieked, and hated herself for it.

"I told you. I won't hurt you." He used the tip of the knife to move the material away from first one breast, then the other.

Her nipples hardened from the cold . . . and maybe from the slow, betraying touch of his hungry tongue to his lower lip.

That blade cut the sleeves. The T-shirt lay beneath her in ruins.

He slipped the knife into the leather holster strapped on the headboard. He used his hands, one each, to press her clenched fists. "So rebellious," he chided. "It won't do you any good. I'm bigger, I'm stronger, and I already know how to make you purr." He wrapped his fingers around her wrists above the bracelets, then slid up toward her elbow, over her straining biceps, and over her bunched shoulders. "So much tension." He used his thumbs to massage her tight muscles above her shoulder blade, and his fingertips to massage the cords at the back of her neck. "You won't be able to keep it up. But definitely you should try. I'll enjoy watching you yield."

Passionate, sharp hatred burned in her stomach.

How could she have welcomed him into her tent, into her bed? He was nothing but a . . . "You're a snake," she said, the accusation dipped in poison.

"No. I am a panther. And you are my mate."

"No."

"We'll see what you say . . . later." He used his thumbs on her nipples. Over and over he rubbed them, first with the pad of his thumb, then with the edge of his fingernail, until she wanted to whimper — and not from fear.

Damn him. If he meant to use her, couldn't

he be a man and get it over with quickly?

Instead he slid his arm beneath her, lifting her, arching her up to his hungry mouth. He suckled softly at first, then harder, taking almost all of her slight breast into his mouth, manipulating it with his tongue and teeth and lips until her eyelids closed and she found her fingernails clawing the pillows under her head.

With careful deliberation he placed his knee between her legs and thrust his thigh against her.

The hard canvas seam of the jeans rubbed against her clit, and her sensation of fullness abruptly became painful.

No, not painful. That wasn't the right word. She was . . . needy.

The bastard who held her, who moved her on him, had chased her down, marked her as his, scared her to death, and now . . . now he was using all his knowledge of her and probably a thousand other women to make her come. Come so fast and hard she'd be ashamed of herself. Of her weakness.

So she gasped, "What's the matter? Can't get it up?"

Slowly he let her down onto the sheets. Rising on his knees above her, he lowered his hands to his worn brown leather belt.

132

She couldn't look away as, with leisurely care, he pulled the two ends apart, then opened the buttons, one by one.

He wore underwear, plain white cotton underwear made, by the looks of it, by some American manufacturer. And as he pushed the jeans down, his erection tented the material. He eased his briefs off — and abruptly the whole business was so much worse.

She'd seen his penis before. Of course. But today it looked longer, wider. It rose from among the curling black hairs, a pale marble veined with blue, and the mere sight of it made her feel a ferocious desire to touch.

But she couldn't. He had tied her . . . his slave.

She closed her eyes and turned her head away. "I wish you'd hurry this up. I don't know what you do all day long, but I'm sure warlords have some duties."

He laughed, and it sounded like a purr. "No. I'm like a hunting cat. There are great, long hours of relaxation, followed by brief bursts of furious activity."

"Which is this?"

"My favorite combination of both." Something soft and luxurious stroked her throat, tickled down her breastbone, slipped under the loose waistband of her borrowed jeans to caress her belly. And for a second she thought she felt the drag of a long, sharp claw across her tender skin.

Her eyes shot open.

Above her Warlord leaned on one elbow and examined her face. "I don't want you to hide behind your lids. I want you completely open to me."

"What *was* that?"

He showed her a glorious, colorful peacock feather and whisked it lightly across her breasts. "This?"

"It felt like . . ." Her gaze fell on him.

His pants were gone. He wore only a tight black short-sleeved T-shirt that clung to his muscled chest. His sculpted body was tense with anticipation, yet still he coolly dusted her skin with the feather, intent on lifting her past the level of suspense to mindless craving.

He laid his palm flat on her stomach, right above the waistband of her jeans — his jeans — and slipped his hand beneath the tough material. He pressed her belly, simply pressed it, and that one point of contact felt so good. Reassuring, kind, as if he cared, not about winning, but about making her happy.

He compelled her surrender based on the

most egregious lie of all.

She yanked at the rope.

He watched with interest. "Testing the knots? That won't help. I was a Boy Scout."

"A Boy Scout? Is *this* what they taught you in camp?"

"No, they didn't offer this merit badge. I imagine camp would have been a lot more popular if they had."

Damn him for tying a good knot. And damn him for making her want to laugh.

Laugh! Now!

She used all her weight to drag herself up the bed, but the rope held, and while she moved up he held the legs of the jeans and pulled them down.

"You're a pig."

"A panther."

"Don't flatter yourself."

"And yet the pants are off."

They weren't really. They were caught at the top of her thighs, and when he teased the feather over her hips, she wanted to kick the crap out of him.

She couldn't, because he'd managed to imprison her legs as efficiently as he'd imprisoned her hands. And her.

Frustration scorched her, so she gave a warrior's yell and walked out of the pants.

What did it matter? He would have her

out of them at his pleasure, and she would not lie there while he did with her as he wished. In a frenzy of temper she kicked at his chest, hoping to catch him unaware and knock him backward and breathless. Instead he snagged her ankle and used her motion to leverage her up and onto her stomach. Her wrists crossed. Her face pressed into the pillows, and she bounded up onto her elbows and knees to scream her defiance.

Immediately he was behind her, between her legs, catching and holding her hips close to his. His erection probed, found, entered, glided.

She grabbed the brass bars. The cold metal against her palms and the heat of his hard-on formed an electric current through her body, making her arch as lightning shot through her spine. "You bastard. You lousy jerk. You scumbag."

"That's right." He thrust hard and deep. "Hate me. Call me names. Be fierce." He reached around, under her belly, and used his fingers to manipulate her clit until she undulated beneath him. "But *care*. By God. *Feel*."

Feel? She couldn't stop feeling. He was deep inside her, controlling her motions with his arm around her hips, making her move for him, with him. Fruitlessly she fought him, trying to establish her own rhythm, to use him like a vibrator, to bring herself to orgasm.

He would have none of that. His motion inside her was deep, small, controlled, inciting yet not satisfying.

Her breath rasped in her lungs. She fought her way forward on the bed — and he let her — until she could pull herself up onto the brass bars on the headboard. Her cheek, her shoulders, her breasts, her belly rested against the cold metal, and still he remained below her, thrusting up into her body in those slow, hot, forbidden motions that made the lightning spread along each nerve. She no longer called him names. She begged him. "Please, Warlord. Please. Deeper. Now. Faster."

"No." His voice trembled as he fought his desires. "You wait. You yield. You call me your master and then I'll let you come."

She was frenzied with lust, but she hadn't lost her mind. "I *won't.*"

He pulled almost all the way out. He leaned against her back and whispered in her ear, "One of us will win. Both of us will suffer."

"I don't give a damn if we both die."

He laughed, his amusement vibrating from his chest to her back, his breath lifting the hairs on her neck. "But what a sweet death it will be."

CHAPTER TWELVE

What was it Warlord had said? *Every time you think of pleasure, you'll think of me.*

He'd made good on his threat. Karen had no idea how long she'd been confined in Warlord's tent. She no longer knew if it was day or night. She knew only that she waged an endless, constant, sensuous battle to keep her pride . . . and if something didn't happen soon, she would give him what he wanted. She would yield. She would call him *master.* She would be not Karen Sonnet but Warlord's slave.

Because no matter what they were doing, she thought of pleasure. When he fed her the meals Mingma fixed them, she watched his long fingers and thought how skillfully they feathered along her spine. When he talked to her, she watched his glorious lips and remembered how they felt as they moved against her mouth in long, leisurely, damp kisses. When he walked away from her, she watched the firm, concave muscles of his butt and remembered how his cheeks felt under her palms as he thrust in and out and in and out.

And when she stared at the bracelets he had placed on her wrists, she thought them beautiful. . . . *Oh, God.* He had drugged her with sex.

She hated him. She hated this place. She hated herself and her own weakness.

Today, as every day, she woke with a single thought — she had to get away. She had to escape before winter set in, for then she would be trapped forever.

Normally in the morning she heard nothing but Mingma's soft murmur speaking to Warlord, and the wind as it whistled a mocking tune. But today she lay very still, listening to a strange man speak from a position just inside the door. "Ye've got to come out, man. There's trouble breaking out among the ranks. The last raid went so well it left some of the men hungry for more. The others are nervous, worried about the reports of trouble."

"Which group are you in, Magnus?" Warlord's smooth, menacing drawl raised the hair on the back of her neck.

Karen heard the sharp sound of fist against flesh, and flipped over in shock.

Magnus was short, stocky, balding, with bandy legs and a wide stance. He had a thin red scar on one cheek, and he was missing the little finger on both hands. He held his fists close to his chest like a boxer in a prizefight waiting for a fatal blow.

Warlord was a head taller, barefoot, dressed in his half-buttoned jeans. He was staring, narrow eyed, at Magnus, and wiping the blood from his mouth. "Shall I kill you now, or should we go outside?"

"Ye'll not kill me." Magnus lifted his chin at him. "Ye know I'm in the right."

Warlord still stared, poised on the balls of his feet, ready to spring. Then gradually, deliberately, he relaxed. "All right. Talk to me."

"Two weeks ye've been in here, man, shaking the tent night and day."

Karen stealthily pulled the covers over her crimson face.

"Ye've got responsibilities. These men follow ye because ye keep them safe and make them rich. But riches will do them no good if the rumors are true."

"What rumors?"

"That the enforcers, the ones the militaries hired to get rid of us . . . that they're led by another like you." Magnus lowered his voice, but she could still hear him. "A beastie who wanders the mountains in animal form."

Magnus thought Warlord was a werewolf? *Oh, brother.* Warlord really had him conned.

"Benjie and Dehqan disappeared while on patrol, and I found a trail of blood headed toward the army camp just over the border. I got close enough to hear screaming down there. They were racking someone. Then Benjie showed up here."

"Unharmed?"

"Hale and hearty. He said Dehqan decided to head home to Afghanistan."

"You don't believe him."

"Not for a minute. No one does. He's jumpy as a cat, and Dae-Jung caught him signaling into the mountains with a mirror."

Karen peeked at the two men. They stood with their heads together, intent on their discussion, and while she didn't know for sure who Magnus was, it was clear to her that Warlord respected and liked him.

"He's betrayed us," Warlord said.

"No doubt about it," Magnus answered.

"Benjie's always been the one to take the easy road. I wonder what they promised him?"

"Money."

"No. Respect. That's what our foolish Benjie craves." Warlord thoughtfully dabbed at the blood on his split lip. "Very well. Bring him to me. Let's see if I can convince him to give me a different version of the events."

"Down by the fire pit?" Magnus asked.

"Oh, yes. Definitely down by the fire pit." Warlord clapped Magnus on the shoulder. "Bring him in."

When the Scotsman left, he was whistling.

Warlord opened a chest, pulled out a long-sleeved T-shirt, and dragged it over his head. He tucked it into his jeans, buttoned up, pulled out a studded leather belt, and slipped it through the loops. Seating himself, he pulled on wool socks and heavy black boots that laced up his calf. Reaching into the chest once more, he extracted two sharp, slender knives and slipped them into his boots. He stood and shook his jeans down, then strapped a large holster around his chest and a smaller one around each arm. He placed a Smith & Wesson 952 in the larger holster, Kel-Tec P-32s in the smaller ones.

The man was gunning for bear.

He pulled on a loose black coat, checked his weapons, then glanced at Karen.

She closed her eyes and pretended to be asleep.

So of course she didn't hear him approach, didn't know he was there until he whispered in her ear, "I won't be long, darling. You're tired. Stay in bed."

She sat up so fast she cracked him under the chin with her head.

He laughed and rubbed his battered face. "It's not my day."

"This is real trouble, isn't it?"

"What makes you think so?"

"Magnus hit you. You don't let anyone hit you unless . . ." Turning her head, she looked up into his face — the pale skin covered by the heavy beard and surrounded by the wild hair, the strong nose, the supple lips, and, dominating the whole, those black, black eyes.

"Unless I deserve it?"

"Yes."

"Do you know what I love best about you?"

"I'm not stupid?" she said tartly, but at the same time she lightly touched the split in his lips.

He corrected her. "I used to lie on my stomach above the construction site and watch you."

"You watched me?" That explained that prickly feeling she used to get at the back of her neck.

"I couldn't tear my eyes away. You work

144

hard. You're smart. You're stubborn. You shine with an inner light, and I hated what you were doing to me, making me realize what I'd become, changing me against my will. I've had other women, but I remember only you. You fill my mind. You fill my soul."

Damn him. How dared he try to enchant her?

"It's a little late for sweet talk." She turned her head away. "Are you going to kill him? That Benjie?"

"It depends on how much he's willing to tell us and how fast he gives out the information." Warlord sat back on his haunches. "Why? Do you feel sorry for him?"

"No. Not if he's betrayed his comrades."

"You don't think much like a woman."

"How does a woman think?" She froze him with a steely cold gaze.

"Women are always all" — he wiggled his fingers and made his voice high and girlie — " 'Ooh, don't hurt him.' "

"You've been watching too many old movies, the ones where the female always falls down and twists her ankle while trying to escape." She bared her teeth in a feral smile. "Try *Kill Bill.* It'll give you a new appreciation of just what violence a woman is capable of."

"You're such a pretty woman. Such a

strong woman. A construction manager." Leaning over her, he slid his fingers through her hair. "What made you decide to become a construction manager?"

Like she was going to tell him about her early private hell. "What made you decide to become a ruthless warlord?" she countered.

His fingers never paused, and his eyes gleamed like obsidian. "I have a natural talent for murder." Yanking her hair, he tilted her head back and kissed her deeply.

She tasted his blood on her tongue and —

The first grenade flew from his hand in a beautiful arc through the bright blue Tibetan sky, right into the convoy, and landed in the lead Jeep. The little pissant of a driver screamed; then the explosion rocked the pass and blew the Chinese general into a million pieces of chicken chow mein. In the moment of shocked silence that followed, Warlord smiled with bone-deep delight; the mean son of a bitch would never again beat a woman to death and firebomb a nomad settlement in retaliation for offering hospitality to an American.

Then the Chinese soldiers sprang into action, spraying the rocks with bullets. His men returned fire. The narrow pass rang with shots. The smell of gunpowder stung his nose, and still he smiled as he fitted the bayonet to his weapon, charged down the hills, and spitted the yellow bastards until blood spattered him from head to toe.

A bullet struck him in the back. Pain exploded in his lungs. He staggered. Dropped to his knees.

But no one on this battlefield could kill him.

Twisting, he looked up at the guy pointing the pistol at him.

Victor Rivera was an older mercenary. He was taking advantage of this opportunity to rid himself of a raw young American interloper. He was from Argentina. And the word he screamed when Warlord speared his gonads was pure Spanish profanity — and the last word he would ever speak.

Warlord lifted Victor's genitals on the tip of the bayonet. Blood dripped down his rifle onto his hands, and into the sudden silence he roared, "This is my enemy! Who else is my enemy?"

The Chinese gaped, then broke ranks and ran.

Rivera's mercenaries moved in.

Warlord laughed, pulled Rivera's pistol from his belt, and shot the lead man in the head.

He was going to hell.

No — he was in hell.

With a gasp Karen returned to the present.

She was in Warlord's tent. Warlord was gone. She lay prone on the bed. Her heart pounded, shaking her chest. Wildly she lifted her hands and looked at them. They weren't covered with blood. She looked down at herself. She wore a loose, pale, sheer nightgown, unstained by gore.

Porcelain clinked softly. Mingma knelt beside the low table, arranging the breakfast dishes and pouring tea into a mug. The scent of her tobacco wafted across the tent. Everything was . . . normal.

Yet Karen was not. She had been somewhere, seen something she should never have seen.

She had tasted Warlord's blood; then she had seen a terrible event long past, and seen it through Warlord's eyes. "Where is he?" she demanded.

Mingma looked up, and Karen's expression must have been alarming, for she stood and backed away. "He left. Said to let you sleep." She gestured at the food. "Breakfast?"

Karen sat up and cupped her head in her palms. What was happening to her? How could she be in Warlord's mind? In his past? Had she truly, finally gone completely crazy?

"Miss?" Mingma touched her shoulder.

In a violent gesture, Karen knocked her

hand away. "Don't touch me." She hadn't forgotten Mingma's betrayal, and right now she didn't need some supernatural acid trip to smell trouble brewing. No matter how sincerely kind Mingma seemed, if the Sherpa had been willing to sell her out to Warlord, she would be willing to sell out Warlord to whatever forces were brewing. Not that Karen cared about him, but she knew he protected her, and in a camp of one hundred men surrounded by hostile territory, protection was a commodity to be valued.

Lifting her gaze to Mingma, she said, "Step out and tell me what's happening out there."

Mingma walked to the tent flap and lifted it.

Karen heard a high, thin scream.

"Benjie," Mingma said.

"Won't he talk?"

"He is afraid." Mingma stared out into the camp, then scanned the horizon.

"Afraid of Warlord?"

"I think . . . afraid of the Other." Mingma's serenity was cracking.

"What Other?"

"The men speak of the Other, a mercenary who will wipe Warlord away and hold this territory forever."

Karen spied the opportunity she'd been looking for.

She stood. She pulled on a robe. She knelt by the table and began to eat. "Leave me."

"Miss, if you try to run again, he will kill me." Mingma's voice shook.

"If Warlord falls, who will pay your fee? Who will support your son in America?" Karen prodded Mingma in her weak spot. "Shouldn't you think about leaving?"

The color drained out of Mingma's brown face, and she backed away from Karen. "Miss, you see the future?"

"Only a fool wouldn't see this future." Karen ate steadily — she would need the sustenance — and didn't look up.

Mingma backed away toward the entrance, paused and lingered, then slipped from the tent.

Karen gave a small, pleased smile. Getting rid of Mingma was the first step toward freedom. For the first time in two weeks Karen was alone. Now she could do what had to be done.

She needed her hiking boots. She needed clothes that fit and that she could hike in. Most of all, she needed her coat.

She hurried to his open clothing trunk. Kneeling on the Kashmiri rug, she sorted through his clothes.

And there it was. Her coat. She dug in the pockets, and as her fingers clutched the icon she closed her eyes in relief.

The Madonna was safe.

She pulled it out and sat there, holding the icon in her hand, looking into the Virgin Mary's large, dark, sad eyes. As she did, the events of that day swam through her brain like a fevered dream. The discovery of the grave . . . the body of the child . . . those eyes, so much like Karen's, sad, dutiful, and a startling blue-green . . . and the dissolution of the fragile body beneath Karen's touch.

Then the thunder of the rockfall, Phil's refusal to leave, Warlord's appearance . . .

Every moment since had been out of her control. But what other course could she have taken? If Warlord hadn't pulled her onto the motorcycle, she would have died. Now here she was, a captive to a man who both frightened and enthralled her.

She had never been religious — she'd had no chance, for her father had no patience with Bible-thumpers — but now, in a prayer that came from her heart, she pleaded, "Mary, please help me find the way home."

Home . . . She didn't have a home. Her father's dark mansion in Montana was decorated with antlers and brown leather, and although she'd been raised there, she was always on edge, looking over her shoulder, waiting for the next sharp criticism, the next impatient sneer.

So why had she begged the Madonna to help her go home?

"What is that?" Warlord's soft voice spoke behind her.

She gasped out loud — when had she become such a girl? — and brought the icon to her bosom, every instinct commanding that she protect the holy object. "I found it," she said. Had he heard her?

"Where did you find a Russian icon?" Warlord caught her wrist and brought the Madonna into the light. He appraised it with a glance. "The style looks as if it was painted early in the history of the Orthodox Church."

"How do you know?"

"In Russia, before the Soviets — and during, sometimes — the icon was the heart of the family, venerated above all things. They're the Gospel in paint, and kept in the beautiful corner, the *krasny ugol,* the red corner."

"The red corner?" What was he talking about?

"In the Russian culture, red means beautiful." He spoke with the calm certainty of an expert. "These icons, especially icons of the Virgin Mary, were considered miracles. Every pose, every color had meaning, and there are folk legends of evil and good fighting for possession of the icons."

"What do the legends say?" More important, how did he know? She had lived through weeks of strange events, but this was perhaps the strangest, that this creature of mystery and shadow should converse with such knowledge about the Russian culture.

"You know, the usual. The devil makes a deal with an evil man. To seal the pact the evil man offers to give the devil his family icon, a single piece of wood painted with four different images of the Madonna. But his mother refuses to let her son take the icons. So he kills her, washes his hands in her blood, and while he drinks to celebrate closing the deal, the devil divides the Madonnas and, in a flash of fire, hurls them to the four ends of the earth, where they are lost." Warlord stared at the icon as if he recognized it. "Hmm. Lost for a millennium now."

She didn't like the glib way he recited the story. She didn't like the way he held her wrist. She didn't like the gleam in his eyes.

"May I see it?" he asked, but it was nothing more than a formality, for at the same time he scooped it away from her.

As soon as he grasped the icon, she heard a sizzling sound, smelled burning flesh.

He tossed the icon into her lap. He stepped back and stared. At her. At the icon. Then at his hands.

"What happened?" Picking up the icon, she cradled it in her palms. It wasn't hot, yet he acted as if it had scorched him.

Walking to the washbasin, he plunged his hands into the cool water. Still in that conversational tone, he said, "Those old legends are rife with superstitions."

She looked at the Madonna, and she suspected the truth. "What deal did the evil man make with the devil?"

Warlord stood with his back to her and stared into the basin. "One that damned his descendants to hell."

"Are you a descendant of that evil man?"

"You're a woman of good sense. You don't believe such a dumb story."

She'd seen the child, dead for a thousand years, open her eyes. She'd lived Warlord's memories. She'd heard Warlord's flesh sizzle when he'd held the icon. In a broken voice she said, "I don't know what I believe."

"It doesn't matter, anyway." He continued to stand with his hands in the water and his back to her. "I'm sending you away."

For a moment, his casual tone muted the impact of his words. Then she understood, and elation tore though her . . . followed by an inexplicable sense of loss. And why should she feel loss? This was the goal she'd wanted, demanded, struggled toward achieving. She could go home knowing she had never yielded to his sexual domination. Leaving now would allow her to keep her pride and integrity.

Yet still the loss was there.

And the fear, for she knew he would never let her go unless something was terribly, horribly wrong.

"Why? What's happened?" she asked.

"My raiding has pissed off armies on both sides of the border, and they brought in an experienced mercenary troop to take me out and keep things under control. The Varinskis are well-known for their terror tactics. It's too dangerous for you to stay."

He'd brought this on himself, then. All right. "I'll need my boots and some clothes that fit me."

He turned to face her, and she was shocked to see him laughing. "Practical, prosaic Karen." Reaching under the table, he found a key, handed it to her, and pointed. "In that trunk."

She rose. "I'll get dressed."

He walked to the tent flap, lifted it, and listened. She could almost see him go on alert. "Hurry."

She didn't need to be told twice. She stripped off the robe and got into the clothes with swift efficiency. When at first he helped, she tried to shove him away, but it soon became clear that he had no lascivious intentions. He worked to place weapons on her body. He strapped a Glock around her chest and a knife up her sleeve, and he loaded her backpack with rounds of ammo and dried rations. He filled a canteen with water and placed it on her belt, and gave her a multitool that matched the one she'd lost in the rock slide. He placed a compass and GPS in her pocket and, miracle of miracles, he hung her passport around her neck.

Her passport . . . she'd thought it lost in the rockfall. "Where did you get that?"

"I stole it from your tent many, many weeks ago."

"You ass," she mumbled, but right now she was grateful. Having her passport would expedite her trip home — and keep her from having to apply to her father for help.

As they worked, she knew he was listening to something outside. At first she heard nothing, the thick tapestries insulating her from the tumult outside. Slowly the clamor pierced the silence in the tent. The noise grew, growled, adding an edge to her haste.

When she had finished lacing her boots, he knelt in front of her. "Head for Kathmandu. Don't stop walking for eighteen hours. Don't trust anyone unless you're in the American embassy, and even then, be wary." He looked up, his eyes dark and serious. "No matter what — survive."

"I will."

"I know." He went to the back of the tent and ripped the seam open.

Noise from the battle blasted into the tent. She heard screams, gunshots, growls of fury, and brutish war cries.

He flipped a section of the walk up and around, then laid it out across the gap. There was the bridge she'd sought when she escaped before. "Remember everything I told you."

"I do."

"When you get back to the States, can you do one more thing for me?"

Call his mother, she supposed, and say reassuring stuff. "Sure. Anything."

Taking her face between his hands, he kissed her. Kissed her deeply, swiftly, with the intent to brand himself on her.

She didn't want to, but she responded. She tasted him, knew him, absorbed him. And, yes, felt loss for a relationship and a man doomed from the start.

Pulling away, he looked into her eyes. "Somehow, someday, I will come for you. Watch for me." He kissed her again. Turned away. Ran toward the front of the tent. Pushed the tent flap open. The last thing she saw was Warlord leaping off the platform and into the melee, a pistol blazing in each hand.

He wasn't there to hear, but she answered anyway: "I'll do anything but that." Picking up her backpack, she walked across the bridge.

She didn't look back.

CHAPTER THIRTEEN

Montana, five weeks later

Karen stood in the doorway of her father's study. The heavy burgundy curtains were closed. The walnut-paneled walls were dark. A new elk head hung above the cold fireplace.

Pen in hand, Jackson Sonnet sat at his desk in a pool of light, a short, broad-shouldered, gray-haired man, scowling as he read the papers before him.

"Daddy?" Her voice broke a little.

He froze. Paused. Without looking up, without a note of welcome or relief or joy, he said, "It's about time you got home."

Her breath caught on a bright shard of broken hope. Just this once, when he didn't know if she was alive or dead, she'd hoped . . . She put down her bag.

It contained her passport, her wallet, enough clothes to last a couple of days . . . and the mangled remains of her slave bracelets. When she'd reached Timbuktu, she'd had a jeweler cut them off. He'd offered her a nice sum for the twenty-two-carat gold; she'd refused. Because she could get a better price somewhere else, she'd told herself. Because she might need the money . . . or because she wanted to cast the bracelets into the fires of Mount Doom, where they would return to the home of evil from whence they came.

She winced.

She might still be a little traumatized.

She advanced into the room. She wanted to fall on her father's neck and weep out her agony, but she knew better. No matter that she'd vanished into the Himalayas; this was no different from all the other home-comings.

So she gave her report. "The mountain collapsed on the site. The rockfall filled the valley. The hotel can't be built."

"You took five weeks to get around to telling me that?" He looked up, his eyes the light, piercing blue that had always, always terrified her as a child.

She'd thought long and hard about what to say to her father. He wouldn't care that she'd suffered humiliation; he would see only that she suffered no crippling injury. So she decided on the truth, or at least the least revealing, least mortifying version of the truth. "I was kidnapped and held captive."

"By whom?"

"One of the warlords who populate the area." *The* Warlord . . . but she wasn't going into that. She ran her tongue around the tender inner flesh of her mouth, and for a brief second tasted the memory of his blood. On the edge of her mind a nightmare hovered, ready to be replayed.

She wasn't going to think about him. Ever.

"Before or after the rockfall?"

"He saved me, then kept me."

Jackson slammed his chair back so hard it hit the far wall.

Karen flinched.

Jackson came to his feet, his heavy hands clenched into fists. His voice low with contempt, he asked, "Do you expect me to believe that?"

"Yes. Why not? What do you think happened?"

"You've been screwing around with this guy because he had a black leather coat and a motorcycle."

"How did you know that?" How did he know *anything* about Warlord?

"You ran away with him and when he was tired of you, you come to me with this cock-

and-bull story —"

Where was he getting his information, with enough truth in it to make her look bad? "Dad. I can't believe you haven't sent someone to take pictures of the hotel site."

"I did," he admitted.

"Did you happen to notice the millions of tons of rock obliterating the base of the mountain? I didn't fake that rockfall." She was incredulous. "Not even you could be that paranoid."

Wrong thing to say. Definitely the wrong thing.

Jackson flushed an ugly red. His harsh voice rose. "Do you know how much that project cost me?"

"It almost cost you your daughter!"

"My daughter," he sneered. "Is that what you think?"

Then he looked surprised, as if someone else had spoken.

The silence in the room was profound, and she found herself listening to the rasp of her own breathing. "What do you mean?"

"Nothing," he muttered.

"You mean, I'm not . . . your daughter?"

His gaze dropped, and he actually looked discomfited. "It doesn't matter."

"Of course." Her hands hung loosely at her sides, but her brain was racing. "That explains everything. The indifference, the impatience, the constant withholding of affection and approval . . . I'm not *yours*."

"What difference does it make? I've had the trouble of raising you. I've paid for your education." His brief moment of remorse faded; he was working himself into a temper.

"Get mad." For the first time, she understood him. "That's the way you deal with everything that makes you look bad or feel uncomfortable."

"What man wouldn't get mad? A wife who's out screwing while I work, and all I get out of it is a worthless child. If your mother had to leave me with a kid, why the hell did it have to be a girl?"

Karen didn't care about his condemnation. She had to find out. . . . "Who was my father?"

"My best friend. Who the hell else?"

She could almost taste Jackson's bitterness. "Who was your best friend?"

"Dan Nighthorse. That bastard Blackfoot Indian."

"I remember him." Barely. He was a shadowy figure hovering in the background of her mind; those early memories were mostly taken up with the recollection of her mother's hands, her mother's smile, her mother's eyes . . . her mother's death.

"He was always skulking around here, in between taking tourists into the mountains to live off the land and see the beautiful scenery. She loved to climb, was an expert, wanted us to go up into the hills to commune with nature, like a couple of hippies. I've got no patience for that crap."

"I know." Jackson might build hotels that catered to trekkers, but unless he could hunt, unless an animal died by his hand, he wasn't interested in camping.

"She nagged me, and finally I told her to stop bothering me and go with him." He looked up at the collection of antlers that lined his walls. "I can't believe she fell for his pile of bull."

A horrifying thought struck her. "Did you kill them?"

"Your parents? No, I didn't kill them, no matter how much they deserved it. I was working while they were out romping around in the wilderness, and a freak snowstorm set in. Your mother stepped off the goddamned cliff —"

"I know." Karen's nightmares had always been of falling.

"Nighthorse broke his neck trying to rescue her, and she damned near froze before the Civil Air Patrol spotted her and brought her in. My father called me and told me to come home and say good-bye to my wife, and *he* informed me then what everybody else knew — that they'd been screwing around behind my back for years."

"I remember Grandpa." A tall, big-bellied, nasty man who abused his son, ignored her, and sent the housekeeper fleeing.

"When I got to the hospital, they told me the internal bleeding couldn't be stopped. Like I cared." He stopped, cleared his throat. He was trembling with some great emotion.

Karen realized he suffered. From humiliation, she supposed.

"Abigail wanted my promise to raise you as if you were my own."

"You gave it to her?" Karen couldn't imagine her father yielding to pressure, not even from a dying woman.

"I gave it to her." He sneered again, but this time he was facing the mirror. "My father said I was a fool, and I was. But I loved her. Bet you didn't know that."

"You . . . loved her?"

"God only knows why. She wasn't good for anything. Couldn't keep the house tended. Couldn't keep the ranch going. She whined because I didn't spend enough time with her. She bitched because I took my pleasures while I traveled. Then she cheated on me with my best friend."

"Imagine that." Everything inside Karen, all the parts that had been unsure, in wonder, seemed to grow strong. Her lungs breathed, her heart beat, her balance was so sure not even an earthquake could throw her off the earth. And all the emotional parts of her, the ones that held on to hope, fell away at the light that shone on her life. "What made you tell me this now? Why, when I've done nothing but work for you, try to please you, perform when no other can — why decide I betrayed you?"

"Phil told me."

"Phil?" She tried to comprehend. "Phil Chronies?"

"Yes, that surprises you, doesn't it?" Jackson surveyed her wide-eyed shock with grim satisfaction. "None other than Phil Chronies, the man who lost his arm in my service. The man you left to die."

"Because he was too greedy to leave the gold —" Suddenly she realized what she was doing, and stopped short. She would *not* justify herself and her actions. Not to her father. Not when she'd just returned from the dead to find not relief, not welcome, but accusations. "How can you believe the worst guy in your whole organization without even asking me what happened?"

166

"You are your mother's daughter, screwing around with some black-haired foreigner instead of working like you should."

She heard the echo of a bitterness so old it had started long ago. "Yes. I am my mother's daughter. I'm loyal until the day when I realize that nothing I do can make you . . . approve of me." *Love me,* she meant, but he wouldn't understand the term.

Warlord had done one thing for her. He had shown her a sort of love — warped, possessive, but given freely. Warlord had bound her with a rope, but now, as she looked at her father, she realized how tightly she'd been bound by his expectations.

Now she was released.

She took a step forward. "You're a fool, Jackson Sonnet. I would have done anything for you. Anything. And you listened while Phil Chronies poured poison in your ear. You took his part against me." She laughed briefly, and with a sense of freedom she'd never experienced before. "Thank you, Father, for making it possible for me to follow my dream."

He shook with baffled frustration. "What the hell are you talking about?"

"I'm out of here." She looked down at her bag. She was wearing her coat. The icon was in her pocket.

Except for her picture of her mother, and she would pick that up on the way out, there was nothing she needed here. Nothing in this house she wanted.

"I'm going to England. I'm visiting the Victoria and Albert Museum. I'm going to Spain to visit every winery in the Rioja. I'm going to eat oranges and olives and tomatoes and bread. I'm going to make friends who know how to play. I'm going to bike, and swim in the Mediterranean, and bask in the sun." She took a long breath, then released it . . . and all the tension of twenty-eight years spent bent and warped by Jackson Sonnet's unending pressure.

He blasted her with all his usual subtlety. "That's the stupidest plan I've ever heard."

"It's not a plan, Father. For the next year, I'm not *planning* a thing. I'm going to let the chips fall as they will."

"How the hell do you think you're going to pull this off?"

"Thanks to you, Father, and your stupid schedules that assured I'd never have time off, I've amassed a small fortune, and I can afford to take a year off." Reflectively, she added, "Or two."

"Are you insane? You've worked every day of your life. What makes you think you can spend time doing nothing but —"

"But what I want? What I've always wanted? I'm going to be civilized. I'm going to be a girl." She tried to think of what would impress him with how serious she was. "I'm going to get a pedicure."

"A pedicure?" He couldn't have looked more outraged — or alarmed. "What the hell do you want a pedicure for?"

"I've only had one in my whole life — and I liked it. Now I'm going to have as many as I want."

"You're fired!"

She thought about it. "No. I definitely think I quit first." She bowed to him in mocking appreciation. "Good-bye, Father. Or should I call you Mr. Sonnet? Enjoy your time with Phil, and try to make yourself believe he's telling you the truth."

The blood vessels that etched her father's ruddy cheeks popped up like scarlet rivers on a map. "I can't believe you're giving up like this."

"I'm not giving up. I'm finding myself." Picking up her bag, she walked out the door.

She didn't look back.

CHAPTER FOURTEEN

Two years later
Aqua Horizon Spa and Inn
Sedona, Arizona

Karen Sonnet stood in the hotel's cool, tall, modern wood-and-stone foyer, talking to Chisholm Burstrom, president and CEO of Texas-based Burstrom Technologies, and his wife, Debbie, about tonight's events, when a new guest stepped through the door — and Karen's breath caught.

The stranger crossed toward the check-in desk. His black hair was cut by a master stylist, and his sculpted face was clean shaven. His stride was long and confident, and his immaculate black European-cut suit fit his masculine form perfectly. His crisp white shirt and blue tie could have belonged to any wealthy businessman who visited Aqua Horizon Spa and Inn to relax and do business.

This guy looked nothing like Warlord, yet

something about him made her heart rate accelerate.

His indifferent gaze swept through the lobby. He focused on her. His eyes sharpened.

They weren't black.

Karen stepped back, her hand on her chest to contain her thundering heart.

His eyes weren't black, but an odd light green.

Hand thrust out, he started toward her. . . .

Behind her, Chisholm Burstrom gave a shout.

Karen jumped.

"Sorry, honey. Didn't mean to scare you." Briefly Chisholm laid a hand on her shoulder, but his gaze was fixed on the stranger. With two long strides he met him. "Wilder, you old son of a gun, glad you could make it."

"Chisholm, thank you for inviting me." The stranger shook Chisholm's hand. "I'm looking forward to the chance to meet your executives and get the scuttlebutt on the new gaming technologies."

"None of that!" Mrs. Burstrom stepped between the two men and flirted little glances back and forth between the two of them. "This hotel is the number one destination spa in the world. I handpicked it specially, I made up the guest list, I chose the activities, and this isn't going to turn into a business conference. Chisholm, you promised! And Mr. Wilder, you don't want to get on my bad side. I'm a fearsome enemy!"

Mr. Wilder held his hands up, palms out. "I would never cross you, ma'am. I'm not that brave!"

The three laughed, comfortable with one another and the situation; then Mrs. Burstrom turned to Karen. "Karen, this is Mr. Rick Wilder, one of our very special guests. Rick, this is Karen Sonnet. She's the force that has been planning our soiree for months."

"She's an invaluable little gal," Chisholm said.

This time the stranger looked at Karen, really looked at her.

Her heart rate accelerated again. She waited, breathless, to hear him ask, *Did you watch for me?*

Instead his eyes warmed with a very civilized appreciation.

She knew what he saw; she had carefully cultivated the laid-back, comfortable image the spa demanded from its staff.

Her blue gown was loose-fitting, sleeveless, knee-length and casual, and "casual" perfectly described her flat, strappy brown sandals and bare, tanned legs. Her brown hair was streaked with blond, some natural, some not, and stylish in a layered cut that swept her shoulders.

She looked like what she was — the events coordinator at a small, very exclusive hotel in a high-desert canyon outside of Sedona.

She put out her hand. "Mr. Wilder, it's good to meet you."

He took her hand and shook it with businesslike briefness.

That surprised her — possibly because she was still half-convinced this man was Warlord. Probably because she'd expected that wild, electric thrill of recognition at his touch.

"It's good to meet you, Karen. I can't wait to enjoy whatever occasions you set up for us." He smiled, his teeth clean, white, and sharp.

Sharp . . .

Warlord kissed her. Turned away. Ran toward the front of the tent. Pushed the tent flap open. Leaped off the platform and into the melee, a pistol blazing in each hand.

She shuddered, then shook off the memory, the madness, and nodded her greeting.

"Excuse me. I've got to check in and

change into something more casual." He nodded at all of them, and smiled at her again.

As he strode away, Mrs. Burstrom said in satisfaction, "That was the smile of a man who likes what he sees."

"Karen, you're in trouble now. My darling girl has that matchmaking gleam in her eyes." Mr. Burstrom laughed, his jowls shivering.

"Hush up, Chisholm." Mrs. Burstrom linked her arm with Karen's and fluttered her fingers at him. "I work under the cover of discretion."

In a polite tone that hid her faint flicker of alarm, Karen said, "Mrs. Burstrom, I don't fraternize with the guests." Her pager vibrated, and she glanced down. *Saved by the bell.* "The caterers have a question, so if you'll excuse me . . ."

"Is there a rule forbidding it?" Mrs. Burstrom walked with her.

So much for "saved by the bell."

Mrs. Burstrom said she trusted Karen's expertise, and Karen thought that probably she did, but she was the kind of hostess who verified every detail, from the welcome baskets in the guest rooms to the flower arrangements on the buffet. She'd worked with Chisholm Burstrom to make this

174

company a success, and she expected this gathering to tie their loyal employees closer to them and bring their honored guests into the fold.

And Karen had worked with her to make sure that happened.

"Is there a rule forbidding fraternization with the guests? No, but wouldn't I be asking for heartache to fall for a guest who's leaving in a week?" Karen gave the same droll answer she always gave to kindhearted inquiries and direct passes.

"You're never tempted?"

"No."

"Not even by a pair of green eyes shot with gold?" Mrs. Burstrom coaxed.

"He has very nice eyes." Eyes that looked positively normal. "But no."

"It's not natural for a girl your age to live alone."

"I'm hardly a girl, Mrs. Burstrom. I'm thirty years old, and except for a yearlong break almost a year ago, I've been in the hotel business full-time for eight years. You wouldn't be the first matchmaker I've thwarted."

"A challenge!"

Karen stopped in the middle of the hallway. "No. Please. My break from the hotel business coincided with the end of a bad relationship. I figure those weeks with him contained enough sex, rage, anguish, and arguments to make up for years of a normal relationship, and I'm not interested in trying again."

"Two years is time enough to heal."

"I haven't felt a niggle of interest since then."

"Yet you looked at Rick hard enough."

Mrs. Burstrom wasn't going to give up, so Karen told more than she usually did. "He reminded me of my ex. I always jump when I see a man like that. It wasn't a healthy relationship."

"Did he beat you?" Mrs. Burstrom asked sharply.

Karen matched her frankness. "Almost as bad. He tied me up."

"All right. I won't push the issue." They started toward the kitchen again. "I want you to know that Rick is an upright, honorable young man who has spent time overseas —"

That quiver of alarm went up Karen's spine again. "Really? Where?"

"India and Japan, and then Italy and Spain."

Karen had to stop jumping to conclusions.

Mrs. Burstrom continued, "He's smart as a whip, speaks a lot of languages, and he developed a computer game that we're marketing in the States and then internationally."

"Really?" Karen couldn't care less about computer games. "What's it called?"

"*Warlord.*"

CHAPTER FIFTEEN

The Aqua Horizon Spa and Inn had been constructed along a cliff, and designed to make the most of the majestic red rock formations and sweeping valley vistas below. It faced south, so it always caught the sun, and the building exteriors, the native plants, and the graveled paths blended into the desert atmosphere with warmth and sensitivity.

Fists clenched at her sides, Karen walked along the trail away from the sprawling, five-story hotel structure. As soon as she was out of sight of the windows she ran, ran as hard as she could toward her cottage at the edge of the grounds. Stepping in, she shut the door behind her and leaned against it.

Usually the eggshell blue walls, cool cream tile floors, and framed Jack Vettriano prints in the studio apartment soothed her, but now nothing could wipe the shock from her mind.

It was him.

Wasn't it?

It couldn't be coincidence that Rick Wilder's game was called *Warlord.*

Could it?

No. It couldn't.

She pulled her suitcase out from under the bed. She kept it packed with good walking shoes, underwear, and sensible clothes, always ready for the moment when she had to flee.

Because although it had been two years since she'd walked away without a backward glance, leaving Warlord to battle for his life, she still believed that someday he could reappear and claim her again.

Somehow, someday, I will come for you.

Going to the safe in the closet, she opened it and pulled out her passport. Then, more slowly, she retrieved the icon painted with the Madonna. For one vital second she stared at the painting. She remembered the child who had protected the icon for a thousand years, the way her eyes had opened and looked at Karen before her frail body crumbled to dust. And although Karen did not want to believe, every morning when she looked in the mirror and saw those same eyes looking right back at her, she knew the child had passed custody of the icon to her.

She had to protect the Madonna.

But she had a life, too, and she needed to protect her own freedom. Grabbing the framed photo of her mother off the table, she placed the picture and the icon in a padded, zippered container and stowed them in the bottom of the bag. She wrapped the glass bell she'd bought in Italy in a lace shawl she'd bought in Spain, and tucked them in one of the side pockets. Then she zipped it all closed and placed it by the door.

She slid her backpack out from under the bed. That contained all the necessities to maintain life in the wilderness — freeze-dried foods, a flashlight, a waterproof poncho, a canteen. A quick visit to her tiny kitchen and she had a selection of Baker's Breakfast Cookies added to her larder, and she was ready to go.

A knock made her swing around to stare at the door as if a rattlesnake stood on the other side. Or Warlord, which was even worse.

"Miss Karen, it's Dika!" the maid sang out.

Fifty-year-old Dika Petulengro had come to work there not long after Karen arrived. She cleaned the two dozen guest cottages that were scattered across the grounds, spoke English with a Russian accent, had beautiful dark brown eyes surrounded by long, dark lashes, and liked everyone. Karen considered her one of the kindest people she'd ever met — but she didn't trust her. Mingma had taught her to be wary.

More important, Karen didn't need a witness to her flight. So she placed her body to block the view and opened the door. "Dika, could you come back in a half hour?" Which gave her time to get to her car and get the hell out.

"Because you have that beautiful man in here?" Dika craned her neck to see around Karen, and her eyes widened. "No. Not a man, a suitcase!"

"I'm doing a little packing for my vacation," Karen said.

Dika bumped the door with her ample hip and knocked it out of Karen's hand. "No, Miss Karen, look. You have packed your pretty glass. The lace mantilla you drape across your dresser is gone." She looked hard at Karen. "And you have that look in your eyes."

"What look?"

"The look of a refugee forced to flee again."

Somehow Dika recognized the expression. Karen set her chin.

"Okay, I help you." Dika pushed her way in and shut the door behind her. "But first tell me why. Why are you afraid?"

"One of the guests . . . reminds me of someone."

"Mr. Wilder?"

Karen grew very still. "How do you know?"

"The staff is gossiping, of course." Dika shrugged. "They said you looked enthralled with the man, but I think maybe they mistake fright for enthrallment."

Karen nodded stiffly. She hated admitting to this overwhelming panic, but Dika seemed to understand.

"Sometime, he mistreated you? Maybe he is your husband?"

"No. And no. I mean, Mr. Wilder is definitely not my husband, and I'm not even sure he's the guy I think he might be." That sounded crazy, Karen knew, so she tried to explain. "The other guy . . . his eyes were black."

"Black. All black? No color?"

"That's right. At first I thought it was drugs, but then I realized he was . . . that somehow he . . ."

"He was the devil's own," Dika suggested.

"Yes," Karen burst out. Of course. Dika understood. She had come from the

Ukraine, from a land as wild and peculiar as the Himalayas. "Mr. Wilder is not him. His eyes are light green, beautiful and not at all frightening."

Dika nodded.

"He indicated that he was interested in me, but it seemed nothing more than any other guy."

"This man, Mr. Wilder, might be . . . You fear him?"

"Yes."

Dika thought for a moment. "You have bitch beer in the refrigerator?"

"A couple."

"I'll open them." Dika indicated the patio door, then bustled to the refrigerator. "Go outside and sit. We need to talk."

"I need to leave."

"First we talk. Then, if you wish, I will help you leave — and I know the secret ways to go."

That made sense. That made a lot of sense. And something about Dika's matter-of-factness calmed Karen's panic and made her think more clearly.

She opened her patio door and went out into the warm, dry air. The encircling wrought-iron fence was thick with shrubs and vines, giving her privacy and the illusion of coolness, and the chairs were made of lightweight blue fabric and reclined to weightlessness.

Behind her the door opened and closed, and Dika thrust an icy beer into Karen's hand. She seated herself with all the assurance of a seasoned counselor and said, "So you don't know if he's actually the one."

"No. When I was in Europe, right after I escaped him, I saw him all the time — on the train, in the restaurants, on the beaches. I'd see some man from behind, notice his walk, the color of his hair, or the movement of his hands, and I would just freak." Karen started to lift the beer to her mouth, then brought it back down. "But it was never him."

"You'd look again, and you were wrong," Dika said. "Then, as days slipped into weeks and weeks into months, you relaxed and didn't see him so much."

"Right. Once, about six months in, I even dated a guy who reminded me of him. This guy was actually a lot better-looking — how could he miss? he actually *shaved* on a semiregular basis — and then he kissed me. I was so bored I almost slipped into a coma." That was a memory she'd just as soon forget.

"Your other man — his kisses were not boring."

"He was a lot of things, but never boring." Karen took a long drink of bitch beer.

"But you don't know what he looks like in the face? You don't remember? You think Mr. Wilder has changed his looks? His eyes?"

Karen told her about the beard and the hair, and the name of the computer game, and finished with, "Mr. Wilder doesn't have Warlord's intensity."

"Yet you, who are a sensible woman, fear that this is the man."

"Sounds dumb, I guess."

"No. Your instincts tell you to be cautious. I believe you should be cautious. This could be a brother or a flunky, someone sent to spy on you."

A chill crept up Karen's spine. She looked around. "I have to go," she whispered.

Dika put her hand over Karen's. "All the more reason you *shouldn't* go. Here you have security men who can defend you. Friends who will believe you when you say a seemingly normal man is a threat."

"Yes . . ." What Dika said made sense, and the clawing sense of panic, the desperate need to take flight, faded.

Dika viewed Karen's relaxation and smiled. "Yes. Good. Let me tell you a story. Almost forty years ago my tribe suffered a great tragedy."

"Your tribe?"

"I am Rom. Romany. Gypsy."

"Oh!" Karen studied Dika's brown eyes, her swarthy complexion, her compact body. "I didn't know the Rom lived in the Ukraine."

"The Rom have wandered across the world, and about a thousand years ago my own tribe made the mistake of wandering into Russia." Dika made a face. "The Russians made persecution into an art form. But we didn't have real trouble until almost forty years ago, when our most precious possession was taken from us."

Karen's mind immediately sprang to the icon. Her icon. "What is your most precious possession?"

Dika sighed. "It was a girl, the one chosen to see the visions that guided us. Our Zorana. When she left —"

"She left? I thought you said she was taken from you."

"The stories differ." Dika shrugged expressively. "The old folks change their tales. All I know is that the luck we'd enjoyed for so long vanished. Our axles broke, our babies died, our young men were killed. My father disappeared into one of the Russian prisons. I was eleven then. In the Ukraine, the militia could be very bad, very corrupt. They took what they wanted, they killed, they burned. My mother taught me to hide when they came, and I always did, until one day when I was fifteen, the general saw me before I could get out of sight. He threatened to burn the wagons if the Rom did not give me into his keeping. So they did."

Incredulous, Karen asked, "How could they?"

"It was me or their own children, and so they sacrificed me."

A ghost of memory slipped through Karen's mind. The child sacrifice . . .

Dika looked down at the bitch beer clasped in her hands. "I never saw my mother again. I was with Maksim five years. The whole time he was mad for me, and eventually, I think, just mad. He said I slept with other men. He accused his soldiers, his brother, his best friend. He beat me, kicked me, made it so I could not have children."

"I am so sorry."

"So finally I did sleep with another man, a powerful man, and when the general came for me I gave the order to have him shot like a dog in the street. Then I came here." Dika looked up, and deep lines etched her upper lip and between her brows. "Even now, sometimes I see Maksim in my night-mares."

"You make me ashamed to complain." Because Warlord had kept her against her will, but he had promised not to ever hurt her, and even now she believed him.

"No. Don't be ashamed. Be proud of yourself that you got away. I thank God every day that I used my strengths to fight Maksim, and I remember with pleasure giving the order to have him killed." Dika lifted her chin. "Miss Karen, you don't want to run forever. If this isn't the man, then you are where you want to be. I will tell the staff to watch him, and if he is the one I will personally fix the sheets to make him break out in a terrible rash and have to go to the hospital."

Karen laughed, and relaxed. "You're right. I've got to stop running from a memory. I've broken the old bonds." And, interest-ingly enough, she meant the ones holding her to Jackson Sonnet, not the ropes Warlord had used to fetter her.

In truth, her break with the man she'd called her father had made her realize how alone she was in the world. She had had no friends, because she had worked too much and didn't have time for them. She had moved from place to place and had no home except the dark, cold, depressing mansion in Montana. And she'd spent her life afraid she was unlovable because of one man's unattainable approval.

So she had changed her life. She traveled. She got pedicures. She made friends, sang songs, drank fine wines. Sometimes she missed the old life; she had been a damned good project manager, and there had been satisfaction in completing the work.

Yet the only true dark spot remaining on her horizon was her fear that Warlord would emerge from the shadows of her old life — and she remembered all too clearly the legend he'd relayed about the Russian villain and his descendents, damned for all eternity. She remembered the way his flesh had sizzled on contact with the icon.

Dika was right. If Mr. Wilder was Warlord, Karen would have little chance to escape him if she ran. So it was time to face her fear. "I'm strong. I'm self-reliant. I'm not the same person I was two years ago. So . . . I'll stay."

"Good!" Dika patted Karen's knee and stood. "My people have gathered again. We have a stake in this struggle against the devil and his minions, and we will help you, Miss Sonnet. So be wary, yet know you have friends at your back. Now I need to go to work."

"Me, too. I've got a buffet to supervise." Karen stood, too.

"Who knows, Miss Karen?" Dika sounded positively perky. "If this Mr. Wilder isn't your lover, then perhaps the demon is dead."

Karen ran her tongue over the inside of her lip. Sometimes, unexpectedly, the taste of his blood filled her mouth, and she saw with his eyes, felt with his heart . . . anguish, darkness, violence, and a deep, desperate, clawing longing. "No. He is most definitely not dead. He's out there somewhere . . . waiting."

As the two women went inside, the stranger stepped out of the shrubbery, dusted himself off, and waited as still as a statue.

Karen left first to supervise her buffet.

Dika worked for a half hour; then she left also, locking the doors behind her.

He climbed the fence. Once within the privacy of the patio, he knelt by the door, picked the lock, and let himself inside.

The cottage smelled of disinfectant. Feminine touches decorated the room. Karen Sonnet had made this place her own.

But she'd been ready to abandon it at the first sign of trouble.

Her bag and backpack were still tossed on the bed.

He started toward them.

She should have run while she could.

CHAPTER SIXTEEN

Jackson Sonnet stared up at his newest trophy — a massive moose head he'd bagged on a visit to Alaska — tapped his fingers on his desk, and waited. And waited.

Finally Phil Chronies appeared in the door of his study. "Here it is, Mr. Sonnet. I found it. I just sort of misplaced it. Forgot about it, really. You get so much mail it's hard to keep track of it all." He sidled up and handed Jackson the detective's report.

Jackson looked at the flat manila envelope. "It's been opened."

"Yeah, those mailmen up here in Montana are real nosy." Phil fidgeted like a kid who needed to go to the bathroom.

"Get out."

Phil fled.

"Don't slam —"

Phil slammed the door behind him.

"— the door!" The little prick did it every damned time.

Chronies wasn't good for anything. After hearing his story about how Karen had been screwing around with some Himalayan biker, how Phil had struggled to keep the job going by himself, and how Karen had left him to die, Jackson had felt bad about the missing arm, not to mention that he'd wanted to avoid a lawsuit, so he'd made sure all the hospitalization and rehab were paid for one hundred percent. That was six months Phil had been out of commission.

Then, when he came back, Jackson had given him a job in his main office in town, answering questions from the field. It made sense; Phil was a goddamned construction assistant. He should have known the business, or so Jackson had thought.

But Phil had been lousy, ignorant of the most basic matters, unable to get materials where they should be when they should be, and his misplaced arrogance had resulted in Jackson's loss of one of his best site supervisors.

Two, if he counted Karen.

So, to minimize the damage Phil could do, Jackson had stuck him in employee relations and told his office manager to keep him busy. After three months Nancy had begged Jackson to get rid of Phil before they had a sexual harassment suit on their hands.

So Jackson had brought him to his home office, and told him to do the filing.

The dumbshit couldn't even do that.

What had Karen said before she walked out?

Enjoy your time with Phil, and try to make yourself believe he's telling you the truth.

It was as though she'd cursed Jackson, because these last two years had been a misery. As far as he could tell, Phil was allergic to work, any kind of work. He made up stupid excuses for his incompetence. Every time Jackson yelled, Phil brought up the story about how Karen had been screwing a biker and left him to be crushed by a rockfall. And every time the guy started in on the story about Karen and the rockfall, it changed a little.

Jackson shouldn't have listened to him in the first place. He shouldn't have told Karen the truth about her mother. He should have kept his promise to Abigail and raised Karen like his own daughter instead of like a convenient employee . . . *Crap.* For the first time in his life he felt guilty.

He was going to have to dump Phil. He'd give him a nice retirement package, threaten him with death and worse if he told secrets about Jackson's personal business, and out the door he'd go.

Because no one had the right to know what was happening with Karen except Jackson Sonnet.

The envelope opened easily — preopened envelopes did that — and he pulled out the report.

Karen had spent almost a year in Europe doing just what she said she was going to do — not one whole hell of a lot of anything.

Sure she'd never be able to stand it, Jackson had kept waiting for her to come crawling home.

But she didn't. The detective agency had sent him photos of her at the Vienna opera, traveling by rail, eating at an open market, lolling on beaches with people he'd never seen before.

Apparently she made friends easily. Just like her mother.

But unlike her mother, she wasn't sleeping with anyone. As far as the detective could discover, Karen was as pure as the driven snow.

That made Jackson wonder . . . was that story she'd told him the truth? *Had* she really been kidnapped by a warlord and held hostage?

Had some son of a bitch hurt his little girl? Had Jackson failed her so miserably?

The paper crinkled in Jackson's fist.

Last year, when she'd finally returned to the States, Jackson had waited to see her walk through the door, looking for a job.

She went to a spa in Arizona instead, stayed there as a guest for a week, then got a job as an events coordinator.

When he read that report, Jackson had almost frothed at the mouth. All those years of college, of training, of learning to survive in the toughest conditions, gone to waste in a pansy-ass spa and hotel taking care of parties for people who lounged around in hot tubs and got massages. And got pedicures, for shit's sake.

According to this latest report, she was still there. They liked her a lot. Every progress report was filled with praise. She'd had a couple of raises. And there were pictures.

Jackson sank down in his chair and stared at the photo in his hand.

She looked good. Not like Abigail; if she'd looked like Abigail maybe he could have forgiven her. Instead she looked like a female version of her father, that goddamned Indian Nighthorse. She'd fixed herself up. Gotten a tan. Let her hair grow and lightened it. Wore makeup and dresses . . .

She was an awfully pretty woman, and she

didn't deserve what he'd given her.

He should have kept his promise to Abigail.

If he had, he wouldn't now be a pathetic old man spying on the girl he'd loved like a daughter.

Phil soundlessly shut the door to Jackson's office.

He'd learned that if he banged it hard enough, it popped back open and he could watch the old fart. It helped to know Sonnet's mood, and it helped to know when to look busy. The old fart threw a tizzy when he caught Phil checking e-mail or playing computer solitaire, and he had really been ugly about that "lost" detective's report. But Phil couldn't help it.

Someone wanted to know all about Karen Sonnet, and *someone* was willing to pay well for the information. And Phil Chronies was pleased as hell to give up that self-righteous bitch to anyone with a cashier's check.

The phone rang.

He smiled unpleasantly as he grabbed his copy of the detective's report and picked up the receiver.

Someone was right on time.

CHAPTER SEVENTEEN

The Burstroms had hired the whole water complex for their opening-night gala, and it boasted a diving pool and a swimming pool, three waterslides, and a quarter of a mile of river that circled the perimeter with a powerful current that propelled the Burstroms' guests from the buffet to the poolside bar and back. There were lifeguards for every five swimmers, two masseuses giving neck rubs on their portable tables, a deejay who played requests, and the Burstroms' guests swam, basked in the setting sun, and marveled at the view.

Karen oversaw the event with a keen eye, and that kept her so busy that she scarcely thought about Rick Wilder and his eerie resemblance to Warlord. Although . . . she never quite relaxed.

When she finally did see him, he was hefting himself out of the swimming pool. She watched, transfixed, as he crimped his toes on the edge, thrust his wet hair out of his eyes, and laughed down at two of Burstrom's older lady employees.

He looked so normal. Not like a warlord or her evil nemesis, but like an American guy dressed in green swimming trunks and a dripping beige T-shirt . . . a really ripped American guy.

She thought she should take the opportunity to study his body, see if she recognized any identifying marks, but it appeared she wasn't the only woman with that idea in mind, and he quickly disappeared under the barrage of four newly minted Burstrom female engineers.

Which made Karen feel sort of funny, like an old girlfriend cast aside.

By the time she got to bed that night she'd been going nonstop for twenty hours, and she slept like a rock, without a single premonition or dream.

The schedule the next morning brought a volleyball tournament and tennis matches, and the afternoon included a wine tasting, and by the time the Burstrom Technologies' first sit-down dinner rolled around, Karen was ready for a moment alone. She saw the dinner through to the dessert course, then left matters in the hands of their very capable caterers and wandered out to her favorite place on the grounds, the Japanese garden. The night was clear — of course, it was the Arizona desert — and the full moon and discreet lighting made the path easy to follow. The white gravel crunched beneath her sandals, and beside the path a tiny brook trickled over polished stones, headed for the edge of the cliff, where it would artfully tumble down in a froth of waterfall. She rounded the corner, descended the stairs cut into the stone — and stopped cold.

The granite bench was occupied. She started to back away, but he turned his head, and the white moonlight shone on his face.

Rick Wilder.

Everything she'd said to Dika about being strong and self-reliant vanished in a flash of alarm.

She lifted one foot, ready to flee.

He stood at once. "Sorry. Sorry! Is this your private garden? I thought I'd excuse myself and not go back, because I knew Chisholm was going to present the annual employee awards. Since I'm not an employee, I frankly don't care. Shall I leave you alone?"

She hesitated.

But he sounded so normal, so all-around-guy-like . . . and she couldn't say he'd followed her, since she'd arrived after him. No one knew where she was, but she had her pager, and it wasn't like she couldn't yell and summon the security guards that patrolled the grounds every moment of every night.

"This garden is for the use of the guests, and if you don't mind my company, I'd love to take a moment to rest." She found an artistically placed boulder in the middle of the raked rock garden, far away from him, seated herself, and groaned. "I have been waiting to sit down for the last six hours."

"I noticed that you run from morning to night."

He noticed? He'd watched her? "Not always," she said cautiously. "Just when we have a large party."

"How often does that happen?" He smiled a friendly, open smile and sat back down on the bench where he'd been before.

"It depends on the season, but in the winter, every ten days or so. People are crazy to get out of the snow, so they come down here and pretend it's July in Chicago."

"Tough job."

"Not really. It's great to watch them. They're almost children, they're so happy."

Without any seeming worry, he faced her, the moonlight on his face. "So this is perfect for you. How long have you been an events coordinator?"

"A year."

"What did you do before that?"

"Before that I wandered around Europe for a year. And before that" — she scrutinized him — "I was a construction project manager for adventure hotels."

"You are kidding." If he was faking it he was good, because she couldn't see a single blink that betrayed anything other than casual getting-to-know-you conversation. "Okay, first — a year in Europe?"

"I like Europe."

"So do I — but a *year?*"

"I got a Eurail pass and went where my whims took me. I ate at great restaurants, I made a lot of friends, I saw a bunch of museums." Again she watched him closely. "I avoided only one thing."

"What's that?"

"The European mountains. I didn't want to see the Alps and the Pyrenees. If I never see a mountain again, it will be too soon."

"You hate 'em."

"I do." She had never meant anything so much in her life.

"You know what I like best about Europe? Gelato. I could make my way through Italy eating gelato."

She was cheering up by the moment. He wasn't interested in discovering what made her tick. He wanted to talk about himself. This guy really was just . . . a guy. "The Gelato Tour of Europe. That sounds magnificent."

"Someday I'll write a book." He looked back toward the ballroom. "The food here is excellent."

"Thank you."

"And the wines are perfect. Did you match the wines with the meals, or did Mrs. Burstrom?"

"I made the recommendations," she said modestly, but all the while she was thinking how much she loved a man with a keen appreciation for fine wine and food. He seemed oh so civilized.

"You're the woman with the schedule. What happens after the awards are given and the dinner is over?"

"It's free time, so I suppose everyone will make a break for one of the bars."

"That sounds about right." He yawned and stood. "I'm going to turn in. I flew here directly from Sweden, and my body clock's still off. May I walk you inside?"

"Yes. Thanks. You may." Because she *was* strong and self-reliant, and able to stroll side by side with Rick Wilder without fear.

"What's the plan for tomorrow night?" He headed toward the hotel.

"Mrs. Burstrom doesn't like me to talk about her plans." She climbed the stairs ahead of him, feeling self-conscious, hoping her knee-length dress covered her thighs. "She likes the element of surprise, and of course I respect her wishes."

"Mrs. Burstrom is quite the character, isn't she? She's got Burstrom wound around her little finger."

"Just the way it should be." Karen grinned.

They got to the top. He stepped up beside her. "What's that? Toward the top of the canyon?"

She halted and looked, too. A light came on and moved, then stopped and went out. "It must be campers, although they're not supposed to be there. Or lost hikers." She lifted her pager, but before she could even speak the spa's chief of security came hurrying up the path toward them.

"Do you need something, Miss Sonnet?" Ethan played his flashlight over Rick.

Rick blinked and brought his hand up to shield his eyes.

Warmth spread through her veins. Ethan had been watching out for her.

"I'm fine, but look." She pointed at the

light that had moved a little closer to the spa. "You'd better send someone up there to investigate."

Ethan stared up at the canyon rim. "Stupid hikers," he muttered. "I'll call the sheriff. He'll take care of it." Before he flipped open his cell phone, he looked into Karen's eyes. "Is everything all right with you?"

"Really, everything's fine, thank you, Ethan."

"Great. Good evening, Mr. Wilder."

As they walked away, Ethan stood looking up at the canyon rim, speaking forcefully to the sheriff's dispatcher.

Rick looked back. "You really have a lot of security around here. I've run into someone every time I've been alone."

"Have you?" She hid a smile.

"Do you have a lot of problems with intruders?"

"No, just the occasional lost soul. But this area is still wild. We have bobcats and hawks, and sometimes a cougar wanders through."

"Wow. I hadn't thought of that." He peered around at the trees as if expecting an attack at any moment.

"But we're perfectly safe. They're more afraid of us —"

"— than we are of them," he finished. "Yeah, yeah, my dad used to tell me that about snakes, but I still hate the big slimy worms."

"Me, too." As she walked, she tucked her hands behind her back. Not that she expected him to make a grab for her, but he was tall, and his broad shoulders made her feel crowded on the path.

The hotel came into sight, and Rick said, "You were telling me about tomorrow night."

"No, I wasn't."

"Come on," he coaxed. "I won't tell. It's the last night, so it must be the grand finale. What have you got planned?"

It was so charming to have a man who was actually interested in what she did. "There'll be a buffet in the afternoon, a ball in the evening, and another buffet at midnight. Then everyone leaves the next day, we have a week of regular guests, and it all starts again."

"We're going to have a ball? So there'll be ballroom dancing? With a live band?"

"They're local, called Good Red Rock, and they play songs from the last six decades."

"I like to dance."

"Really?" She raised her brows in disbelief.

"Yep. Women will do anything for a guy who knows how to dance."

He made her want to giggle. *"Anything?"*

"Trust me."

"So you don't really like to dance; you merely like to reap the rewards." To her amazement she realized she was flirting. Lightly flirting. With a guy who had sort of reminded her of Warlord.

Maybe this was a sign that she was healing from the horrors of that time in the Himalayas. "Well . . . yeah. Do I sound like a sinner?"

He seemed so amused, she didn't stop to examine the words for hidden meaning. "You sound like a very smart man to me."

"So, my evil plan is working. Tomorrow night would you dance with me?"

"Yes . . . but for no more reason than the pleasure of the dance. There'll be no *anything* between us."

"Fair enough. Because by tomorrow night I'll have entranced you enough for *anything.*"

She snorted softly. "You can hope."

"I do." He smiled at her, an open smile, and something inside her relaxed.

Surely if he were Warlord he wouldn't expose his face so utterly. Surely if he were Warlord she wouldn't feel so lighthearted.

"They say when a man dances with a woman, all his secrets are revealed."

"In that case . . . I'd better try to get more interesting fast."

"You don't think you're interesting?"

"I do think I'm interesting." He stopped.

She stopped, too, and looked up at him.

He tapped her nose like an admonishing older brother. "But I'm a computer nerd. I think binary numbers are interesting."

She laughed aloud, and enjoyed the sensation of his hand as he cupped her cheek and rubbed the high point of the bone with his thumb. "Why does a computer nerd know how to dance?"

"My parents are immigrants. Dancing is required."

She spoke without thought. "Then I will enjoy myself in your arms."

Softly he said, "That would be the best *anything* you could give me."

CHAPTER EIGHTEEN

As Karen dressed for the Burstroms' big dance, she was pleased with herself. For the last three days every event had gone off perfectly. The Burstroms had raved about her to the hotel manager, so much so that they had somehow given him the impression that they intended to offer her a position in their firm.

She foresaw a plump bonus in her immediate future.

The woman she saw in the mirror pleased her, too. Her black knee-length gown was plain, with an asymmetrical neckline and a six-inch slit up the back of the body-hugging skirt. The cap sleeves showed off her toned arms, and she'd done her hair in an upsweep, with blond strands that dangled around the face she had so artfully made up. Not that she didn't always look her best when she attended these events, but today she glowed.

How could she not? All day Rick had been courting her, not blatantly, not ostentatiously, but with subtle attentions that made her feel special. Flirtatious. For the first time since she'd fled the Himalayas, she could laugh and talk with a man without wondering if captivity and sexual bondage would follow. Yet for all the comfort she felt in Rick's presence, her senses still hummed. He was dangerous. Not like Warlord, but he was not a man to be lightly dismissed. Any man who successfully ran his own international company had to be dangerous in his way. But she doubted his way involved gunshots, mercenaries, icons, and pacts with the devil.

She opened her jewelry box. She reached for her amber earrings, and instead found herself stroking her slave bracelets with one fingertip.

Oh, they weren't really slave bracelets anymore. They'd been roughly cut off her wrists. She'd carted them around Europe in the bottom of her bag for ten months. Then, one day in Amsterdam, she'd stood looking in a gold-working shop at a man who was pounding a sheet of gold with a sledgehammer. And she knew what she wanted to do.

She'd brought back her mangled bracelets. She'd sweetly asked him to let her pound on them. At first he'd been startled, and the two of them had argued in his broken English and her wretched Dutch. Finally he had conceded that the almost-pure gold could be shaped, even by an amateur like her. Standing in that window, she'd pounded both bracelets flat. Each slam of the hammer had made her smile. With vindictive delight she'd pounded into oblivion the marks that proclaimed her a slave. With a little more care she'd worked the panthers into artistic, vaguely amorphous shapes. Then she had smoothed the edges, let him reshape them into bracelets, and tried them on.

They looked fabulous, heavy and gloriously barbaric. She had admired them, taken them off, and never touched them again.

Now she took pleasure in the slick gold surface. Gingerly she lifted them from the box and slipped them around her wrists. She stepped into her black satin pumps with puffy black satin bows, and walked to the full-length mirror.

The dress was chic, the shoes were sexy, and the bracelets were loose, cool against her skin, and breathtaking. She looked the antithesis of a slave.

Without allowing herself a single thought

of warning, she caught her turquoise silk wrap and tossed it over her shoulders. She left on the lamp in the sitting area, and walked out the door.

Tonight she would put the past behind her and never look back.

The ballroom was sumptuous, decorated with flowers and silk hangings, and the French doors that lined the patio were open to let in the dry desert air. Inside, sixty people were dressed in their best. She saw sequined cocktail dresses and red chiffon evening gowns, designer tailored suits and formal tuxedos. Champagne and tequila flowed freely, and Good Red Rock played while every single person took to the dance floor.

Texans knew how to party.

But Karen was working, keeping an eye on the waiters who circulated with trays of champagne and hors d'oeuvres, drying off a guest who had leaned against the small decorative table and knocked off a large vase full of flowers. She called for staff to pick up the shattered ceramic and the broken flowers and wipe up the spilled water. She pinned up the hem of Mrs. Burstrom's full-length gown when Mr. Burstrom stomped on it while they danced the Cotton-Eyed Joe.

And all the while on the periphery of her sight, she watched Rick Wilder's dark head. He talked, he smiled, he danced with female after female. As the ballroom grew warmer he stripped off his jacket and tie. His crisp white shirt and suit trousers showed off his broad shoulders and flat belly, and when he unbuttoned his cuffs and rolled up his sleeves, the corded strength of his tanned forearms made Karen's mouth grow dry. Packaged like this, he was a gorgeous model of a man.

Yet apparently he never glanced her way. While he held a woman in his arms he was aware of no other. . . . And last night he'd told her the truth: Every one of those women would have done *anything* for him.

Late in the evening, when the party was running smoothly and she was standing alone behind a ficus, he found her. His gaze swept her approvingly, and lingered on the bracelets. "You look magnificent."

Magnificent. She liked that.

"Would you do me the honor?" He held out his hand, palm up.

Old-world elegance in a gorgeous package . . . and a man who observed her astutely enough to know when she was finished with her duties.

For all her suspicions, she had not yet

linked him to Warlord, yet to know that he watched her while she was unaware . . .

At her hesitation, his green-and-gold eyes crinkled in amusement.

And that made her realize she needed to make a decision and stick with it. Either he was Warlord or he wasn't. Last night she'd decided he wasn't, and nothing had happened that should change her mind.

Overcoming her reluctance, she placed her hand in his and stepped into his embrace.

The band played a swing tune, and he stumbled a little as they started to move to the music.

Definitely not a Warlord move.

Despite the first misstep, Rick led well, keeping up with the lively beat until she was gasping with exertion — and pleasure.

And that did remind her of Warlord.

I promise that before I am done with you, every time you think of pleasure, you'll think of me.

And she did. Fool that she was, she did.

When the song ended, Rick asked, "Did you enjoy yourself in my arms?"

"Very much." She looked down, away from his teasing glance, then up and into his eyes.

He scrutinized her face, her gown, her shoes. "Beautiful," he breathed.

She was flirting, dragging out every last breath as an enticement, and he responded.

"The next dance is a slow one." He offered his hand again.

"Sure." *Take that, memory of Warlord. I'm going to dance twice with the same sexy guy.*

She let him pull her close. She put her arms up on his shoulders, his reassuringly broad shoulders, and together they swayed to the music.

This wasn't Warlord. She would know Warlord by his touch. She would know when he held her like this, their bodies moving together in a rhythm that carried them in slow steps toward intimacy.

Wouldn't she?

But she couldn't see Warlord dancing at all, ever. Dancing was such a civilized procedure, and . . .

She had to stop thinking about him. Now.

Rick Wilder was not Warlord, so maybe . . . Rick Wilder was the cure for what ailed her.

She pulled back and smiled up at him, into his reassuringly light eyes. "Where are you from, Rick?"

"I was raised in a tiny town in the Cascade Mountains. My parents are foreign immigrants, and they raise grapes for wine, and we've got a fruit stand. We're very organic. Worms don't dare invade our apples. My father would curse them."

"Your parents sound delightful. Any siblings?"

"Two brothers and one sister." He moved with the music seemingly without thought, leading her confidently. "What about you? What's your family like?"

"I have a stepfather. He raised me, but we're estranged."

"Bummer." Rick cocked his head. "Or not?"

"I don't know. All my life he's been such an asshole, but I haven't spoken to him for two years, and I sort of miss him." She blinked in surprise. She didn't know why she'd said that. She hadn't even realized she thought such a thing. "I think he might be lonely."

"I know where you're coming from. My dad is an old-world disciplinarian, and I was always the wild child." Rick offered the information easily, like a man who had no secrets to hide. "When I was a teenager, I resented his always telling me to do the right thing, but now I've done the wrong thing enough to realize that he wanted me to be a good man. When you do the wrong thing often enough, you turn evil."

"Evil?" That took her aback. "That's a harsh word."

"That's what my father would call it. For him there is no gray, only black and white."

She supposed immigrants had a different view of life.

"In fact, I'm going on from here to visit them."

"A family gathering?"

"They don't know I'm coming. I'm going to surprise them." He smiled, but it wasn't his usual open, easy smile. This one was a little twisted, a little pained.

She probably looked exactly the same when she talked about Jackson Sonnet.

"You should come with me," he said impulsively.

At least, she supposed it was an impulse. "What? Why?"

He sighed. "Because my father's going to nag at me. I can hear him now. 'Adrik, you're almost thirty-three years old. What? You don't even have a girlfriend? You should be married. You should have babies.' "

Karen started to laugh.

He watched her glumly. "Oh, sure. You think it's funny."

"I think you're grabbing at straws."

"But what a lovely straw you are."

They smiled at each other in perfect accord.

"So, Adrik is your real name?"

"A name from the Old Country."

On impulse, she said, "Would you like to walk me to my cottage?"

"I would like nothing more." He took her hand and pulled her from the dance floor.

"Now?" She hadn't meant now.

He stopped by the doors. "My darling events coordinator, the guests are headed for the midnight buffet. Mrs. Burstrom is giving us the glad-eye. And if I stay here much longer, I'll be good for nothing but a bout of loud snoring."

"What do you think I want you to do in my cottage?"

"Have a drink while we whine about our parents."

"In that case . . ." She took his hand and led him outside.

He made it so easy for her. There was no pressure. She knew she was doing the right thing, using him to flush Warlord out of her mind.

As soon as they stepped off the patio he stopped her and kissed her cheek, then slid his lips along her jawline and down her throat.

People saw them. Women saw them. And the gusting sighs almost blew Karen off her feet.

Yet the kiss was so sweet, so gentle, Karen

could do no more than chuckle and run her fingers through the pelt of his dark hair. "Do you know you just made me the envy of every woman here?"

He wrapped his arm around her waist and led her down the path toward her cottage. "No, I just made myself the envy of every man here."

In some distant portion of her mind, she realized he was saying exactly the right thing.

But so few men bothered. She had to give him points for that. And points for finding out where her cottage was . . . That made her steps falter.

"How do you know where to go?"

He looked indignant. "Do you think after that encounter with the security guard last night, and seeing those lights on the canyon rim, that I would let you walk to your cottage without watching to make sure you got home safely?"

He was a sweetie. *Such* a sweetie. Mr. Burstrom had given her the thumbs-up as they left the ballroom, and Mrs. Burstrom had looked positively mushy.

Karen stopped and lightly kissed his lips.

He kissed her forehead and leaned his cheek against the top of her head.

She snuggled close. They walked in tandem along the path.

Taking her key, he unlocked the door.

The whole situation was so normal, like an everyday date with everyday people who might or might not go to bed together, and she would not think of Warlord or slave bracelets or men who were condemned by an ancient deal with the devil. . . .

She opened the door. The lamp she'd left on gleamed in a stream of light. A whisper of a breeze filled the air with the fragrance of mesquite, a gift from the window she'd left slightly open. She gestured him inside. "Would you like a drink?"

"No. What I would like . . . is you."

Since the day she'd walked out on Warlord without a backward glance, she hadn't wanted a man. But she wanted this man. She didn't understand what combination of body and spirit, sinew and soul made him attractive to her, but she wasn't afraid. There was nothing about this man that spoke of possessiveness, of the mad need to hold her captive. He seemed like the kind of guy who would dance a dance, take his pleasure, and be on his way.

And that was just what she wanted.

She pushed the door closed behind him.

This was not a man of earth and air, fire and magic, but a completely normal guy who danced with women in the hopes of getting in their pants. And while she'd never been much for quick and easy couplings in college — the little experimentation in which she'd indulged had convinced her that casual sex was just, well, casual, and her time was better spent reading or working out or even studying — right now, casual sex was just what the doctor ordered.

Rick leaned against the wall and pulled her close. He had a lovely erection beneath those trousers, and she lifted her mouth to his, thinking he would get right down to business.

Instead he kissed her eyelids and shut her eyes, then slipped his tongue around her ear until she shivered with delight. He repeated the caress to her cheek and jaw, and followed his finger with the warm touch of his lips.

With each touch her body stirred until she wanted to shout with triumph.

Warlord hadn't marked her as his own. She could feel pleasure without thinking of him. This was what she needed to wipe him from her mind — the passionate embrace of a normal man.

And then Rick kissed her, deeply, warmly, while the world swirled around her and the earth moved beneath her feet.

When he lifted his lips she stared into his green-and-gold, deceitful eyes, raised her hand, and slapped him as hard as she could across the face. "Warlord. You complete and utter bastard."

CHAPTER NINETEEN

It was him. It was Warlord. She knew him as soon as she tasted him. "How *dare* you? How *dare* you play this game with me?"

Warlord watched her, his deceptively pale eyes never leaving her face.

"Get out." She yanked herself out of his arms. "Just get out, and never come back." She reached down to page her chief of security.

His reflexes had not slowed. He plucked the pager from her hands and tossed it at the chair, placing it right in the cushion, where it bounced and came to rest.

Blind with rage and disappointment, she wound up to hit him again — and he picked her up and swung her around. He pressed her back to the wall and slid his hands beneath her legs, wrapping them around him as confidently as he'd moved her across the dance floor. As confidently as he'd lulled her suspicions and made her think he was a trustworthy, unassuming piece of fluff of a man, when in fact he was the most intense, savage creature who ever donned a business suit.

She shoved at him. "Put me down. This isn't the Himalayas, and I'm not some wimp of a woman who's too afraid to get up and go."

"You do yourself too little justice." He no longer bothered to disguise his tone. The way he spoke, the purr in his voice, that was all Warlord. "You were never a wimp, Karen. You were a creature of fire and passion, and you showed me the light when I was far gone into the dark."

"What a pile of crap." She was so angry her heart pounded in her throat. Her cheeks burned. She squeezed the cords of his shoulders between her fingertips. "You came here to make a fool of me."

"I came here to save you."

"From what? Myself? From my foolish desire to be a normal woman who lives in the US, wears dresses and heels, and has a girl job?"

With acid in his tone, he said, "You seem to have mistaken me for your father. But you called him your stepfather, didn't you?"

"What do you know about my stepfather?" Her voice shook with fury.

"Only what I could glean from *hours* of Internet research." He sounded both sarcastic and knowledgeable. "Add to the discovery that after you got back from Nepal, you went home for an hour, left, and never returned, and that was enough."

She hated that he'd invaded her private life, nosed around, assembled enough information to make good guesses on her relationship with Jackson Sonnet. "Now I realize I should have done research on *your* family, seen if I could figure out what makes *you* tick."

"My family keeps a low profile." He slid his fingers along the edge of her neckline to the dip in her cleavage.

She took advantage of his distraction and slammed her forehead toward his nose.

He dodged to the side. "Why are you fighting me? This is what you want."

"How the hell do you figure that?"

"Did you think you could wear my bracelets and not face the repercussions?"

"Your bracelets!" She lifted her wrists so they were before his eyes. "Have you looked at these babies? Have you seen what I *did* to them?"

"You made them into a decoration for your wrists, a decoration that ensured you could never forget the man who gave them to you."

His presumption made her jaw drop. She remembered how she had beaten on the gold, slamming it with the hammer over and over until her arm ached and the malleable metal was damaged, changed from the look of the hated slave bracelets to mere decorations. "You're insane."

"No. I just know you better than you know yourself. I know you because you took me inside yourself, and I touched the deepest part of you. No matter how much you hate the idea, you've spent the last two years waiting for me to come back to you."

"I've been waiting in fear."

"No, honey." He put his forehead to hers. "You've been waiting in anticipation."

She stared into his eyes, his light green eyes shot with gold. Her heart hammered in her chest, and she could barely breathe. From fury. Absolutely not from anticipation. "If I had recognized you . . . *How* did you do it? Change your eye color? Before, did you wear black contacts?"

He gave a crack of laughter. "You don't believe that."

She didn't.

"My eyes were black because I had fallen so deeply into the heart of evil that my soul was black."

"Sure," she mocked him. "And the eyes are the windows to the soul." But a chill of goose bumps crawled up her spine. The sacrificed child . . . the icon . . . the tale he'd once told about the family bound by the devil's pact . . . and he held her in his arms.

"Yes. They are. Look at your eyes. Pure and deep, like a glacial pool."

"Cut . . . it . . . out. I'm not buying a word."

"Good, because I don't want to talk about that now."

"That's *all* I want to talk about with you."

"That leaves us only one thing we both want to do."

She felt his body tighten, and she knew. "No, we don't!"

But she was too late.

He kissed her. She wanted to bite him, but first . . . she wanted to taste him. The flavor was piercingly sweet and poignant beyond belief. Whether she wished it or not, he tasted of memories, of passion . . . of pleasure.

That pleasure sent her hurtling into space, into him. . . .

The wind from the open window beside the bed lifted a strand of her hair and wrapped it around his chin like an embrace.

She heard the bump of his shoes as he kicked them away.

He opened his fly, dropped his pants, rubbed himself between her legs. His bare cock rubbed against her panties, the silk making him slip and slide.

The friction was like kindling to start a campfire — and she burned in immediate response.

She wrenched her head back, banging it on the wall. Banging some sense into her pea-brained head.

How could she have not known? How could she not have recognized his scent — leather, cold water, fresh air, and that peculiar aroma that was his alone — the smell of wildness? Yankee Candle could use Warlord as a scent, and women would flock to light that wick.

"Damn you." She struggled in his arms like a butterfly pinned against the wall. "I have friends here, and they won't let you get away with this."

"Your friends watched you lead me to your cottage. Do you think they're out there waiting to hear you cry out in ecstasy?"

She took a long breath, ready to scream.

And he kissed her. Really kissed her this time, taking advantage of her vulnerability, absorbing her taste, reacquainting himself with her essence . . . coming alive with passion.

This was the man she remembered, intense, fiery, so alive desire leaped from his body to hers. In all the history of the world, no man had ever wanted a woman the way he wanted her.

He held her as if she were precious. One hand supported her; the other caressed her waist, her breasts, her throat, like a collector who adored each facet.

And she absorbed his adoration, responded to the pure excitement of being close to him again. Her toes curled. One black satin pump clattered on the tile floor. Dimly, as her muscles clenched and her breath quickened, she knew she was revealing too much of her long, lonesome craving. Yet sensation swamped her, rising like a tide to fill the desolate, lonely parts of her, the hidden corners of her soul that had withered from loneliness. From wanting him. With him between her legs, against her body, she bloomed again.

When he tore his mouth away from hers, she gasped, eyes closed, trying to regain some composure before meeting his gaze. Because he knew, had always known, that she couldn't resist him. He would be mocking her. Of course.

The change, when it came, came quickly.

As if he were no longer aware of her, he doused the fire between them and stood stiff, still, cold. He let go of her legs, put both hands on her waist.

She opened her eyes and saw his head slowly, so slowly, turn to look toward the bed.

Warlord was motionless, on edge, a wary, ready predator. His nostrils flared as he smelled the air. His eyes moved back and forth, trying to see what was hidden, and in their depths she saw a red flame glow.

Something was wrong. Something was here.

Her gaze flew to the window.

She'd left it open an inch, with a lock stop holding it in place. Now it was open wide.

She heard a slithering sound.

In a flash Warlord let her go.

Her feet hit the floor hard. She staggered sideways on one high heel.

As he twisted, his eyes changed. *He* changed.

In his place stood a panther, black, snarling, hunched, and facing the bed.

CHAPTER TWENTY

She screamed and backed against the wall.

Warlord . . . Warlord was a panther? Or the panther was Warlord?

Huge, black, sleek, threatening . . . but not threatening her.

Two years ago in Nepal, she had witnessed the supernatural when she touched the long-dead child, the villagers' sacrifice to the devil . . . and the little girl had opened her eyes. Those unforgettable aquamarine eyes that had so completely matched Karen's.

Karen had hoped never again to see anything so eerie, hoped never again to be so close to that other world where fantasy took life and evil held reign for a thousand years.

But Warlord had returned, and now . . . from beneath Karen's bed, a king cobra lifted itself from its hiding place. Its skin was shiny and glorious with color: black and red and gold. The evil thing was ten feet long, as round as her thigh, its hood spread wide-open, its segments glinting like jewels of death, its intelligent black eyes tracking the movements of the panther. Of Warlord.

Yet she knew with terrifying certainty that the snake was aware of her, and anticipated murdering her with keen relish.

How did this thing get in here?

Why was it so big?

How could it have such an intelligent and malevolent intent?

Only one answer was possible: This snake was like Warlord, a man who became a creature from hell to stalk, hide, take life with intelligent efficiency.

Warlord said he had fallen into the heart of evil.

She flattened herself against the wall. Her nails scraped along the wallboard.

Now he'd pulled her in with him.

With a flash of intuition, she realized — the deal with the devil. Warlord had told her the legend on the day he'd touched the icon and burned hemself.

The deal with the devil . . . This was the result.

Incongruously, the panther wore Warlord's shirt, open at the neck, sleeves rolled up.

The serpent swayed hypnotically.

Not a muscle moved on the great cat's sleek body.

Without warning the cobra spit. Silvery drops of venom struck the panther's face.

The panther screamed, a shriek of agony, as his flesh sizzled.

Poison dropped to the floor, thick as mercury and just as deadly.

The panther staggered backward, then leaped straight up and twisted in midair. Its back claws slashed the cobra's wide-open hood.

Then the panther landed on the bed and jumped out the window.

In a night of horrors, that was the most horrible thing of all.

The snake reared up, dodging wildly back and forth, seeking the cat. Its blood spattered the walls and the floor. Its coils knocked over her speakers, trashed the stand full of her DVDs, smacked her clock across the room.

Karen inched along the wall, eyes fixed on the deadly, writhing reptile, desperate not to attract its attention, even more desperate not to get in its way.

Gradually the serpent's agitation calmed. It fixed its gaze on Karen and seemed almost to smile, its tongue flicking in mocking anticipation.

It seemed to believe that Warlord had abandoned them both.

So. The snake was not as smart as she had previously feared.

Yet where was Warlord? Had the venom splashed in his eyes? Was he blinded?

Did she have to save herself by herself? She would try. Of course she would try, but as this thing lifted and balanced itself with serpentine dexterity, she realized its giant head reached as high as her throat.

She dashed toward the door, but the snake blocked her.

The fangs gleamed.

She backed away.

The eyes glowed red with flame. The body slithered toward her in great waves.

She wanted to scream but had no breath, wanted to run but had nowhere to go. She put one foot behind the other, groped behind her, desperate to avoid obstructions, to stay on her feet. Her mind raced. If she could jump onto the mattress and throw herself through the window, she might be hurt, but she would be free. She would run and scream, and security would arrive, and —

She stumbled backward over something hefty, inflexible, something that rolled under her foot. She tried to catch herself. Her foot slipped on the tile. She sat down hard. Warlord's leather dress shoe was on the floor. Warlord's shoe had brought her down. She looked up, saw the cobra rising above her, its eyes black and elated, its two fangs bared, glaring white and ready.

She grabbed the heavy shoe and flung it, aiming for the long lift of the creature's body above the floor.

The snake collapsed, off balance. Instantly it rose again, furious at her assault. She was going to die —

The panther leaped back inside, onto the bed, then bounded off the mattress and onto the serpent, smashing its head toward the floor. With its teeth the great cat flipped the cobra up in the air, then snapped its spine with an audible crack.

Blood spurted. The ghastly thing writhed on the floor in its death agonies.

The great panther stood panting, its mouth crimson with blood — and marks seared by the venom into his right cheek and both eyelids.

Rick. The cat was Rick, and Rick was Warlord, and her most bizarre nightmares had taken form in real life. She backed toward the window, knowing that flight was futile, knowing she had to try to escape from this nightmare where giant cobras spit lethal venom, and the man she knew so well . . . wasn't really a man.

The snake's flopping became more frantic, an unnerving rhythm of serpentine death.

At the same time the panther groaned and changed. She couldn't tear her fascinated, horrified gaze away as the dark fur slid back into skin, shoulders and chest filled the shirt, leg bones stretched out straight, the paws grew fingers and toes, the face developed a strong chin, a prominent nose, and . . . one pale green eye sparked with life, while the other was swollen shut, with the skin peeled back and oozing. Rick — or Warlord, or whatever it called itself — was almost human once more. Almost.

She shook her head and muttered, "No, no, no," as if the chant would somehow return her to reality.

Behind him, the snake's upper body rose, fangs bared, its black, lidless eyes fixed on Warlord.

Horror froze her in place. She yelled, "No!"

But it was too late.

The snake buried its fangs deep into Warlord's thigh.

Triumph gleamed in its eyes — but only for a second.

Warlord finished the change. Grabbing the

cobra by the back of the neck, he jerked it free and slammed it against the wall. The skull cracked. The snake fell, dead at last.

And Warlord was completely human.

Too late.

She lunged toward him. "Are you all right?"

He fended her off with one hand. "Don't!"

"Let me get an antivenom kit." She reached for the phone.

"It wouldn't help with this venom. You have to go. Now."

"You could die!"

"Unlikely," he snapped. He held his leg in both hands. One eye was swollen shut. The skin over the other was scoured red and covered with dirt, as if he'd violently rubbed the venom off. "They're after the icon."

Nothing he could have said would have commanded her attention like that single word. "What icon?"

"The icon of the Madonna. The one you found in Nepal." When she still pretended ignorance, he said impatiently, "You've got it packed in your bag with your mother's picture."

"How do you know what I —" *He'd searched her room.*

This was Warlord, all right. And Warlord was a panther.

She had guarded that icon, kept it secret, never told anyone about the child's body, and her eyes, and the way they had looked into Karen's . . . and only one man had ever seen the icon.

This man. "You told them I had it."

"No. I did not."

"Right." Her ire rose. "Because you're the bastion of honor. How do you know that's what they want?"

"I spied on them. I heard them. I came here to warn you."

Remembering the last few days, she said, "You took your own sweet time about issuing the warning."

"I don't know how they found you so quickly." He lifted his arms, then dropped them. "But you don't need to repeat my mistakes. Listen to me. Get dressed."

She looked down at her crumpled black dress. "All right." She headed into the closet, stripped off her dress, and dropped it on the floor.

"My plane is waiting at the airport," he called. "You can fly, right?"

"You know every other thing about me. Don't you know that?" She pulled out her stack of tough clothes, the kind she had worn when she was building hotels.

"Your pilot's license is up-to-date."

He really did know everything about her.

"I'll call and tell them to get it ready to go. I've filed a flight plan for California."

"What's in California?" She dressed so swiftly, she pulled her black T-shirt on inside out. She didn't take the time to correct it.

"My brother. He owns Wilder Winery. Smart guy. Powerful. He can protect you. When you get to the airport, search the plane. Make sure you haven't got any extra baggage in the form of another Varinski."

She walked out wearing jeans and a heavy belt, her inside-out black T-shirt, her hiking boots, and a light jacket — and, beneath the long sleeves, her gold bracelets.

She couldn't bear to leave them behind.

"What's a Varinski?" she asked.

He nodded toward the snake. "That's a Varinski."

She shuddered, grabbed the comforter off her bed, and flung it over the long, twisted body.

Warlord continued, "I'll call my brother. When you land at Napa County Airport, he'll take care of everything."

"Like I would trust your brother?"

"You have to trust someone sometime, Karen Sonnet." Sweat broke out all over Warlord's body, and he shuddered and grimaced in pain. "You've got no choice.

Now go."

She knew how to walk away without a backward glance. Once before, she'd walked away from him. She'd walked away from her father.

Now she grabbed her bag and her backpack, strode to the door, opened it wide, stepped through, and quietly shut it behind her.

CHAPTER TWENTY-ONE

Warlord watched Karen disappear out of his life.

Good for her. He was glad she took the Varinski threat seriously. He was glad she was willing to do anything to protect the icon.

He deserved this, to die alone, half-blind, and in agony.

But . . . after all that had happened, he didn't want to bite it here on the floor of her cottage. She *needed* him to survive.

He needed to know that she *did* survive. She was his light in this world, and she had to go on.

Thin threads of agony shot through every nerve in his body, and he breathed slow, deep breaths until he'd vanquished the pain.

During that year he'd spent in hell, he'd learned to control his pain. In fact, he'd learned a lot. He'd learned to survive eternal darkness and stifling heat, a lack of air and constant beatings. More important, he'd learned patience, he'd learned to plan, he'd learned self-discipline.

Self-discipline. The one thing his father had yammered at him to learn, and Warlord finally had it. Except when it came to Karen.

He'd planned this whole operation: Get close to her, alleviate her fears, seduce her, show her that he was a different man, then gently explain the danger that stalked her and get her the hell out of there and to his parents.

Only one thing had thwarted him.

Karen. Karen, with her professional distance and her pink toenails and her wary courtesy. Karen, with her black dress and her upswept hair that bared the nape of her neck and her willingness to sleep with Rick Wilder while she wore Warlord's bracelets around her wrists. Karen, and her one moment of high-octane, head-on, passionate kissing — right before she knocked his dick in the dirt.

She was the only woman who had ever managed to hit him, and she'd done it twice.

He wasn't bragging about it. But that said a lot for the way she affected him.

The cobra, that stupid fucking cobra, had spit poison at him, bitten him, and filled him with death. The Varinskis' pact with the devil was falling apart, and they would do anything — sabotage, torture, murder — to prevent that from happening. Warlord was passing into the next world. And all he could think about was Karen and how much he wished he could have loved her once more.

So, dumbshit that he was, he would do everything in his power to live. He had to struggle. He had to fight. He wouldn't simply lie down and die.

He set his sights on the pair of his dress trousers crumpled on the floor eight feet away from him — the trousers he'd shed when he'd thought, incorrectly, that he was going to get lucky tonight. Keeping his breath even and his blood pressure down, he slowly pulled himself along the floor until he touched the cuff of one leg. He pulled it toward him, crumpling the material until he could reach into the pocket and pull out the switchblade he kept there.

With the touch of a button the short, sharp blade sprang out. It glinted in the light, his savior if anything could save him. He twisted around, trying to see the puncture points where the snake had bitten him. He couldn't; the fangs had pierced him in the upper thigh on the back of the leg.

Nevertheless, he'd give a poke and see if he could spill the venom out, along with a lot of blood. What had he to lose? He flexed his wrists and prepared to blindly operate — when Karen opened the door and walked back in.

She was gorgeous. He wanted her. So he said the only thing that made sense: "Get the hell out of here."

"Don't tell me what to do." She lifted both of her bags as high as she could, dropped them, and slammed the door with her foot. "Give me that stupid knife."

"You have to leave."

She marched over and extended her hand, and her eyes sparkled with outrage. "I'll leave when you can leave with me. Now, are we going to get this done before another of your stupid, slimy friends pops out of the woodwork, or are you going to loll around on the floor and whimper?"

She was furious with herself for returning. And the fact that she had returned warmed his heart and strengthened his resolve.

He *would* live.

"When you put it that way . . ." He handed her the knife, handle first, and hoped she wasn't mad enough to take the opportunity to stick it in his heart.

She rolled him onto his stomach. "Gonna

sting," she said.

"Already stings." He could feel the venom dissolving the cells, the threads, the strength of his muscles in his leg.

With two sure strokes she sliced his skin and into his muscle.

The pain made him arch in agony.

Blood spurted and ran down his leg.

"Did I hurt you?" she asked.

"Yes."

"Good." She reached up to the end table beside the bed and flipped on a reading light. "Remember what the venom looks like?"

"Thick, silvery, beads together like mercury." When it hit his cheek and eye it had burned like acid, ripping his skin and . . . well. He could do nothing about his eye. No use thinking about it now. But he'd been able to shake the venom off onto the floor, and outside he'd rubbed his face in the flower bed. If anything had saved his vision, that had, but he could still feel the remaining molecules eating away at his skin. . . .

"The poison is nestled in there, clinging to the strands of your muscles. So roll back onto your side." Karen gave him a shove.

He did as he was told. "Why are you doing this?"

"Because I'm sick of worrying about you

and when you're going to pop up again."

"So you're going to take care of me so I don't surprise you anymore?"

"Also, I need help living through the night, and you're my best bet."

"Not in this shape."

"Shut. Up." She used the tip of his knife to push first one drop of poison, then the other out onto the floor.

They rolled and beaded like mercury.

"Not good," she muttered.

"Because?"

"They left a silvery coating along the strands of your muscles. Stay here." She ran for the bathroom. He could hear her slamming through the drawers.

Karen made him feel almost . . . hopeful.

She came back with a bottle of hydrogen peroxide, rolls of gauze and first-aid tape, and a bottle of Listerine.

He didn't even want to know what she intended to do with the Listerine.

"I haven't got a snakebite kit. Or a suction cup. So we'll try this." She knelt at his side. She tilted him onto his stomach and poured the hydrogen peroxide into the wound.

It hurt like a son of a bitch.

She tilted him back and let it drain out.

"No change. The silver's still hanging in

there. Let's try it again." She did, and all the while she talked to him, trying to keep him focused.

He knew it. He appreciated it. But she was getting increasingly frantic, and finally he gasped, "I'm no good to you. Go on now. Remember, my plane. My brother —"

She rolled him onto his stomach. "I know perfectly well how to walk away." She sounded livid that he dared suggest she didn't.

Thank God. If he pissed her off enough, she'd do her disappearing act and maybe save herself and the icon and his family.

Instead, in the most courageous act he'd ever witnessed in his life — and the stupidest — she stuck her knee in his back, put her mouth to the bite, and sucked the poison out of his wound.

CHAPTER
TWENTY-TWO

Karen spit the blood and venom onto the floor.

Warlord knocked her off, shoved her away.

Dimly she heard him shout, "Are you crazy?"

The poison hit her first, ripping into her senses like acid.

Then she tasted his blood, and —

The Varinski wore a helmet and a Kevlar vest. His earlobes hung low, each pierced by a three-eighths-inch countersunk bolt. He had a knife in a holster strapped to his side, and steel covered his knuckles. His arms were muscled and massive, and he had a face like a Neanderthal — wide jaw, heavy brow, and one cheekbone that had been broken and shoved up toward his eye. He waded through the battle, throwing Warlord's men aside as if they were toothpicks. He was massive, indifferent to pain, fast as lightning . . . and his gaze was fixed on Warlord.

A fight to the death. Warlord deserved this. He rushed to meet him.

They met in a clash of cruelty.

Warlord slashed at the Varinski, ripping him with tooth and claw, but this was no ordinary demon. This guy had a flair for killing. He didn't bother with his knife or his pistol, but pounded on Warlord with his metal-clad fists, taking pieces of flesh with each blow.

Warlord slashed with his knife, ripping the Varinski's neck, his legs, his face, but the Varinski shook it off and kept coming. He moved quickly, used his hands as well as his fists, showed the kind of technique only a self-defense master should know.

Warlord panted, his breath heaving in his lungs. He was losing. For the first time since he was a boy with his brothers he was losing a fight. Quickly, he weighed the options. If he changed, became a panther, perhaps he could escape, but . . . his men were over-whelmed, wounded, dead, or prisoners.

No. He would stay with them. He would get them out.

The Varinski circled him; then, at a shout from the field, he looked away.

Warlord made a lunge for the Varinski's belly — and one mighty fist slammed him in the chest.

Warlord blacked out, woke to find himself

flying through the air, blacked out again as he bounced down the cliff . . . and hit the rocks.

The brisk, antiseptic taste of Listerine splashed in Karen's mouth. She sputtered and spit, shoved Warlord's hand and the bottle away. "Son of a bitch!"

Warlord held her in his lap. He shook her shoulders. "Are you all right? Do you know how potent that poison is? Are you crazy?"

"Yes. Yes. Yes." Launching herself out of his arms, she ran to the bathroom. Her stomach heaved, and she tossed her cookies in the toilet. She hung there for a moment, her mind whirling as she tried to think, to comprehend what was happening to her.

Bracing herself, she rose and went to the sink, leaned against it, and looked into her own haunted eyes.

She'd tasted his blood . . . and been transported. It had happened before, in his tent in the Himalayas, but only briefly.

This time she'd seen, smelled, felt that dream, that vision. She'd lived in his skin, and what had occurred had been her nightmare. She'd bounced down a cliff and hit the rocks, and suffered horrible internal injuries. She should have . . . no, *he* should have died a slow, painful death.

He hadn't.

She shivered.

But he had suffered. She knew that now. He had suffered in a myriad of horrible ways. Yet he had survived to save her life, and if she didn't move, didn't push her own shock aside and deal with the situation *now*, he would die on her floor. Even Warlord deserved better than that.

That snake man out there wasn't the only one of those things. They had to escape.

She splashed cold water on her face, brushed her teeth, and went out.

Warlord was on his feet. He had managed to wrestle his way into his trousers, and now he fought with the fastenings.

"First let me look at the bite again."

"It's fine." His complexion was gray; his pupils were pinpoints.

"I can see that." A little more gently, she pushed at him. "Let me look. It needs to be bandaged. You're dripping blood on the floor." She pointed at the pool by his feet.

"I suppose. Just *don't* touch it again." He lowered his pants.

She wiped the wound clean with the gauze. "The blood's washed it out. I can't see any more of the venom." She pressed another gauze pad over the bite, taped it in place, and glanced up at his white-knuckled grip on the bedpost. "You have to fight whatever's in your system."

He looked down at her. Red, painful blisters spotted his cheek, one eye was sealed shut, and a fine sheen of sweat covered his forehead. Yet the hand he reached out to her was steady, and he stroked her cheek as if she were the one who needed reassurance. "Don't worry. I'll hang in there long enough to get you onto the plane and to safety."

"I didn't mean . . ." But she'd told him she was saving him because he was her best bet for safety.

Did he believe that?

Did she?

He tugged up his pants.

She helped him with the zipper and the belt, then pushed him into a chair and shone her reading light on his face.

Carefully she cleaned the dirt out of the wounds. "This one eye should be okay. How about the other one? Can you open it?"

"No. But the eyeball didn't take a direct hit. There's a chance I'll retain my sight."

He was so calm. So sure of himself.

He continued, "I called ahead. They're getting the plane ready. We have to get to the airfield and head toward the mountains."

"I'll order a car." She started to lift the phone, then paused. Hotels had operators, and phone conversations were not always private.

She paged Dika, then helped him on with his shoes and socks.

A soft knock sounded on the door. She looked through the peephole.

It was the maid. She was smiling, nodding. "Miss Karen," she called. "I brought the bottle of wine you requested." She held up a bottle for Karen, and anyone else who was watching, to see.

Karen let her in.

As Dika took in the mess — the scattered DVDs, the smooth, jewel-colored tail of the snake protruding from beneath the comforter, the man in the chair — her smile disappeared. "What happened?"

"We were attacked."

Dika lifted her chin at Warlord. "Is this the man you were afraid of?"

"Yes, but he saved my life."

"Again," Warlord interjected.

"You took your payment last time," Karen snapped.

"So in return you're saving his life?" Dika looked him up and down. "Handsome devil. I can see why you might."

"You told me to trust my instincts. In this case, my instincts tell me to get him out of here without anyone seeing. Fast." Karen waited, wondering if Dika would mock her.

Instead, the soft, smiling maid was gone, replaced by a hard-faced, determined, and intelligent woman. "Right. Give me five minutes. I'll be back." She left.

Karen pulled two water bottles out of the refrigerator and started to hand him one.

He shook in a hard burst, and gave off a flash of fever so hot she felt it where she stood.

For the first time she took a breath, and realized how inadequate she was to this task. She didn't know anything more than basic first aid. She wasn't capable of fighting demons who turned into beasts. She placed the bottle against his neck, hoping to cool him, and said, "I'm a normal, sensible woman who is good at planning chocolate buffets and dealing with flower arrangement emergencies. How am I going to help you now?"

"Sensible, yes." He took the bottle, opened the cap, and drank. "But you are anything but normal. You can build a hotel, beat up a man, survive a trek through the Himalayas. Right now I can't think of anyone I'd rather have at my side."

She didn't want his tribute — but it touched her heart. "Drink it all," she said tartly. "It'll flush the venom through."

As he drank, he was grinning, and he reminded her of someone. Someone she liked.

Oh, yeah. He reminded her of Rick Wilder.

"I've got survival gear on the plane," he said. "With the stuff you've got in your backpack, we'll be okay."

"Did you go through everything I own?" She drank, too, grimly aware that she had also taken in a few fatal drops of the poison . . . and a few frightening drops of his blood.

"Right after your little conversation on the patio." He nodded toward her sliding door.

She jerked the bottle away, spilling water down her front. "Dika? You *heard* us?" He'd heard every word she'd said? About him? About her? About her fears?

Even now, sick as he was, he watched her, smiling. "Dika was very helpful. If she hadn't convinced you to stay, I would have had to take stern measures."

"Damn you to hell. I should walk out right now and leave you to the vultures."

Taking her wrist, he kissed it. "It's too late for that. Even if I die from this — and I may — somehow I would come back for you."

"Shit kicker." She paced from one window

255

to another and twitched the curtains aside to look out.

What was wrong with her that his confession both flattered and compelled her? Why, of all the men in the world, was she in thrall to Warlord?

Dika hurried toward Karen's cottage, pushing her housekeeping cart ahead of her.

A year ago, when Karen found employment at Aqua Horizon Spa and Inn, Dika had arrived from her people with a mission — to make sure Karen Sonnet remained safe and the prophecy could be fulfilled.

Now the Varinskis had struck suddenly, viciously, and Dika had to get Karen and Wilder out.

She rapped on the door, and in her perfect maid's voice she sang out, "I'll clean up that spilled wine now, Miss Karen."

"Come in, Dika; we appreciate your doing this." Karen sounded as pleasant as Dika. The bright girl completely understood the reason for subterfuge.

Dika closed the door behind her and locked it. She opened the side of the cart and said to Wilder, "Get in."

Wilder nodded and stood slowly, moving as if his joints ached.

Karen saw his disability and cursed colorfully, in a variety of languages.

So. The girl might not like him, but she couldn't stand to see him in pain.

Wrapping her arm around his waist, Karen helped him fold himself up and in. Dika loaded Karen's bags on top of him, closed it up, and Dika and Karen and their hidden passenger headed out the door.

Karen helped Dika push — Wilder weighed a ton, and the wheels sank into the gravel paths — and they chatted lightly as they walked, for all intents and purposes two women who worked at the spa and were friends.

Yet Dika's skin crawled. *They* were out there, the Varinskis, moving in for the kill. . . .

Dika, Karen, and Wilder reached the parking lot without incident.

Karen looked at the brightly lit entrance of the Aqua Horizon Spa and Inn, then at the white laundry van as it pulled up. She looked down at her hands as she clenched them into fists over and over. She faced the danger, and she feared the trial.

Dika couldn't help her with her fear, but she could help her take the next step down the road.

Two men jumped out and lifted the cart into the back of the van.

"These are my people, the Rom, my tribe. They will get you to the airfield." Dika placed her hand flat on Karen's head. "Blessings, luck, and strength be with you."

Karen hugged her, jumped in, and waved as they peeled across the asphalt and into the darkness.

Dika turned back toward safety. Toward the brightly lit entrance to the lobby.

Yet as she walked, the sense of being watched grew. She slid her knife from up her sleeve. She glanced behind her. Strained to listen. Her steps got shorter and faster. She almost reached the doors — and someone stepped out of the bushes. Or, rather, some*thing.*

Pointed ears spouted from the top of its head. Fur covered its neck and cheeks, yet its nose and eyes and body were definitely human.

He was what the Rom feared — the new and evil Varinski curse, a being who straddled the line between predator and human.

"You shouldn't have done that." He spoke slowly, as if words were hard for him.

Dika's only safety was inside. She stepped sideways. "Excuse me, please." She tried to go around.

He moved in front of her, half grinning. "I

said you shouldn't have done that."

"I need to go in."

"We're going to get them anyway . . . and now I'm going to get you." He sprang at her, fangs bared.

With a swift slash of her knife she cut his face.

He howled in agony.

She darted toward the entrance.

As the automatic doors opened, she shrieked with all the force of her lungs.

She saw the bell captain look up in horror. Saw the manager on duty start around the check-in desk.

Then the beast caught her in his claws. His fangs gashed her neck. And while she screamed, he ripped her to shreds on the pristine sidewalk of the Aqua Horizon Spa and Inn.

CHAPTER
TWENTY-THREE

As the van sped down the road and dawn tinged the sky with the purest, lightest blue, Karen opened the cart and helped Warlord climb out.

He moved with excruciating slowness. "It's the venom." The ceiling was low; he bent to avoid bumping his head. "I feel as if I'm one hundred years old." He shot her a hard look. "Are you feeling any effects?"

"My fingertips are tingling as if they've got frostbite."

He took her hands, turned them palms up, examined the skin, took her fingers into the curl of his. "You're doing really well."

"I didn't get much."

"You saved my life."

The guy was running a fever, had probably lost an eye, could scarcely move, and he was worried about her. He was warming her. Physically. Emotionally. "So now we're even," she said. "No obligation on either side."

"I saved your life. You saved mine." He smiled. "But I tied you up. So for us to be even, you should tie me up."

"I will." She yanked her hands free. "And throw you off a cliff."

"Uncharitable." In a sudden paroxysm of chill, he shivered and paced away from her. "You may not have to."

"I know," she muttered, and rooted around in the cart until she found a pile of clean towels. She wrapped two around his shoulders for warmth. Used one to wipe the sweat off his face.

And slammed against the back door of the van as the driver put the gas pedal to the floor.

"Varinskis." Warlord stood immobile, braced with one hand on the ceiling and one on the side, and looked out the back windows.

Inching her way to her feet, she looked out, too.

A black Hummer H2 with dark-tinted windows swung in behind them and was gaining fast.

The private airfield was ten minutes from the hotel.

"We'll never make it," she said.

Then the guy in the van's passenger seat

opened his door — at eighty miles an hour — leaned out, and dropped something on the road.

Karen watched a small ball roll, break open, and spread steel stars across the asphalt.

The Hummer drove over them. The tires blew. They swerved off the road.

Karen breathed a sigh of relief, started to turn back to Warlord — and the Hummer doors opened. A wolf sprang out. Another. Another. A peregrine falcon flew out and after them. And in an impressive show of sleek strength, a great panther leaped from the vehicle.

His body flowed as he ran. His spots glistened in the rising sun.

Her heart leaped with the horror of knowing . . . knowing the truth about these beasts, these things that came from the heart of evil, who would murder her, murder anyone who got in their way. "Who *are* these guys?"

"Varinskis," one of the guys in the front said aloud.

She glanced at Warlord.

He was one of them.

She glanced behind them. The wolves were falling behind. They were just too slow to keep up. But they kept running, knowing they'd get there.

The panther ran ahead, looking almost leisurely in his pursuit, but his green eyes seemed to glow.

"How much longer?" Warlord asked.

"We're almost there."

She saw him push aside the pain and the fever. Saw him gather his strength.

He flexed his knees, his arms. Coming to the back, he looked out. "Wolves. Bad choice. Their top speed is forty-five miles per hour. What else have they got?"

"A peregrine falcon."

"Which dives at speeds of over one hundred miles per hour. These Varinskis aren't all stupid. Someone in this part of the organization has brains. I wonder who?" He scrutinized the panther. "Innokenti. Of course. Wouldn't you know he'd be a panther?" Taking a breath, he quietly said, "The bird'll be on us before we can get on the plane."

She looked out on the runway. A Cessna Citation X sat on the runway, ready to go.

"That's yours?" She was impressed. Fastest small jet in the world.

"Can you fly it?"

"Try to stop me."

He nodded. "The bird will go for me. Take your bags and get on that plane."

"These guys are like you. A mixture of man and animal." She ought to be over the shock by now.

She wasn't.

"Except they're the bad guys and I'm the good guy." Warlord sounded so calm, so reassuring.

The van screeched around the corner and into the airfield, throwing her into Warlord's arms.

He held her, hard, for as long as it took them to clear the gate. "If I don't get on the plane by the time you're ready to go, shut the door and take off."

She could. She should. He was sending her away. She knew her way around the world better than most people did. She had money. She had his plane. He might not have faith in her, but she knew she could run from him and his freaky enemies, hide from them, keep the icon safe, and if she did that, she would never have to confront her passion for this . . . beast.

But the same stubborn *stupidity* that had made her go back in her cottage and save his life still held her in its grasp. "No."

"They want the icon."

"They can't have it, so you'd better win this fight."

Blood flushed his cheeks. He visibly shook

264

off the poison. He gazed at her with the old Warlord determination — how could he ever have fooled her? — and said, "You're right." As the driver slammed on the brakes, he held the door handle, and her. Before they'd come to a full stop he flung himself out. "Have the plane ready to go as soon as I've finished," he shouted. He landed on the asphalt with the lithe grace of a . . . a panther.

She saw a blur streaking toward him from above.

The van fishtailed, stopped, and both guys leaned back and yelled, "Out! Get out! Get to the plane!"

She grabbed her backpack and bag and went.

The van screeched away.

The small, beautiful blue and white personal jet sat waiting. She raced to the wheels and shoved the chocks aside, leaving the wheels free to roll. The stairs, part of the outer shell, hung there, open and inviting. She took the steps three at a time, got to the top, and turned in a tight whirl.

Below her, Warlord fought a slender man who handled a knife with deadly accuracy.

And out beyond the gate the wolves were loping along, their eyes fixed on Warlord, and glowing red.

"Fine," she muttered. She had her weapons, too.

She dumped her bags in the passenger seat and ran to the cockpit. She'd never flown one of these babies. Yet her father had trained her well. It took only a minute to familiarize herself with the controls. Then, with a grim smile, she began the preps for takeoff.

Battery — on. Fuel pumps, gangload — on. Right engine starter engage, rpm coming up. Ignition — on. Throttle around the horn. She could feel the vibration of the engine spooling up and hear the whine somewhere behind her.

Left engine starter switch in hand, ready to activate . . . As soon as Warlord was on board.

As she ran through the checklist, the tower radioed, "What the hell's going on down there?"

She grabbed the mike and put a note of panic in her voice. "They're fighting with knives. Send the airport police!"

Not that the police would do much good, but they'd provide a diversion, and she needed all the help she could get.

Behind her the engines purred, sweet and low. She moved the plane a few inches, feeling the way it handled.

The two men wrestled on the ground, and Warlord was visibly losing strength as they rolled.

The wolves were through the fence, all their attention focused on the battle.

The cops were running toward the fracas, their pistols in their hands.

Karen gunned the throttle and, with the engine screaming, headed for the wolves.

They hadn't expected that. They looked up, saw her illuminated face through the windscreen, and kept running, playing chicken with an airplane because they thought that a woman wouldn't really run over them.

Arrogant, egotistical, dumbshit thinking about this girl.

She swerved fast enough to mash one into wolfie roadkill.

The howls, composed of equal parts fury and anguish, reached her ears even over the sounds of the screaming engines.

She turned the plane again and chased one of the remaining wolves. It might be some supernatural being who changed from man to wolf and back again, but she was pretty sure she could make a dent in his ego with the wheels of her plane.

The wolf veered off toward the grassy edge of the runway.

She headed toward Warlord and the other, the falcon Varinski.

She'd made her point. The Varinski lost his concentration and watched her from the corners of his eyes.

Warlord gathered strength and, with a swift wrench of his hands, snapped the guy's neck.

"Yes!" She slowed and swerved, putting the steps close to Warlord. She heard a clatter of feet, looked and saw him pitch head-first into the cabin, and yelled, "Secure the cabin!"

Left starter — engage. Left throttle — advance.

Warlord looked up toward her, and as his will drained away his face became skeletal.

"Get up and do it!" Because the wolves had disappeared from her view, and she knew that at least one of them was going to try to catch their plane.

Picking up the microphone, she transmitted, "Tower, November eight-seven-eight-seven-six, taxiing, ready to copy clearance."

Warlord heaved himself to his feet. He looked out and blanched paler than death.

"There's a pistol in the side pocket of my backpack," she called.

He found it, pulled it out, and shot in one smooth movement.

She heard a yelp. "You killed him," she yelled.

"It takes more than that to kill a Varinski." He pulled the steps up and sealed the plane; then, as she moved onto the runway and accelerated, he staggered up to the cockpit and heaved himself into the copilot seat.

The Cessna neared takeoff speed, and a man, a human, stepped onto the runway.

She recognized him.

She shouldn't, but she did.

She'd seen him in a vision.

A face like a Neanderthal — wide jaw, heavy brow, and one cheekbone that had been broken and shoved up toward his eye. His earlobes hung low, each pierced by a three-eighths-inch countersunk bolt. He waded through the battle, throwing Warlord's men aside as if they were toothpicks. He was massive, indifferent to pain, fast as lightning —

No. No! She couldn't go into one of those trances now. She had to *focus*.

The Neanderthal stood with his massive hands on his hips, his eyes drilling into hers, silently commanding she stop.

The little Cessna accelerated like a slingshot dragster. She saw the mark on the airspeed indicator indicating single-engine speed as the airspeed needle flashed past it. Immediately she pulled the control wheel back slightly.

Airborne, gear up, flaps up, turn to departure heading.

Right before she hit the Neanderthal, he moved aside.

"What was that?" she whispered.

"My idea of hell."

CHAPTER TWENTY-FOUR

The rust-colored desert and its dangers fell away and the blue sky embraced them.

"What are you doing?" the tower screamed at them. "You did not have takeoff clearance! Return to the field immediately! A violation has been filed!"

Warlord reached down, flipped a switch, and the speaker went silent. Elevating the long middle finger of his clenched right fist, he rotated it with a flourish and pointed straight ahead.

"What does that mean?" Karen asked.

Warlord grinned. "Screw them. I filed visual flight rules."

Karen grinned back. "Where are we going?"

"Turn the pointy end of this aerial vehicle to northwest. Three-three-zero should be about right."

As they arrived at a nice, safe, mountain-clearing altitude, she engaged the autopilot and turned to Warlord.

He looked like hell. A long cut on his chest oozed blood onto his crumpled two-hundred-dollar shirt, and his eyes were closed hard, the skin over them crusting over, as if he were trying to keep evil visions at bay. One fist rested over his heart, the other over his gut, and his legs were braced as if he were fighting a grim battle.

She was sorry, but she didn't have time for sympathy. "What's the plan here? You're in bad shape, and to tell you the truth, I'm not feeling so good myself."

He stared at her through one dull green eye. "It's the poison. Even a trace is toxic to someone like you."

"I'm not dead, just feeling ill."

"You also swallowed a few molecules of my blood, and that will fight the venom."

"Why? What's so special about your blood?" *Other than the fact that it makes me see things you've seen, hear things you've heard, fall into your memories, your mind.*

He grimaced and didn't answer.

"It's because you're one of them." And that made her furious all over again. "You're a . . . a Varinski."

His unwounded eye sprang open, and he glared fiercely. "No, I'm a Wilder. My name is Adrik Wilder. Remember that."

"Why should I?"

"Because if I die of this, I want one person to remember my name."

"You're not going to die." Not after all this, he wasn't. She wouldn't allow it.

"No?" He groaned and moved his long legs as if the joints ached. "Go back in the cabin. Get in the right overhead. Get out my clothes."

She did as he commanded, and when she came back in he was naked, huddled on the seat, his formal wear crumpled on the floor beside him.

She sized him up with a single glance. His body looked longer, thinner than it had been in the Himalayas, and yet the muscles were sculpted. He had scars on his shoulders, pale and crisscrossed, and across his chest and down his arm, a vibrant tattoo, two thunderbolts of glorious red and gold.

Despite her fervent hopes while they were apart, his genitals were still intact.

"When did you have time to get a tattoo?" She touched the thunderbolt lightly.

"It's not a tattoo. It's the mark that came to each Wilder boy at puberty, the one that proves he's part of the pact with the devil." He winked. "It's a swell gift to get along with a cracking voice, body hair, and inconveniently timed erections."

273

"But you didn't have it before."

"I did, but as I grew more evil, the stain shriveled and became black."

"Like your eyes."

"Yes. Like my eyes. And as with my eyes, as I've stepped back into the light, the color has returned." He shivered, and goose bumps spread over his skin.

She started to shove his arms into the black T-shirt, but when he leaned forward she caught a glimpse of his back. The crisscrossed scars covered him from his buttocks all the way up his spine and from shoulder to shoulder. Some were deep, cutting ridges through his skin. In outrage she asked, "What happened to you?"

"It doesn't matter." He took the T-shirt and pulled it on.

"Doesn't matter!" She pushed him into the black flannel shirt and wrapped him in the thigh-length camouflage coat. "How could that not matter? Someone beat you!"

"Doesn't matter," he repeated.

Kneeling at his feet, she fed his legs into long underwear and a pair of camouflage combat pants. "It was that Varinski, wasn't it? The guy who defeated you in battle."

"How do you know that?" he snapped.

So she was right. She had seen into his mind. Into his memories.

Every time she tasted his blood, their minds' connection grew stronger. . . .

But he didn't realize it, and she didn't want to explain what she couldn't comprehend herself. "Doesn't matter," she imitated him.

"You are an aggravating woman." He pulled up the pants, dug in the pocket, and found a piece of paper. He shoved it at her. "In an hour, call that number. You'll get Jasha. Give him these coordinates and tell him Adrik needs him."

"Who's Jasha?"

"My brother."

"Why don't *you* call him?"

"There's a pretty good chance he hates me."

"You have that effect on people."

He caught her by the back of the neck, held her as he leaned down, and kissed her hard. "But not on you."

"I do hate you," she said automatically.

At least, she had hated him for two years, and for good reason. But no matter how hard she'd tried, she hadn't forgotten him.

Now, as she stared at his face, so close to hers, as fever flashed through him, as his pupils narrowed and he shuddered in agony, she knew what he'd risked to rescue her.

Maybe she still hated him. She didn't

now. But death pumped through his veins — through her veins, also — and she would not let it take them.

They had unfinished business.

Warlord sat back, his face twisted. "Whether he hates me or not, there's a pretty good chance Jasha will come. *If* he believes you."

"I can't wait to make *that* phone call."

"I prefiled the flight plan with the FAA. We're about to change it."

She remembered the guy on the runway. "Good idea."

"Descend as low as you can comfortably fly and turn north, across the Great Basin."

She disengaged the autopilot and did as he directed.

He continued, "We're headed for the Sierra Nevadas just south of Yosemite."

"And then where?"

His mouth set in grim lines. "That's all."

"What do you mean?" She wasn't going to like the answer, she could tell.

"We're flying this baby right into the side of Acantilado Mountain."

CHAPTER
TWENTY-FIVE

"No. Oh, no." Karen clutched Warlord's arm. "Have you lost your mind?"

"We'll jump in tandem so we don't get separated." He handed her a sheet of paper.

She glanced at it. It was written instructions to get them to the site where they would meet Jasha . . . if he decided to come.

"Are you afraid?" he asked in apparent concern.

"No, I'm not afraid! Why would I be afraid?"

"You're afraid of falling."

"I'm not afraid of jumping!" Did he think she was some kind of coward? "But look around you. This is a Cessna Citation X. It's a beautiful bird. Crashing her would be a crime!" Karen frowned. "Actually, it probably really is a crime."

He considered her as he might consider a butterfly. "I've been a mercenary. I've killed and robbed. Do you see me as someone who is worried about the criminality of crashing my own airplane?"

"I suppose not. But the Cessna . . ."

"Did you see him?"

At once she knew who he was talking about. The guy in her dream. The guy who had stood there and watched the airplane come at him without a sign of fear. She nodded, her gaze fixed on Warlord.

"That beast is Innokenti Varinski. Remember that deal with the devil? His ancestor made it. Their ancestor . . . they're trackers. They're mercenaries. They find their prey wherever it runs. And they're after you."

"But . . . !" She patted the perfectly functioning, beautifully sleek controls.

"I know." He caressed his leather seat. "We're going to crash it in a remote location in the High Sierras. It's winter. Rescuers will have a hell of a time finding us."

"They'll follow the homing signal from the emergency locator transponder."

He looked at her incredulously.

And she knew. "You removed the ELT."

"Disabled it," he said. "When they do finally locate the crash site, it's going to appear that our bodies have been incinerated in the fiery crash. The Varinskis will be suspicious, but this is the only chance we have of putting them off our scent, of buying ourselves time to escape."

Questions and protests whirled in her head. "If the Varinskis are mercenaries, who's paying them to find me?"

"No one. They're hunting you for themselves."

"Why? Why me?"

"Because you've got the icon."

"Why? Is it that expensive that they have to have it?"

"No. It's powerful. If it is united with the other three Varinski family icons, the pact with the devil will be broken and they will be like other men." He pulled on the socks she'd brought him.

"How do you know this?"

"After I held the icon, after it burned me, I was haunted by the realization that I was in league with the devil. That whether I liked it or not, I was the same as Innokenti, distasteful to heaven." Warlord watched her steadily. "And not worthy of the woman who obsessed me in my dreams."

She shook her head. She didn't want that responsibility.

"Oh, yes. You kept me alive in the dark, and somehow you possessed one of the Varinski icons. I didn't believe that was coincidence. Those icons have been hidden for a thousand years. So after I . . . after . . .

about a year after you left, I got myself together and I made it my business to find out what was happening. I visited the old Varinski home in the Ukraine." Warlord laughed. "That place was a joke, a huge old house with rooms added on wherever, broken windows stuffed with rags, cars in the yard overgrown with weeds. There are at least a hundred Varinskis living there. They'd killed their leader the year before and were fighting among themselves to see who would take over the family business."

"Who would hire these . . . assassins?"

"Mostly dictators and military leaders, but really, anyone who can afford their price. And don't forget the Varinskis have been doing this for a thousand years. They've got the reputation to charge whatever they please."

"Is this big business?" she asked incredulously.

"Is war big business? Is murder big business?"

That was answer enough. "So the Varinskis are rolling in money."

"Let's say they have good reason to fight like hell to maintain the status quo." He was fumbling with his hiking boots, acting as though his fingers were numb.

She put the plane on autopilot again, knelt

at his feet, and pushed first one, then the other, into his hiking boots. "So you sneaked in the house somehow?"

"No." He grinned. "I walked right in like I belonged."

She had to admire his guts.

"Apparently I look enough like the rest of the family that no one paid a bit of attention. I wandered around, listened while they talked, and found out someone had made a prophecy —"

"Who? A medium?" She wavered between sarcasm and belief.

"Sort of. Uncle Ivan is this old Varinski. He's blind — the first Varinski ever to go blind."

"No Varinski in a thousand years has gone blind?"

"The deal with the devil guaranteed good health and long life, but now there's illness, and that is a sign the pact is disintegrating. From what I could tell, Uncle Ivan has these white, cloudy eyes, he drinks all the time, and pretty much is incoherent and drooling. Except every once in a while he speaks in Satan's voice." Warlord shivered. "He warned their leader that he'd better find the icons or else, and when Boris turned out to be a failure, he had the Varinskis kill Boris."

Nothing made sense; legends and mythical beasts were playing on a great big plasma screen that made the monsters — and the heroes — look more real than anything in the real world, and she was scared.

"What about you?" she asked. "Will you be like other men, and never change into a cat or . . . ?"

"I assume." His good eye became a fevered slit, and he looked . . . hungry. Anguished.

Warlord said she shone with light. She didn't believe that, but she tried for a little optimism. "If the Varinskis are in such disarray, you've got a good chance of winning."

"Yes, except . . ."

"Except what?"

"There's one kid, name of Vadim. He smells like . . . evil, and I swear, when I was there he was the only one who knew I didn't belong. He's young, so at first he couldn't seize power. But the old men who oppose him are dying, not by any natural means, and when I was there Vadim was gaining ground. Since then I've talked to other mercenaries, listened to the rumors, watched his progress on the Internet, and he's in charge now." Warlord was grim. "If he succeeds in stopping us — my family, the Wilders — the devil will keep every Varinski soul for another thousand years."

They were flying over the western edge of Nevada. To the east was the dry, brown, flat Great Basin. To the west the mountains rose, shocking white and snowy against the lowering gray sky.

She looked around at the luxurious Cessna. She looked out at the Sierra Nevadas. And she did not want to abandon this airplane. "You've got a brother," she said persuasively. "You were sending me to him. Why don't we go to him together?"

"He's not happy with me, and he will be less happy when I bring my battle to his doorstep."

"That battle is your family's battle." She finished tying his boots and sat back on her heels.

"Innokenti is fighting for the Varinskis, yes. But he is stalking *me.* I made a fool of him. He beat me in battle. He imprisoned me. And all the while he thought I was nothing more than a mere human."

"So what?"

"Do you realize how much the Varinskis would love to get their hands on a son of the current Konstantine? Of the American Konstantine Wilder? No, of course you don't. If they held one of us, me or one of my brothers, or, God forbid, my sister, the battle would be over." He grinned unpleasantly. "Innokenti had me and never realized who I was. He never realized that burying me a thousand feet underground wouldn't be enough to keep me confined. He didn't realize I could generate a revolt that would make the Varinskis a laughing-stock among assassins and mercenaries around the world."

"It's personal between you two." The sting in her fingertips was spreading up her arm. Her toes tingled painfully.

"And you're caught in the middle. I'm sorry." He sounded sincere.

"Not that I like being caught in the middle, but I rather like —" She stopped.

"What?"

"Nothing." *I rather like that you refuse to bring the wrath of the Varinskis down on your unsuspecting family.*

"We'll parachute out of here together. We'll survive somehow, and there's a good chance this maneuver will fool Innokenti completely."

"Really? A good chance?"

"A decent chance. The best chance I can make for us. If he believes his mission is complete, that we're dead, then we'll be safe."

"Okay. Winter in the High Sierras." She thought of the icy peaks, the snow measured in feet instead of inches, the avalanches . . . the cliffs waiting for the unwary to slip, plummet onto the rocks below, and die. "Goody."

He took her hand. "You won't fall."

When she was his captive, she had hated that he knew her weakness. Now, when danger nipped at their heels and he was scarred by the past and threatened by the future, his words comforted her.

"I know. I really do. I think it's just a natural fear of falling combined with . . ." She could almost hear Jackson Sonnet's voice snap, *God damn it, Karen, stop being so melodramatic.* "Well, just a natural fear of falling."

"Combined with your mother's death," Warlord finished her thought.

"You did your research." How uncomfortable was this? He knew about her mother. He was analyzing her. Seating herself in the pilot's seat, she busied herself with the controls.

"It wasn't tough to find that news report." Then he surprised her. He put his arm around her shoulders. "I am sorry. I can't imagine the pain of losing your mother so soon."

To have him talk about her mother and hold her at the same time . . . that made her choke up. Choke up over a death that occurred twenty-six years ago. She furtively wiped a tear off her cheek. "I've never really gotten over it. I should have, but I haven't."

"I did some research on your father, too. He doesn't sound like the most sensitive guy in the world. Maybe you were never given the chance to get over it."

She turned her head and looked at Warlord. She should be incredulous — this man who had held her captive, who placed slave bracelets on her wrists, who spent two solid weeks inflicting the best sex on her unwilling body — he was making aspersions about Jackson Sonnet and his lack of sensitivity.

But Warlord was so close his face almost touched hers. And this feeling that welled up in her — it wasn't lust. It had nothing to do with sex. It was the recognition of one wounded human soul for another. "When did you last see your mother?" she asked in a low voice.

He answered as quietly, "Seventeen years ago."

"Do you ever miss her?"

"Every day. And when I see her again, I'll go down on my knees and beg her forgiveness for leaving and never letting her know I was alive."

"What will she do?"

"Probably pop me a good one to the back of the head. Then hug me. Then feed me. I hope we get stuck on the 'feed me' stage for a while. She can really cook."

Karen smiled. He sounded so affectionate. So hopeful. "What about your father?"

Warlord's arm fell away. "My father and I always clashed."

"Why?"

"It's hard. I love being a beast. I love stalking my prey. I love fighting with tooth and claw and knowing I will win," Warlord said fiercely. "But my father is named Konstantine, because he was the leader of the Varinskis. Then he met my mother and fell in love. They married — from the stories they tell, the Varinskis and her Romany tribe opposed the match — and immigrated to the United States. They changed their name to Wilder, had us three boys, and then ten years later, a miracle girl, the first girl born in a thousand years. . . ." Warlord half smiled.

Karen watched him, fascinated to see him lost in his sentimental recollections.

But Warlord caught himself and straightened. "The thing is, as the leader of the Varinskis, my father did some unspeakable stuff before he married Mama, and he was strict like you wouldn't believe. He said . . .

he said every time I turned, I slid down the long path to hell, and you know what? He was right. I know it now. The mouth of hell almost swallowed me before I turned away, and even now it beckons me."

He scared her when he talked that way. "What do you mean?" she whispered.

"I should never become a panther. I should never step into the shadow. But when I do, I feel so strong and sure. It must be like cocaine. It creates an illusion of power so addictive, I can never stop. Yet I have to, or I'll be like . . . them."

"The Varinskis."

"Yes. Like the Varinskis. So you see, for a lot of reasons we have to save the icon."

Furtively she stroked the gold bracelet around her wrist, then straightened her shoulders. "I'll throw it away."

"Will you?"

She couldn't. Of course she couldn't. She couldn't betray that child with the beautiful blue-green eyes, the eyes that looked so much like hers. Karen turned her gaze away from him.

"No, of course not." His skin took on a stretched look, as if he were swelling all over, and as if his head were too heavy he leaned it back against the headrest. "Because one woman is meant to possess that icon, one woman only. And that is you."

"Because I found it."

He rolled his head and looked at her. "Do you know why you found it?"

She shook her head.

"Because according to Uncle Ivan's damned vision, only one woman can find and hold that icon — and that woman is the woman I love."

CHAPTER
TWENTY-SIX

"What a pile of crap." Karen sat stiff and furious in her seat. "You don't know what love is, if you think what you feel for me is love."

Warlord closed his good eye and thought about it. "I guess I can follow that. You think that if I loved you, I wouldn't have kidnapped and held you."

"Or come for me at the spa and lied about who you were."

She was so angry. And so beautiful. If he weren't sick, the beast in him would rise to claim her, and she would have reason to hate him once more. As it was, the snake's venom ate at his liver and ripped at his skin. Only by concentrating on her and their conversation could he keep from wailing in agony. "In my own defense, I had to lie or you would have run. You almost ran anyway."

"You mean when I saw you the first time

and I thought you were . . . who you are?" She pointed a finger at him. "And that's another thing. You eavesdropped on Dika and me." Obviously she was leaping from one resentment to another. "Running away would have been a good idea. A solid plan."

"I would have followed you."

"You didn't follow me last time."

"Out of the Himalayas, you mean. I couldn't." Reaching out, he took her chin and turned her face to his. "You believe me, don't you?"

"Yes. You could never stand to let me win."

With her snaps and sulks, she made him want to laugh. With her spirit and bravery, she made him want to protect her. With her body . . . she simply made him want. "In Nepal I grabbed for you like a selfish boy. But on the day I lost you, I started a long walk through hell." He turned his face toward the sun.

In the past year, it seemed he could never get enough sun.

"When I came out on the other side I'd learned a few lessons. I knew what I didn't want, and I knew what I did want. So at the spa I courted you, and actually thought I did a pretty good job. You were going to sleep with me until . . . Damn it! I shouldn't have kissed you."

"Do you think I wouldn't have recognized you at some point?" She sounded more than a little testy.

"If I could have gotten your clothes off and my head between your legs, you would have been too far gone to care." He wasn't as ill as he feared, for the mere idea worked on him like an aphrodisiac. "At least until morning."

She went from testy to totally pissed off. "You have never suffered from either modesty or lack of confidence."

"Honey, I serviced a lot of women before I brought you to my tent, and for one reason — so I would know how to make you happy."

"That was so kind of you." She was really ramping up the sarcasm now. "You sacrificed yourself on the altar of love, and just for little ol' me, waiting in your future. What a sweetheart you are. And to keep in practice, I'm sure you've serviced a lot of women since."

The brief flush of excitement faded, leaving him chilled. "No. There hasn't been another woman since you."

She stared at him, her mouth half-open.

He didn't give her time to recover. He pulled himself out of his seat and staggered toward the back. "I'm going to put on my jumpsuit, get ready to go, or I'm afraid I won't make it." He opened the overhead, knowing perfectly well she'd turned to watch him. "I've been with a lot of women, but other than you, I've only ever loved one woman."

That gave her back her power of speech. "Who was this paragon?"

"She was just a girl. Emma Seymour. We met at a band competition. She was from the opposing school."

"High school?" By the tone of Karen's voice, he knew he'd surprised her.

"Yeah. I'm an all-American boy. I went to high school. In Washington."

"You're really from Washington?"

"I might kill and steal, but I don't lie." He pulled down his parachute and the survival gear he'd stowed, knowing this day might come. "I remember Emma's face so clearly. The dark brown eyes, the long, dark hair . . . her complexion was perfectly clear." Considering what a pimply-faced kid he'd been, that had been a real marvel. "She didn't want me to tell anyone about us, so I didn't. When we talked on the phone, it was in low voices so no one could overhear. We met down in Burlington twice a week for coffee, and we discussed books we liked and the computer I was building and where she wanted to go to college. We did not talk about our families. The whole affair had a thrilling kind of *Romeo and Juliet* secrecy." He glanced toward the cockpit to see how Karen was taking it.

Her mouth was hanging open again. She snapped it closed and asked, "Did you sleep with her?"

"My first time ever." Talking about it made him feel marginally better. "We did it right below the bleachers after the football game was over and the other kids had left, and I remember I was so scared I was trembling."

"That's . . . well, that's cute."

"I didn't think so. I really hoped she didn't notice, because it wasn't her first time."

"Was she an upperclassman?" Karen sounded both amused and fascinated.

"She was a senior." He pulled on the jumpsuit and barely kept from groaning at the pain in his joints. "She was a goddess."

"Especially since she made you feel like a god?" Karen was chuckling now.

"When I did something dumb, she didn't make a big deal of it. She made me forget to worry about coming too soon. She made it good for me." He stopped and stared straight ahead. "Which is why I killed her father."

Karen's laughter stopped as if it had been cut with a knife.

"After we'd . . . had sex, I went home and my mother was up." Even the memory made him squirm. "If there's one person a guy who's just been laid for the first time doesn't want to see, it's his mom. But I must not have looked any different, because she informed me that Emma was on the phone and told me to tell her not to call so late. Then Mama kissed me and went to bed."

"Is that the last time you saw her?"

"Yeah." He nodded. "Yeah."

"What did Emma want?" Karen watched him, her eyes troubled.

"The first thing I thought was that she was pregnant. Then I realized we'd just done it two hours before and it was too early to tell, plus we'd used a condom. She asked if I still loved her, and I said I loved her a lot. And she said she didn't want me to think she was a slut, and I asked if she still respected me." Seventeen years later, and he remembered the conversation as if it were yesterday. "So I told her I was coming over, and she said no, her dad would kill me. The way she said it bugged me. Like she was really scared. So I told her to unlock her window. I hung up and ran over."

"She lived close."

"No. Not really. By road her house was about forty miles away. But a panther doesn't travel by road. I took the straightest line possible — up the hill, down the hill, through the creek. Her place was small, an old farmhouse, and the place looked like hell — rot in the siding, broken step on the porch, missing shingles." He brought his fully loaded backpack down and set it on a seat. "She'd opened her window, and I could smell her scent."

"Her scent." Karen looked out at the high, thin clouds streaking by. "Like in Nepal, when you could smell mine? Because you're a panther?"

He nodded. "But along with Emma's scent, I could smell the faint tang of blood. She'd had her period the week before, and I knew this wasn't menstrual blood. She was hurt."

"Her father?"

"I didn't realize what had happened right away. That kind of behavior was so foreign to me — my dad worshiped my sister, cherished my mother. I'd never seen anything like that." The memory of Emma's pain still made Warlord sick — and so angry his eyes glowed with flame. "He'd hit her so hard her nose was broken. Swollen. He split her lip. She was holding her left arm. I asked if she had any broken bones, and she thought maybe her wrist. I wanted to take her to the hospital. She said no, they didn't have any money, and he . . . he wouldn't let her out of the house. She said some school-teacher saw her and me together, called her dad, and when Emma came in he was waiting for her."

"Did he —"

"Rape her? No, not that time, but the way she acted . . ." Warlord wanted to punch something. "I told her that it was my fault she was hurt, and I'd take care of it."

"What did she do?"

"She cried. And begged. Her father was a farmer, a big guy, and I was still a skinny kid. She thought her father would beat me to death." Warlord checked the parachute, made sure it would open, then repacked it and pulled it on his shoulders.

"How did you . . . ?"

"I made a lot of noise. He came into her bedroom. I challenged him to a fight. He laughed. Because, you know, he was one of those guys who didn't beat up on people who could hit him back. I taunted him, made him good and mad, and jumped out the window. I told him I'd meet him at the end of his driveway. That was clear out by the road, out of sight of the house. The guy lumbered out after me. Man, he was big. Fists like hams. When I stepped out of the shadows, all he saw was a boy. He was so cocky. He thought he was going to kill me with one hand tied behind his back."

"He was in for a surprise."

"When I leaped at him, I changed. He saw the panther and screamed. He didn't stand a chance."

"Neither did Emma."

"Just what I thought." Warlord pulled on his helmet. "I killed him. Ripped him to shreds. Dragged the body away. Hid it in the mountains. God only knows if it was ever found. Then I ran away. Went to Seattle, stowed away on a Philippine cargo ship, and never looked back."

"But your family?" Karen's voice trembled.

Karen was too sensitive, too soft for him. But God help him, he couldn't let her go. "My dad always said that if I wasn't careful, if I didn't control myself, I would kill, and kill again. I figured I had fulfilled my destiny."

"You became Warlord."

"Being a mercenary was a good — and very profitable — job for a man like me." The story ended, his need to tell Karen the truth was discharged, and the sickness returned with a vengeance. He sat on the floor, stretched out in the aisle, and relaxed. "I've done a lot of things I've regretted since then, but no matter what has happened since, no matter what I've done or where my crimes have led me, when I remember poor Emma, I'm not sorry. If I could, I'd do it again."

When the phone rang in Jasha Wilder's bedroom, he tightened his hold on the woman in his arms and said, "Leave it."

His secretary tried to wiggle free. "We can't, Jasha. Darling, it's probably the winery. We're already late. Honey, come on, stop. You know I can't think when you do that."

"That's why I'm doing it." But when she groped for the phone, he rolled away, lay flat on his back, and cursed whoever had interrupted a lovely interlude.

She settled against the pillows, carefully covered her breasts with the covers, and picked up the receiver. "Ann Smith."

"Ann Wilder," he muttered. When he'd hired her as his administrative assistant, she'd been quiet, modest, and shy. Now she was his wife, and to that list of qualities he had to add stubborn. She was plain stubborn about not changing her name to his, and it irked him.

She probably refused to do it *because* it irked him.

"Ann Wilder," he said again.

She ignored him and spoke into the phone. "May I ask what this is in reference to?"

He faintly heard a reply.

Ann's spine snapped into an upright exclamation point. In a crisp tone that made him sit up, too, she said, "There is one word that will make all the difference in this phone call. I will either let you speak to Mr. Wilder or I will hang up. What is that word?"

Whatever the answer was, it made Ann say, "Just a minute, please." She put the caller on hold and turned to Jasha, her color high. "Her name is Karen Sonnet. She says she's in a plane with Adrik. When I asked for a word, she said, 'icon.' "

Jasha took the receiver.

Ann got up, put on her robe, and fetched the laptop. She searched for "Karen Sonnet" and brought up a screenful of possibilities.

Jasha took the phone off hold and said, "Jasha Wilder. You'd better make this good."

"I have no intention of making this good. I don't know what your family problems

300

are, and I don't care." This Karen wasn't bothering to subdue her irritation. "But Warlord insisted I call and give you these coordinates —"

"Warlord?" Jasha didn't know whether to smirk or groan.

Ann lifted her brows.

Jasha nodded.

She typed *Warlord* into her search engine.

"Rick," Karen said. "Rick Wilder. Or Adrik. Whatever."

Ann typed on her laptop, *Adrik Wilder.*

Karen continued, "Anyway, he asked that you come to help us because we have Varinskis tracking us, and he believes we need help."

"Why isn't he on the phone?"

"He's unconscious in the back of the plane."

"That's convenient." In a flat, furious voice, Jasha said, "Karen Sonnet, or whoever you are, I don't know what the hell stunt you're pulling, but when he was seventeen my brother Adrik disappeared from our lives. Two years ago we received a letter from Nepal notifying us that he was dead, and his remains were returned to us. We buried those remains."

"Did you think to check the dental records?" For someone who was asking for

301

help, Karen was damned sarcastic.

"There wasn't enough left for dental records."

"You should have checked the DNA." He heard Karen take an annoyed breath. "Look. We're crashing the plane in a remote location in the High Sierras and making our way on foot to these coordinates. You can take them down or not. You can believe me or not. You can help us or not. But as I understand it, there's a prophecy about *your* family, *your* cousins want *my* icon, and the giant snake that bit Warlord isn't nearly as horrible as the extreme fighter who's tracking us."

Whoever she was, she knew a hell of a lot about a hell of a lot. Jasha gestured to Ann for a pen and paper. "Give me the coordinates. Maybe I'll be there."

Ann handed him the paper, and on her laptop typed, *Rick Wilder.*

"And maybe if you're not up for it, you ought to send help." Karen rattled off the coordinates.

"I'll call you with my decision."

"Not on this phone you won't. It's going down with the plane."

Jasha heard a beeping.

"Gotta go," Karen said. "We're jumping in three minutes."

"I thought you said Warlord was unconscious."

"He is, on and off. If the slap of cold air doesn't wake him up, I'm flinging him out anyway."

"What if he doesn't come to?"

"Serve him right."

Maybe it was *Adrik.*

"Although sometimes he's not so bad. You know?" As if she didn't like admitting to softness, she snapped back into annoyance. "Don't worry; we're jumping tandem. I'll get him on the ground. Then . . . God help us if you won't."

The line went dead.

Jasha stared at the receiver in fury and astonishment. He was the president and CEO of Wilder Wines. He was married to the finest woman in the world. He was the oldest Wilder son. He was a warrior. He was a wolf. No one talked to him that way. "Does she think I'm so dumb that I'm going to drop everything and go running into what is obviously a Varinski trap? I cannot believe the nerve of that woman."

"It's been two years since your mother had that vision," Ann reminded him absently as she flipped through Internet pages. "Two years since I found the first icon and Tasya found the second one. Your father's

303

illness is accelerating. If we don't find those last two icons pretty soon, he's going to die, the pact will go on forever, and —"

"I know. I know!" Jasha hated being so helpless. "He'll go to hell for all eternity."

"And your mother will be in her own hell without him." Ann tapped his arm and handed him the laptop.

There, on a tech business news page, was the announcement of a hot new computer game set to sweep American gamers, and under the headline, WARLORD, was a photo of its designer, Rick Wilder.

Even after seventeen years, Jasha recognized his brother Adrik.

Tears sprang to his eyes. "The little shit," he said.

Ann hugged him. "I know."

"Seventeen years without a word. He broke Mama's heart. The news of his death almost killed Papa."

"I know."

"For God's sake, we buried Adrik's remains."

"I know."

"I ought to leave that snot to freeze in the wilderness."

"You should." Ann looked at him. "Do you want me to charter you a plane to Yosemite?"

"Right." He kissed Ann and jumped out of bed. "I'll call Rurik and tell him we've got to go get our little brother out of trouble — again."

CHAPTER
TWENTY-SEVEN

The autopilot was on heading hold/altitude hold as it flew them low through the Sierra Nevadas. Snowy peaks dwarfed the tiny plane. Twice a mountain came so close Karen flinched in the pilot's seat. Grimly she hoped Warlord's calculations were right. If he was off the slightest bit, the beautifully sleek Cessna Citation X would never have a chance to smash into Acantilado Mountain. Instead it would smash into a different mountain, probably too soon, and take Warlord and Karen with it.

She finished her preparations, pressed a kiss of apology to her palm and then to the instrument panel, and stepped back into the cabin.

Warlord was stretched out in the aisle, dressed for the jump.

She touched his forehead, pressed her hand against the vein beating in his throat.

He was still alive. *Thank God.* She'd

wondered. She'd feared . . . and why, she didn't know. Of all the men in this world who deserved to die, in her book he had been number one.

She pulled on her coat, jumpsuit, goggles, and full-face helmet. She strapped her bag to the front of her, then pulled on the bare piggy-back harness. She could not believe she was going to abandon this beautiful plane.

Yet she couldn't really whip up indignation about the loss of the airplane, not after hearing the story about his first love. . . . *If I could, I'd do it again.*

He'd lured a man to his death. He'd killed him with tooth and claw.

Emma's father had deserved it. And if he'd been turned over to the courts, sooner or later he would have walked and gone back and beaten Emma again. Or killed her.

So who was in the wrong?

She stepped over Warlord's body. His camping backpack bulged, with snowshoes strapped to the outside.

She looked down at his unconscious face. "You were ready for this, weren't you?"

Going to the door, she located the emergency door-release handle and activated it. The door blew out and down, disappearing under the Citation's wing. Wind blasted a tornado in the cabin. She turned and started.

Warlord was standing behind her, strapping his backpack to his waist.

The first alarm sounded; the plane's computer recognized that it was too low, recognized that it was approaching an obstacle.

"Is Jasha coming?" Warlord shouted into the wind.

"I don't know," she shouted back. "I probably said the wrong thing." She glanced at the rapidly oncoming mountain.

Another alarm. And another.

"There isn't a right thing to say to my family. I've burned too many bridges." He hooked her to him.

"He said they'd buried your remains." She looked back at him. "Ready?"

"Let's go."

The alarms were sounding continuously now. Frigid air blasted them in the face.

They jumped.

They were free-falling less than a thousand feet from the ground.

She counted to three, then yelled, "Do it!"

Warlord pulled their rip cord. The updraft snapped them from full screaming downward fall to a slow, peaceful descent. A slow, peaceful, freezing-ass-cold descent.

Behind her, Warlord maneuvered them to face the impact.

He wrapped his arms around her as the glorious, sleek bird of a Cessna cascaded into the stark, rocky cliff of Acantilado Mountain. The ball of flame exploded, then disintegrated. The concussion blasted them across the treetops and down a slope.

With the two of them hooked together, and all the weight they carried, they descended fast. Too fast. They had no clear space to land. "Cross your legs!" Karen heard, and complied just as the snowy forest reached up to snag them. She flinched as her boot hit a tree limb.

Then they were in the woods, snow spilling off the branches that slapped them for their impertinence. The scent of pine filled the air.

They were headed for a tree trunk, the biggest tree trunk she'd ever seen. Warlord's arms tightened around her. She threw her arms up to protect her head.

And something grabbed the parachute and jerked them to a stop.

The jolt knocked the breath out of her.

Then, with a huge crack, the branch that held them broke. They plummeted to the ground, smacking boughs, until Karen landed facedown in a snowbank, Warlord on her back. The impact broke through the crust. Ice packed in under her face guard, filled her eyes and her mouth, and brought her to immediate full consciousness. The weight of Warlord and the supplies made her flail helplessly, desperate to take a breath.

He rolled over, pulling her out of the snow, and while she yanked off her helmet he unhooked the strap that bound them.

While she spit and wiped, he came to his feet, pulled off his helmet — and laughed.

She couldn't believe it.

"What's wrong with you?" She cleaned a chunk of hard-packed snow out of her cleavage. "We almost died — more than once we almost died — we're still in serious danger, and you're *laughing*."

"But we didn't die, and what a ride!" He laughed again, and shrugged out of the parachute harness. "Wasn't it spectaular?"

"No."

"Come on, Karen." He hugged her to his side. "Gravity won. We got to the ground. That's a good omen."

"You're crazy."

"One of us has to be. And look." He pointed to his face. "The cold brought the swelling down. I can open my eye a little —

and I can see."

He was right. Where the venom had touched, his skin still looked appalling — crusted-over and red. But his lid was better, and his eye was clear and moved freely.

Her relief made her admit, "Then I guess all this snow is good for something." He watched her wiggle around, pulling snow from places that should never have seen snow. "Need any help digging that out?"

"No."

"Really. I'd be glad to help."

Sick as he was, he was smiling. Flirting. Happy to be on the ground, glad his eye was undamaged, and somehow shored up with the unshakable belief of idiotic manhood that if he could just put his warm hands on her freezing body, she'd collapse into his arms in a passionate heap. "You're incorrigible."

"So I've been told." With a carefree shrug, he gave up . . . for the moment.

He put on his snowshoes, then helped her on with hers. Glancing up at the broken branch above them, he said, "If the Varinskis search, that's going to betray us."

"We're over seven thousand feet. It's twenty degrees. The storm is starting." She held out a gloved hand and let a snowflake drift into it. "The Varinskis are the least of our problems."

"True. The snow will cover the wreckage and our tracks."

"If we don't get to a safe place, the snow will bury us alive."

He collected the parachute. "Come on, while I can walk, and let's find somewhere to set up camp."

"And then what?"

"And then we will live through this . . . or die together." He kissed her cold cheek. "If I have to die, I want it to be with you."

She pulled a hat and scarf out of her bag and wrapped herself up. "Let's make sure we live. I've got unfinished business with the Varinskis." She shot him a meaningful glance. "And with you."

CHAPTER
TWENTY-EIGHT

Karen saw Warlord stagger, go down on one knee. Lines of pain etched his face, and the venom's mark etched his skin.

She stopped, gasping. "We have to set up camp."

"We haven't gone far enough." He rose to his feet. He sank back down. "Not far to the rendezvous point."

The excitement of the jump had kept them on their feet, but after a mile in the snowy woods with a snowstorm closing in, that excitement had failed. Everything about Warlord — his fading color, his dull eyes, the sweat that beaded on the exposed part of his brow — mirrored her own adrenaline crash, and the creeping pain and paralysis of the venom.

"It doesn't matter. We simply can't go any farther."

"We've got to. We're too close to the spot where we landed. We're too easy for the

Varinskis to find."

"Right. You go ahead. Let me know how that works out." She looked around for the best place to set up camp. When she looked back, he'd quietly pitched forward on his face.

She dragged herself over, flipped him onto his back, and checked his pulse. He was giving off flashes of fever that should have melted him right through the snow. "What did you expect?" she asked his prone body. "Five hours ago a magical big-ass cobra bit you. Four hours ago you beat up Wonder Falcon. An hour ago we crashed your plane. Did you think you were Superman?"

He did. She knew it. She'd be surprised if he didn't own Superman sheets. In some ways he was such a guy. In others . . . well, this wasn't the time to contemplate his past or his ability to turn into a panther, or she'd leave him out in the snow.

"At least the cold has reduced the swelling on your face." She squinted into his eyes. "I think your vision will be okay." She patted him on the shoulder. "Good work."

She picked a flat spot nestled into some boulders where the towering incense cedars would protect them from the snow. She looked up at the sky and saw only billions of snowflakes rushing toward the ground.

She didn't want to be buried alive.

She searched his backpack. She found dried rations, rope, snap links, a folding shovel, two semiautomatic pistols, ammunition . . . Jackson Sonnet would approve. The guy was prepared.

She dug a shallow trench, took the parachute from Warlord's stiff hands, and layered it over the snow. She pulled the two-man tent out of his backpack. Thanks to Jackson Sonnet, she'd learned to set up a tent in the dark in subzero temperatures, with the wind blowing. Good thing, for she erected this one in a haze of pain and desperation. She didn't have a lot of time. The numbness was spreading inexorably up her arms and legs.

She laid out the sleeping bags — good to forty below, she noted approvingly — in the cramped space inside the tent. She zipped them together to make one big bag, and stacked their backpacks in the corner. With a shiver she went back out into the snowstorm, dragged Warlord's prone body to the entrance, and rolled him inside, knocking the snow off him. She fastened the tent flap closed. She stripped him down to his underwear, shook him awake enough to drink water from the canteen. She took a drink herself, and zipped him into the bag.

Then she sat, panting, stared at his black,

tousled hair, and tried to remember why she'd worked so hard at saving his life. He was Warlord, the mercenary who'd kept her as a slave and forced her to acknowledge helplessness in the face of her own sexuality. This was Rick Wilder, the jerk who pretended to be an innocuous businessman to get in her pants again. And when she had saved his life, he would still insist that he should be part of her life. If she left him out in the snow to die . . . She shuddered.

Okay, she couldn't do that, because . . . She opened her bag and dug through until she'd found the icon. She stared at the rendering of the Virgin Mary, broken by her son's sacrifice. The Madonna looked right at Karen, silently reminding her of the precariousness of life, and her painted-on tears glistened anew. Karen couldn't sacrifice Warlord, no matter what he'd done or what he would do.

She knew a lot about Warlord's defeat. She'd seen it herself, and in a corner of her brain, she played and replayed that scene she had witnessed in her mind: the battle, the fight with the Varinski, Warlord's loss.

Where had he been the last two years? In a hospital? In a prison? In a coffin? It was possible, she supposed. When that Varinski had hit him, he'd been flung through the air onto jagged rocks. Most men would have died. Yet Warlord was here and, until tonight, he had appeared to be hale and hearty. How was that possible?

How was any of this possible?

His rough voice grated across her nerves. "Karen. Come to bed. We need each other's warmth."

Karen woke with a start.

Warlord was unconscious.

The icon was in her bag.

She was delirious. If she didn't get in the sleeping bag soon, she never would.

Outside, the storm's fury made the trees creak and groan.

In here, in the dim light, she could see her breath.

She fought her way out of her outerwear, sweating from exertion and fever. When she was down to a T-shirt and underwear, she gave a sigh and slid in next to Warlord. She ought to take off her gold bracelets, but right now, for no reason she could understand or admit to, they gave her comfort. They connected the past and the present, and she needed a bridge back to the time when Warlord was healthy . . . for now he burned beneath her touch.

Placing one hand on his chest, another on his brow, she whispered, "Please, God. We have to live through this."

As if she'd prayed the perfect prayer, she sank into Warlord's mind and his heart.

Warlord woke in a panic. He tried to stand. His legs were broken. His ribs were broken. He was blind. He could barely breathe, and his thoughts stuttered in his head. Panic beat at him, and he shouted, "Hey!"

"Shut him up. Shut him up!" The flashlight shone directly into his face, and he flinched away.

"Ye leave him alone. He's hurt."

Warlord recognized the voice. "Magnus?"

"Hush." Magnus sounded funny. Hoarse and anguished. "We've got to be quiet."

"You shut him up," the flashlight said, "or I'll finish him."

Not likely. You're not a Varinski. But Warlord obeyed Magnus. His second in command sounded so frantic, and Warlord didn't understand where he was, why he hurt, what had happened to them.

The flashlight went away, once more leaving them in absolute pitch dark.

"Where are we?" Warlord whispered.

"In Siberia, in the deepest gold mine in the world." Magnus groped up Warlord's arm and held his shoulder. "I can't believe ye're alive. How did ye survive that fall? When that

318

monster hit ye, it was like ye'd been blown from a cannon."

A face popped into Warlord's mind, blazing like a demented Halloween mask, a face composed of a Neanderthal brow and jaw. Involuntarily, Warlord shrank in his skin. "Who was he?"

"Name of Innokenti Varinski. He's the new enforcer for the armies on the border where we used to reign." Magnus moved, and groaned. "Did ye know ye had a cousin like him?"

"No." In all Warlord's years as a mercenary, he'd never met a Varinski.

Now he never wanted to meet another one. "Who did they capture? Who did they kill? Who's hurt?"

"There's a lot of injuries — Bobbie Berkley's in here with us; he's not going to live — but we lost only eight men." Bitterly, Magnus said, "They have a use for us."

Warlord didn't guess; he knew. "We're the new slave labor."

"Gold miners, that's us."

All of his men, but especially Magnus, hated to be confined. These were men who walked their own paths, and now they would dig . . . until they died. Warlord felt sick with guilt. "How far down are we?"

"Only eight hundred feet. They're pampering

us until we're healthy —"

"Healthy? What's wrong with you?"

"I lost an eye, and I can't stand up straight enough to run a drill."

This was his fault. "What happens when we're healthy?"

"They'll send us below."

"Below?" Warlord moved painfully, slowly. "We're at eight hundred feet. Just how deep is this sucker?" He healed quickly, more quickly than normal men. His bones were mending, but there had been a lot of damage. He had to get on his feet. How much longer until he could stand?

"Sixteen hundred feet straight down. They say they won't let helicopters fly in the area because the downdrafts suck them in. The deeper you go, the closer to hell you are, the hotter it gets. They say the air down there is full of poison and men die where they drop, and not even the worms are there to eat them."

This was his fault. His fault. His fault. He'd neglected duty to touch Karen, to hold Karen, to hear Karen's voice and make love to Karen. His men trusted him, they followed him, and he'd led them right into slavery. He'd failed them.

He knew what damage his uncontrolled lust had caused, yet he had to ask, "Did Karen

320

escape?"

"Yer woman?" There wasn't an ounce of reproach in Magnus's voice. "I never heard that they caught her, and no reason why she shouldn't have. The damned Varinskis were too occupied with crushing our bones to bother with a woman."

Warlord closed his eyes in relief.

Karen was safe.

Then, lifting his head, he said, "Listen to me, Magnus. I'll get better fast. And you know what I am. I'll get you and the other men out of here; I swear I will. . . ."

Karen struggled, trying to get away from the horror of this vision, but it gripped her and wouldn't let her go.

Four days Warlord had been down here. He knew that because once a day someone shoved food and water into their cell. Bobbie Berkley had died on the floor beside them; the guards had left him for twenty-four hours before they dragged his body away. The heat, the dark, the sense of being trapped in the womb of the earth with billions of tons of rock pressing all around like a grave . . . it never changed. Nothing changed down here.

Magnus twitched and groaned in his sleep, and once when the guards shone a light in the cell, Warlord saw his injuries.

He hadn't just lost an eye. He'd lost half his face.

His fault. It was all his fault.

Now Warlord heard the guards at the door, and jerked away at the light.

"He's fine. Get him up and send him down." Warlord recognized that voice. Innokenti Varinski.

He broke into a cold sweat.

As if he were a puppy, the Neanderthal picked him up by the collar. "I see you remember me."

"I remember you."

"I am Innokenti Varinski. I am your conqueror." When Warlord said nothing, Innokenti shook him. "Say it."

"You are Innokenti Varinski. You are my conqueror." Warlord told himself he obeyed because it was the smart thing to do. But more than that, he obeyed because he was afraid. Afraid of this beast who had defeated him in battle, hurt him as he had never been hurt before, and who would delight in the chance to do it again. And again.

Innokenti sniffed him as he would a moldy piece of bread. "You smell funny . . . for a human."

"I need to wash." Warlord did not need this massive Sauron imitator to figure out they were related by blood. As long as Warlord's abilities were secret, his men had a chance.

"Would you like us to draw you a bath? And put rose petals in the water?" Innokenti grinned and showed a mouthful of black and missing teeth.

"When did the Varinskis start rotting like normal men?" It was a fair query, maybe a little rude, but still a fair query, for the deal with the devil had guaranteed them long lives without the problems that plagued mere mortals.

But evidently Warlord had hit a sore spot.

The Varinski's smile disappeared. He smashed his forehead against Warlord's face until blood spurted from Warlord's nose and mouth. "You insolent little prick. I'll show you rot." He flung him against the wall, picked up the guard's steel prod, and slashed Warlord across the back.

Warlord screamed. Five times the rod fell. Then Innokenti threw it across the room. He hit a guard, who shrieked and fell to the ground. "Chain his hands and feet and put him to work." Picking Warlord up off the floor, the Varinski said, "I'm Innokenti Varinski. When you die, remember me and curse my name."

"Innokenti," Karen muttered. "Innokenti." The scene shifted and . . .

Days and months without end, without light,

without enough food or water.

Warlord didn't have the breath to curse In-nokenti Varinski. He didn't have the strength or the will. The depths of the mine sapped his energy. The work shattered his body. The constant loss of his men, one after another, broke his will.

This was his fault. His fault. His fault.

Once a month Innokenti arrived with his steel rod and beat Warlord. At first Warlord didn't know why he'd been singled out. Had Innokenti realized that Warlord was related to the hated rogue branch of the Varinskis, the Wilder family?

Then Warlord recognized the source of In-nokenti's frustration. No other man could have lived through a single one of those beatings, yet every month when Innokenti returned, Warlord was working again.

Innokenti would take his rod and beat Warlord, and one day would succeed in killing him, for only another demon could kill a man bound by the pact with the devil.

But not yet. Not yet.

If Warlord hadn't neglected his duty to his men and spent all his time with Karen, he and his men would still be free. Yet the memory of Karen was the only thing that kept him alive. When the guards had beaten him with the steel rod, and he could no longer imagine what sunshine and fresh air felt like on his skin, he would bring Karen to his mind.

Karen, glimpsed on the train from Kathmandu.

Karen, in her tent in the depths of night.

Karen, clutching him on the motorcycle as they raced the rockfall.

Karen, dancing in the meadow, kissing the ground, naked under the waterfall.

Karen, tied to the brass bed and writhing with pleasure . . .

Sometimes, she was so close he could smell her scent, touch her skin, hear her voice crooning to him.

That was when he knew he was hallucinating. Karen would never croon to him . . .

In a year's time half his men were left. They died while blasting the rock. They died in cave-ins. And worse, one by one, they lay down and died of starvation, from the beatings . . . and because all hope was gone. Nothing he said made a difference. They didn't trust him anymore.

Even Magnus had given up.

He had to lead them out. They couldn't wait any longer. He couldn't wait any longer.

Because he had given up, too. He didn't realize how low he had sunk until one of the guards poked him with a steel rod and said, "Hey, titty-baby. Guess who's coming tomorrow? Your best friend, Innokenti Varinski. And you know what he's going to do? He's going to beat you half to death. Better get ready to scream, titty-baby."

Warlord sank to his knees and cried. Cried with fright, cried for the release of death, cried and begged the guard to kill him, when he knew it was impossible.

The guard laughed and poked him again. "Do I look insane? If I killed you, he'd kill me. No, titty-baby, I'll just wait to hear you sing soprano tomorrow."

The tears leaked down Warlord's cheeks all the way through that guard's shift and into the next. None of his men would look at him. Magnus wouldn't talk to him. He had let them all down . . . and still he cried.

Then, with the change of the guard, opportunity presented itself. He didn't recognize it — until Karen's voice snapped in his mind, *Pay attention!*

Two guards instead of the usual four. Both were drunk — somewhere up above the mining company had thrown a party. One guard passed out and never heard the roar of the drill before it pierced his chest. The other fell from Warlord's swift and slashing chain.

"See, boys?" Magnus said. "He did it." But his voice was weak, and he collapsed when he tried to collect the weapons.

Warlord picked up his friend and placed him in the elevator.

Magnus had shrunk down there. His bones almost pierced his skin, and in the harsh light his lips looked blue.

Thirty-eight men crowded into the elevator.

"I'm going up the stairs to the next level. Give me a couple minutes, then follow. While I finish the guards, you collect their weapons." Warlord leaned in to push the button. "We need the weapons to break out of here."

"Who the hell are you to tell us what to do?" Logan Rogers demanded.

"He's the guy who got us out of there," Magnus said.

"He's the guy who got us in there, too," Logan retorted.

"Do you have a better plan?" Warlord asked.

Logan subsided.

"Then shut up." Warlord looked around at the remains of his band of mercenaries. "Free the other prisoners, but don't let them on the elevator. It won't take the weight. When we're done with the management, those miners will have their chance."

His men nodded solemnly.

"Horst, before those assholes up above realize what's going on down here, you might want to figure out how to override the controls."

"How are you going to take out the guards by yourself?" Horst asked in his ponderous Swedish accent.

Warlord looked at the chains on his wrists. He was emaciated, so thin he looked like a starvation victim. Would the panther be able to slip out of the cuffs? If not . . . well, in this dark they would never see a panther, even a chained panther.

He smiled his first smile in a year. "They haven't got a chance."

They didn't. He moved from level to level, silent, invisible, striking without warning. His men arrived behind him and gathered the weapons until every one of them held rods and whips and guns.

At five hundred feet, when someone on the surface got wise and tried to cut the power, the elevator continued to rise. Horst had done his job.

But Warlord was falling behind. He was weak, too weak to run so many stairs. He couldn't make it.

When his men reached the top, they couldn't just go running out of the elevator. A single machine gun would mow them down.

He had to stop them before they reached the top.

Then he heard it. Gunfire from above.

CHAPTER
TWENTY-NINE

Karen caught her breath. She came up with a gasp. She found herself struggling, trying to sit up in the sleeping bag.

Warlord held her in his arms, saying over and over, "It's all right. It's all right."

"It's not all right. I can't breathe. I can't . . . it was dark. There was no air. It was hot. They beat me." Tears leaked from the corners of her eyes.

"The venom has made you ill." He trickled water into her mouth and onto her forehead. "But you're better now. You can breathe. Take a breath now."

She looked wildly around the barely lit tent. The weight of the snow made the nylon sag around them and hid the sunlight.

"See? We're in the mountains. Together. This is now. That time and place is past."

"But I saw it." And yet . . . she was here. He was here.

He wrapped her close. "You were there. I

saw you . . . but I figured I'd gone crazy."

"I'd wake up at night and it was so dark, and I'd know you were alive somewhere. . . ." She was sore in her bones and muscles, as if she had been beaten. "Oh, God, how did you stand it? All that time with no hope . . ."

"When you walk through hell, keep walking," he said wryly. "A year in the dark in the heat gives a man a long time to think, and I did. I reviewed my life a thousand times."

"I know." She had been in his mind every minute.

He gave her the canteen.

She drank.

"At first, when I remembered, I was defiant. I was proud of what I'd done, walking my own path, ignoring my father's admonitions, being free." He fed her pieces of an oatmeal-raisin Baker's Breakfast Cookie.

She ate slowly, filling the empty places.

"But at about review three hundred, I started remembering my brothers and my sister, thinking about what it would have been like to know what they were doing, who they loved. I remembered my mother, the kiss she gave me the last time she saw me. I even remembered my dad and every word he said to me, over and over, all the time I was growing up." He mimicked a deep voice with a pronounced Russian accent. " 'Don't change, Adrik. Keep your heart pure, Adrik. Every time you give in to the panther, you put yourself into the devil's hands, Adrik.' I remembered how much I hated all that good advice, and how dumb I thought he was, and the way I swore that when I was an adult I'd do whatever I wanted."

"And you did."

"And I did. Eventually in the dark I faced the fact that my dad was right." Warlord's eyes narrowed. "Man, I hated that. But I also figured it didn't matter. I had to get my men out any way I could, and if that meant sitting on the devil's right hand, I would. When the chance finally came, I became a black panther, silent as a shadow, and every time I killed a guard I knew I'd saved a hundred prisoners. And every time I killed a guard, I had the blood of another man on my hands."

She knew where she was. She could breathe without obstruction. Yet she still ached . . . for Warlord.

"The closer my men got to the top, the more excited they were. I knew why. I could almost smell the fresh air, and I wanted to feel the sun on my face." His green eyes glowed as he relived his anticipation. "I couldn't control them. They got ahead of me. When I heard the shots I wanted to shriek at them for being such fools."

She hung on his every word. "What was it?"

"Five floors from the top they ran into an ambush."

"Which wouldn't have happened if they let you go first."

"I pointed that out later, I can tell you. By the time I got up there they had the guards down, but four of my guys were shot, and it was a hell of a mess. I figured the main attack above would be ready to launch, but I also knew the way the guards drank. Their reflexes had to be off. They had to be in disarray. Most important, they were used to dealing with men too starved and dispirited to rebel. So — it was a mine; we used dynamite every day — we rigged an explosive in the elevator. My men sent it up while I took the stairs and cleared the way. They followed, and everyone was on the surface in time to see the explosion." Proudly, Warlord said, "I took control of the mine with thirty-eight very pissed-off mercenaries, and we didn't stop until we'd hijacked a plane bound for Afghanistan."

"Innokenti?" She shivered.

"I assume he arrived soon after." He laid her flat and tucked the sleeping bag close around her neck. "I would have hated to be one of the surviving guards."

"Magnus. Is Magnus alive?"

"He is, and living very well for a one-eyed former mercenary with eight fingers and twenty-nine teeth. He's the consultant for the *Warlord* game."

"He likes video games?"

"He hates them. He always thought it was stupid that players sat and stared at a little screen and exercised their thumbs, so when I was talking about turning the whole experience into a game, he said build it so the action happened in a room all around the player. In *Warlord,* the player has weapons strapped to his body and sensors hooked to his hands, feet, and head, and he has to defend himself against the oncoming threats." His enthusiasm grew as he spoke. "The higher the level, the more difficult the battles, the more attackers involved. It's actually a training setup for mercenaries."

"A video game in a room?" She watched him with an indulgent smile. "Where will it be played?"

"Pizza places. Paintball galleries. Burstrom has his finger in a lot of pies, and he's buying up property to build actual game houses.

But in addition, Burstrom and I see potential for training in any kind of fighting and self-defense. Karate schools will build them in. We've already started work to modify the idea for training boxers. The preliminary sales have brought in over seventy million dollars."

"Seventy million dollars." Her indulgent smile evaporated. "You've got to be kidding!"

"My cut is only ten percent."

"Only? That's seven million."

"That's just the beginning. Projections for next year are for five times that."

"Wow." She had never figured him for a financial wizard.

"As with every venture, there is always a chance projections will fall short," he warned her.

She didn't see that happening. Not to this smooth-talking entrepreneur.

He continued, "In addition, I put the money I made as a mercenary in a bank in Switzerland, and with the help of my financial adviser —"

"You had a financial adviser?"

"I would have been a fool not to." He let her absorb that. "So with the help of my financial adviser, my personal worth tops thirty million. That amount is completely separate from the money involved in the development of the *Warlord* game."

She was in shock. She remembered how he lived, in a tent with the spoils of a hundred raids . . . and he was worth thirty million? And counting? "Why are you telling me all this?"

"I want you to know that if you will do me the honor of marrying me, I will always take care of you."

It was a good thing she was prone. Otherwise she would have collapsed on the spot.

"My sins are beyond count. The memory of you was the only thing that kept me alive for the whole wretched year of my captivity." He leaned over her and smoothed her hair away from her face. He stroked her cheek with the back of his fingers and smiled into her stunned eyes. "We have a connection. More than one." He grasped her wrists, brought them out from beneath the covers, and held the gold bracelets between them. "Look. You wear my badge of ownership."

"I wear them to show I escaped you!"

"You wear them like a wedding ring."

That struck home, and she winced.

"You can visit my mind," he said persuasively. "Marry me."

She remained absolutely still, absorbing

his words, knowing the truth, but too afraid to acknowledge it.

"Search your brain," Warlord said. "What do you see?"

Immediately she knew the answer. But in knee-jerk defiance she said, "Nothing."

But he wouldn't let her get away with lying to him.

Leaning toward her, he put his forehead against hers. He looked into her eyes. And he placed his hand against her heart.

It was dark. It was cold. And she wanted her mommy.

But her mommy didn't come.

The servants whispered and looked at her. Her grandpa came in and stared at her, then scowled and shook his head. But mostly she was alone in the dark, cold house, scared and hearing whispers, wisps of words. . . .

Poor child. No mother at all. Lover dead. Jumped off a cliff after him.

Tears leaked out of Karen's eyes.

Mommy. Mommy.

Poor child. Dan Nighthorse dead. Mother fell off the cliff, landed on the rocks, and can you imagine? She bled there for a day, her internal organs destroyed, and when they rescued her she screamed.

Karen heard her father come home. She came out of her room and ran to the balcony, waiting for her daddy to visit her. And she saw her grandfather grab her daddy by the scruff of the neck and carry him into the office. She was with that Indian guide. She's been with him for years. Do you know what this means . . . ? *The door slammed behind them.*

What does it mean? Daddy. Daddy.

Poor child. Five years old. Dan Nighthorse dead. Mother fell off the cliff, landed on the rocks, and can you imagine? She bled there for a day, freezing in the cold, her internal organs destroyed, and when they rescued her, she screamed in agony. Poor child. Her mother died. Poor child. She's alone.

Forever alone . . .

Karen woke up crying.

Warlord had tears in his eyes, too. "My poor little girl. My poor little girl. I can't stand it. You're not alone. Not anymore."

She tried to push him away. "Stop it. I don't want this. Stop it."

"It's too late to stop it. You swallowed my blood, and it gave you the strength to fight off the effects of the venom. It gave you a window into my mind. And what else, Karen?"

"Nothing," she insisted.

Gathering her into his arms, he pressed her ear to his chest, and as she listened to the thump of his heart she fell into another memory.

The sun burned down on her. The horizon stretched forever. And she had one chance. One chance to make good, to make her father see her, really look at her, finally notice how hard she worked, how smart she was . . . one chance, and this was it.

Karen approached the sullen framing crew, two dozen men lounging against a pile of lumber.

They were mad, every one of them. They'd been working Jackson Sonnet's Australian adventure hotel, they were less than halfway through construction, and their project manager had had a heart attack. They were getting the boss's twenty-three-year-old daughter as a replacement, and without saying a word they managed to let Karen know what they thought.

One chance, and they wanted to take it away from her.

She smiled, because smiling always disarmed the guys, stuck her shaking hands into jeans pockets, and asked, "Who's the crew boss?"

One man, tall, thin, brown faced, raised his hand. He didn't stand.

Okay. One chance, and if she handled this guy right, if she could get him to work for her . . . One chance. "Alden Taylor. Experienced in framing, plumbing, electrical, Sheetrock, finish carpentry. You've been with my father for how long?"

"Twenty-five years with the mean old son of a bitch." Alden had a pronounced Australian accent, and he was trying to shock her by abusing her father to her face.

Instead he'd played right into her hands. "Would you say the mean old son of a bitch is given to acts of kindness?"

Alden snorted.

The other guys grinned and stirred.

"Charity? Generosity? No?" Karen didn't bother to wait for a reply. "There's one thing and one thing only my father cares about — getting his hotels built and operational so he can make a profit. Right?"

This time Alden tried to answer.

She brushed him aside. "That mean old son of a bitch has had me working on hotels every summer since I was fourteen. I can do everything you can do, plus finish concrete, plus design plans, plus I can talk to the hotshot investors and impress them with my construction management degree. I'm here as project manager because I'm the best Jackson Sonnet has got. He doesn't care that I'm his daughter; he offered me the same deal he offers everyone else. If I get the hotel in on time and under budget, he'll pay me well. If I screw up, I'm out of here."

Alden's lips twitched as if he wanted to grin. "He never changes."

"I beg to differ. He does change. He gets meaner every year." She was nervous, talking too fast, but she had everybody's attention. "I'm shaky when it comes to electrical, and my finish carpentry stinks. That's why I asked that you be my assistant project manager." She walked over and offered Alden her hand.

He looked at it, took it, and let her tug him to his feet. "You promoted me?"

"Yeah. Congratulations, and welcome to twenty-hour days." She looked up at him. "This morning, before I even stepped onto the job, Dad called to let me know we're behind schedule, and he chewed my ass for it. So while I walk the project, you get these guys to work. Then come find me; we'll talk about your pay raise and go over the plans to figure out where we can make up some time." She started to walk into the half-framed hotel, then looked back at the stunned Alden. "I mean . . . if you want the job."

Warlord's voice startled her out of her trance. "Did he take it?"

"Yes." Then she realized what she'd admitted. "Don't."

"So you got your one chance to make

good. Did your father ever notice?"

"Please. Don't." She couldn't have him know all her secrets.

He tilted her head up and brushed his lips across hers, over and over, until her eyes closed. "My blood in you gave me a window into your mind."

"No." His touch, his kiss dulled the sharp edge of reality, but she knew the truth.

Over the last few days she had seen his weaknesses. She had witnessed his pain.

She had lived in his skin. She had sinned his sins. She had killed men. She had exulted in battle. She reveled in sex with a thousand women. . . .

With his eyes she had seen her own face for the first time.

She had gloried in her capture, in the hours and days and weeks of unrelenting pleasure. She had been determined to win the sensual battle between them.

She'd survived, barely, the battle that put him in the mines. There she had dwelled in hell with him, known his remorse as he watched his men die, felt the pain of his beatings, and suffered the slow dwindling of his spirit. And she had seen that no matter how oppressive the darkness and the heat and smells, no matter how deadly the work, Warlord had never given up. Not for his sake, but for his men's, he had been determined to gain their freedom.

Warlord had redeemed himself. Warlord had proved he had strength and a soul of honor.

Karen had no such strength, no such honor. Her life was small, her fears exaggerated. She had never wanted him to witness her anguish at her mother's death, the lonely days of her childhood, the futile attempts to please her father, the difficulty of her construction work . . . the anguish and joy of living as Warlord's slave.

Yet he had. At some point in the last few days he had been in her mind and witnessed it all.

"Marry me," he said.

She turned her head away. "Why would you want to marry me?"

"The sight of you, the scent of you, the heat of you go right through to my bones. You warm me, the hard, cold core of me, and when I saw you across the foyer at the spa, for the first time in two years I was alive and healed." Swiftly he added, "I will never hold you against your will."

She glanced at him from the corners of her eyes.

"I didn't say I wouldn't try to convince you. I didn't say I would ever give up. But I will not ever again hold you against your will. I have been held against my will. It was a hard lesson, but I learned it." He bowed his head to her. "Please forgive me."

They were trapped in a small tent, in a sleeping bag, in clothes they'd worn for five days. Yet he begged her like a courtier before Queen Elizabeth.

She didn't want to marry him. But she enjoyed the begging. She enjoyed it even more because she knew — she *knew* — that although he meant what he said, he'd had to fight his own possessive nature to make that promise.

"Please?" he said again.

She put her hand on his head, mostly because the pure black silk of his hair enticed her. "I forgive you."

"Will you marry me?"

That was Warlord. Always swift to follow up an advantage. "No."

"I would be a good husband to you. Karen, I love you."

"But I don't know if I . . ."

"Love me?"

"I don't know if I love you." Her father had taught her she couldn't depend on any man for the truth, and Warlord had confirmed that lesson. "I do know I don't trust you."

Yet she watched him with troubled eyes. Was she unfairly burdening him with the wrong baggage?

"Shh." He lifted her, stripped her T-shirt off. "You worry too much."

She ought to stop him. Tell him that she could never forgive him for the time she spent as his captive. Tell him that she knew even the long year he'd passed in hell hadn't vanquished the devil in him. She'd seen it at work in the last week, when he had hunted her down, lied to her about his identity, tried to seduce her.

Warlord removed his clothes, then held her with a hand on either hip, pressed himself against her, and closed his eyes, as if the mere touch of her body on his skin moved him to ecstasy. His erection strained against her belly. His chest, beautifully decorated with the blazing thunderbolt, rose and fell with his breaths. She held his arms in her hands and coiled her legs around his . . . because the ecstasy enveloped her, too.

He lifted himself. He wrapped his thumbs under the elastic of her panties and slid them down her legs. "Kick them off," he whispered. "Please get rid of them."

Like a fool, she responded to his pleading.

In reward he slid deep into the bag to kiss

her shoulders, the tender inside of her elbow, her palm, her fingertips.

How she had missed the way he worshiped her body, every limb, every inch of skin, with his touch and his mouth!

No matter what, she was now bound to Warlord, for while she was in his mind she had learned that he loved her. Loved her with all the passion of a man who had lived in hell and now saw a chance for heaven.

That was why she allowed him to caress her belly and between her legs.

That was why she stroked the deep scars across his shoulders.

That was why she would let him make love to her, and would make love to him in return.

He ran his palms down the sides of her body, learning her curves once more.

Outside, the wind peeled the dry snow off the tent layer by layer, letting the daylight seep through the nylon structure. The tree boughs sang as they swayed, and the rich odor of pine mixed with the scents of their bodies.

They had almost died of the venom. They had been through hell together.

His warm, soft lips kissed her nipples, tasted them, made her realize how sweet this affirmation of life could be.

Wrapping her fingers around his head, she held him, reveling in his breath on her skin, then pulled him up onto her. "Please," she whispered. "I want."

"What do you want?" He smiled and kissed her lightly, over and over. "Tell me."

She showed him. She dragged her hands down his chest, down his belly, and enfolded his penis in her fingers.

His breath hissed between his teeth. He arched his back. His eyes closed in agonized gratification.

In mockery and delight, she said, "Before I am done with you, every time you think of pleasure, you'll think of me."

He opened his eyes, looked down at her, and said, "I do. My darling, I do."

Then they moved together until the snow blew off the tent, and the bright sunshine leaked through the thin nylon, and the light illuminated his gorgeously sculpted and dearly beloved face.

After three days of unending snow and wind and blizzard conditions, the weather cleared, and the Civil Air Patrol and the mountain rescue team went out to find the Cessna Citation X. It took them two days of hard searching to locate the wreckage, but when they did, Innokenti and a dozen of his handpicked men were with them as civilian rescue experts.

Innokenti stood watching as the rescuers combed the wreckage for any sign of survivors, and shook their heads pityingly. They thought every person aboard had been killed.

Innokenti withheld judgment. He was waiting for a report from his best spotter. When Pyotr was on the wing, nothing got past his sharp eyes.

Some of the Americans murmured in amazement when a brown hawk circled Innokenti's head, then flew into the trees. Innokenti followed.

There was Pyotr, jumping up and down with excitement. "They're here," he said. "I saw the proof. A new broken branch on a cedar."

"Maybe it was wind damage."

"Something hooked on it. The bark is broken in the middle, and the needles are stripped off the end."

"Good work."

Innokenti's other men gathered around.

"We're going after them." He sternly viewed their anticipatory faces. "You can have the girl, but leave Wilder for me."

"What about the Americans?" Lev jerked

his head toward the rescuers.

Innokenti started down the hill, changing as he went. "Kill them all."

CHAPTER
THIRTY

Warlord ducked out of the tent, dressed in layers and layers of dry clothes, and walked out into the snow.

The day was perfect, high, wispy clouds against a bright blue sky, a brisk wind, and a temperature that hovered around ten degrees. Or perhaps the day wasn't so much perfect as he felt perfect. Wonderful. Better than he had in two years. No — better than he had in his whole life. Karen wasn't his yet, but he had gained ground.

Of course, she'd had to view his complete castration first — and that didn't make any sense at all. When he had realized she was in his brain, living with him the dark days of his imprisonment, he had wanted to shout out his refusal.

He had died every day in the mines, and every time Innokenti Varinski beat him he'd screamed in agony. Worse, the last time, when he heard Innokenti was coming, he had cried. Cried like the titty-baby the guard had called him.

But Karen didn't seem to care that he'd broken down, that he'd whined and whimpered. She almost liked him better for acting like a girl.

He didn't understand women. He never would. But he thanked God for putting them — especially Karen — on this earth.

Karen stepped out of the tent and stretched, and didn't look at him. Because she was shy about the passion she'd been unable to hide, or embarrassed that he'd been in her mind, or pissed that she'd surrendered.

Not that she'd completely surrendered, but she would. She would. She couldn't fight him *and* her own desires, and when she realized that, he would get his ring on her finger as swiftly as possible. Then he'd spend the next hundred years teaching her to love him, and showing her she could trust him.

"You look beautiful." He took her in his arms.

"No, I don't." She managed to make him sound as if he were an idiot. "I haven't had a bath in five days."

"Absolutely beautiful," he repeated, and kissed her, and kissed her again.

She kissed him back, then pushed away as if she'd betrayed too much.

He pretended not to notice. "I wish I had a cell phone so I could call Jasha and see if he's at the rendezvous."

"He didn't sound too enthused," she warned.

"Jasha is the oldest. He may not be enthused, but he's the most responsible human being you'll ever —"

A thin, sharp sound sliced through the air.

He shoved her back against a tree and, holding her there, scanned the sky.

"What was that?" she asked.

"We're going now." He reached in the tent and brought out his backpack and her bag. "I should never have let us linger here."

"That was a gunshot."

"Right." He'd packed two Glocks and a hundred rounds of ammunition. When he'd loaded the bag, he'd thought that if he didn't kill the Varinskis with a hundred rounds, he never would. But with Karen with him, one hundred rounds seemed pitifully few. With Karen here he wished he had an M16 machine gun. Or a tank. Anything to keep her safe.

"You think it was the Varinskis." She helped him load the weapons. "But couldn't it be a hunter?"

He strapped one pistol around his chest under his coat, and all the while he worked the possible scenarios for attack and defense. "Anything's possible."

"You're right." She acknowledged the words he hadn't spoken. "But not probable."

"You're a marksman, right?"

"My father made sure of that."

As Warlord strapped a pistol around her, under her coat, he smiled into her face. "Your father had his good points."

"He prepared me for survival, that's for sure. The old son of a bitch." She sounded wistful.

He understood why. He'd seen the conflicting emotions that roiled in her. She hated Jackson Sonnet for raising her without sentiment or softness. Yet at the same time he'd been her only parent, the constant in her life, and although she didn't want to admit it, she understood what a blow to his pride her mother's infidelity had been . . . and his best friend's betrayal. "You miss him."

She nodded. "I guess I do."

"When this is over we'll go see him." He put his knife up his sleeve. He hung the ropes on his belt by the snap links. Opening her bag, he said, "Get the icon." He wouldn't touch it. He still had the burns from the first time.

"We're not taking the rest of our stuff?" She sorted through her clothes.

"We've got to move fast." He laid out their snowshoes.

She didn't argue. She didn't complain. She didn't lecture him on the environmental impact of leaving their equipment. She brought out the icon, then the picture frame. With swift motions she stripped out her mother's picture. She tucked them both in an inner pocket with a Velcro catch. Her skinning knife went in a pocket; her camping ax hung on her belt.

He strapped on his snowshoes.

She followed suit. "I'm ready."

"You're a woman in a million." He glanced at his portable GPS, and they moved out.

The going was downhill, but rugged. He kept them under cover where he could, avoiding deep snowbanks, watching the skies, and listening for pursuit.

"Where are we headed?" she asked.

"The rendezvous with Jasha."

"If he's not there?"

"That spot is the best defensive high ground I could find. That's why I chose it."

"How did you foresee all this?"

"I prepared for every scenario." He

glanced back at her. "When you meet my father, you'll understand."

"Am I meeting your father?"

"He'll want to meet my bride."

"I haven't said yes."

"I'm hopeful." He grinned at her mulish expression, and faced front.

"How far do we have to go?"

"Are you tired?" The exercise was burning off the last effects of the venom. He felt good, yet the high altitude made his lungs fight for enough air. For all Karen's stoicism, she was completely human, and a girl.

"I'm fine."

"I can carry you."

She caught up with him. "Look. I grew up hiking around the Rockies, and they make the Sierra Nevadas look like an overpass." She fell back. "So don't patronize me, mister."

"Touchy." He grinned as he felt the blast of her fury warm his back. "We're probably twenty miles from the wreckage. The bird hasn't found us yet."

"The bird? You mean the falcon? I thought you killed it?"

"There are more. When they're tracking they'll always bring at least one bird. Once it locates us we're prey, and it's just a matter of time before the pack arrives to finish the job. If we can get to the rendezvous first, and Jasha is there, we'll have a chance. If he's brought reinforcements, that would be better."

"How many reinforcements?" She began to sound hopeful.

"My brother Rurik."

"Oh." She was deflated.

"Don't discount my brothers. My father coached them. Coached us all. They're smart and vicious fighters."

"So we've got a chance?"

"Sure. There's always a chance." Not much of one, but the prospect of the fight cheered Warlord. He wanted that icon safely with his family. He wanted Karen where he could protect her. Most of all, he wanted to finish Innokenti. It was time to free himself of the fear that haunted his every footstep. "Depends on how many men Innokenti brought. More than eight and we're in trouble."

"Great," she muttered.

"Remember — *you* can't kill a Varinski. They're part of the pact, essentially demons from hell."

"Then what am I doing with a gun?"

"You can hurt them. You can protect yourself." They were making good time, but the next stretch was an old rock slide, clear of cover, with barely a tree to protect them from watching eyes, and a great, sheer pack of snow.

Warlord stopped at the top. "No way around."

"But a great way to make speed." She pointed at a great old downed cedar. The bark was loose, and with a few swipes of her ax she held a piece as tall as she was and half as wide. She put it on the snow, pointing downhill, and took off her snowshoes.

"A sled." He couldn't believe his clever girl.

"Get on," she said.

He almost took the front, then realized it was her idea. He took the back. "How did you think to do this?" He tucked his snowshoes under his arm.

"You've never built one?"

"No. We always bought them at Wallyworld."

She got on the front. "My dad didn't see the sense in play, so my toys always had a practical purpose."

The old son of a bitch, indeed.

She continued, "That meant I had to get innovative. I got pretty good at picking out the appropriate tree and —"

They pushed off. The bark was rough on

the bottom, and at first it was slow, but as the snow packed on underneath they moved faster and faster. And, Warlord quickly realized, they couldn't steer. By the time they reached the bottom they were flying — flying toward the pile of boulders and downed trees left by a rockfall. He was horrified, terrified, wondering what maggot had suggested he do the gentlemanly thing and let Karen sit in front . . . when a splinter flew past his cheek. Another, and then half the sled. The whole thing disintegrated beneath them and they came to a skidding stop.

While he sat there in shock in the snow, Karen stood and dusted off her seat. "I was starting to wonder if that would break apart in time." She offered her hand. "We should get out of here."

He jerked his gaze toward the sky.

A single brown hawk circled high above them. Another joined him.

"They've nailed us. Let's go."

The next two miles were a hell of haste and worry. The wind blew in their faces, freezing their exposed skin and making the going hard. Their trip on the sled had cracked one of Karen's snowshoes. They abandoned them. Every fifteen minutes he made her drink water and eat a few bites, but they never slowed. Every moment he strained to hear the sound of paws racing across the snow. "We're getting close," he said.

Before she could answer, a wolf howled half a mile behind them.

The color drained from her face.

He pointed. "Run straight ahead."

She watched him shed his coat, his hat, every bulky bit of clothing, stripping down until he should be shivering. Yet he burned with the heat of battle. "What are you going to do?"

"Fight the back guard. When you get to the top of the cliff —"

"A cliff?" Her eyes accused him. "That's your defensible ground?"

He handed her her rappelling equipment. "There's a cave two-thirds of the way down. Get in it." Grabbing her, he kissed her with all the love and desperation in his heart. "Whatever you do, stay safe. I can't bear the thought of a world without you."

CHAPTER
THIRTY-ONE

Karen recognized a good-bye kiss when she received one.

Warlord pushed her away.

She grabbed him by the front of his thin T-shirt and pulled him back. She kissed him hard, branding him with her taste. "Be safe yourself. Fight well." Turning, she sprinted down the hill . . . leaving her love behind.

Hell of a time to decide that.

"A cliff," she muttered. "Good thinking, Warlord." Of course, from a purely strategic point of view, it *was* good thinking.

She could see the long stretch of ground ahead, dotted with giant incense cedars, then the break in the earth where the cliff fell away. If she and Warlord reached the bottom first, as Innokenti and his men came over the cliff they could pick them off. But Warlord wasn't with her, the bottom was a long way down, and how did he think she was going to rappel when the only time she'd ever rappelled was when her father had forced her into a harness and flung her bodily off a training wall. She walked faster, her gaze on the edge of that cliff. If she concentrated very hard on the memory of Jackson Sonnet yelling at her, "Get your ass over, Karen!" that might get her in position —

A man stepped out from behind a tree and in front of her.

A Varinski.

She recognized him by his height, his strength . . . the red glow deep in his eyes.

In one smooth motion she brought her pistol out of her holster.

He put his hands up. "I'm Rurik!"

She didn't lower the pistol.

"Rurik Wilder."

"You might be." Because he looked a little like Warlord, but with brown hair.

"Did he tell you about me?" The red glow faded a little, and the guy who called himself Rurik tried to look meek.

It didn't work.

"He told me about you." This guy was dressed for combat, too, in a minimum of clothing.

"Jasha's going to help Adrik."

Up the hill she heard a shot, then the shriek of a bird as it spiraled downward.

The supposed brother tensed, and the red glow intensified.

"Why aren't you helping Adrik?" she asked coldly.

"Because Jasha put me here to help you."

"You *are* Adrik's brother." She put her pistol away.

"Yeah." He frowned. "What convinced you?"

"You think I'm a girl, and you want to protect me. Instead, why don't you give me some credit? Go help your brothers."

"You sound like my wife," he said in shock.

"She must be a remarkable woman."

"That's one way to describe her," he mumbled.

She started downhill.

When she looked back he was gone.

She ran the last steps to the top of the cliff, ran so quickly she almost skidded off — which would have solved the problem of protecting her, for the cliff was seventy-five feet high, with great boulders at the base. Solved the problem, yes, but would have ruined her day.

Behind her, she heard another shot, a human scream, and the deep-throated howl of a wolf.

Stupid to know that battle was joined, that

361

her man and his brothers were fighting for their lives, and hers, and yet her mouth was dry and her hands shook as she hooked herself into the harness and fastened the rope to a tree.

Shouldn't the bright, new, shiny fears trump the old, silly, worthless fears?

In the logical part of her mind, she noted that the cliff was sheer granite, with almost no handholds and no way to save herself if she fell. Which was ridiculous, because she had tested the rope. She hoped she managed to keep her eyes open long enough to find the cave. As she inched her way over the edge of the cliff —

"Go! Go! Go!" She heard Warlord yelling, and looked up to see him racing toward her. "Jasha and Rurik are holding them, but Innokenti split the group. They've found a way down. We're surrounded!" He climbed into the harness and fastened his rope to a rock. "I'm your defense in the cave."

She found she was over the edge, in the L shape, her feet firmly planted on the cliff face. She launched herself with a jump, let the rope play out, launched herself again. Her heart thrummed frantically. Her hands sweated. But she could do this. She could definitely do this. "I'm fine," she yelled. "Hurry!"

Below them someone gave a deep, ululating war cry. The hair rose on the back of her head.

Her hand slipped. She froze. She looked down. Five Varinskis swarmed out of the woods.

One had a face like a Neanderthal, a body like a tank, and wore machine bolts for earrings. He looked up at her — and grinned.

Innokenti.

Midair, Warlord passed her, speeding down the rope face-first, shooting with cool marksmanship.

No way would she let him be braver than she was; perhaps Jackson Sonnet wasn't really her father, but he'd imbued her with his competitive spirit. She leaped as hard as she could.

At the top of the cliff she heard shots, dog-like growls, and the sounds of battle.

Below, Innokenti gestured to his men. They spread out.

One took wing as an eagle.

Innokenti staggered back as one of Warlord's bullets hit him in the chest, then straightened again.

Kevlar vest, she thought, and hoped it was true.

He took up a position, legs braced. He lifted his pistol, took aim, and shot.

Warlord collapsed. Began to fall. Brought himself up. Collapsed again. Blood covered his forearm, and he struggled to control his descent.

Infuriated, Karen screamed like a banshee. "Asshole. Innokenti, you asshole!"

Warlord struggled to stay in place.

She leaped toward him. Realized the futility. Vaulted toward the cave.

She was rappelling like a pro.

Below her Innokenti laughed, great, booming roars of amusement.

Hail struck her face. No, not hail — bullets riddled the cliff around her, and rock chips blasted her.

"Hang on," she screamed at Warlord.

She jumped hard enough to land in the cave. Stripped off her coat. Freed her pistol. Stepped out on the ledge.

Warlord struggled with the ropes. If he lost tension, he would fall right into Innokenti's arms.

Innokenti aimed at Warlord.

The eagle dive-bombed toward her, cruel eyes fixed, talons out.

She looked down the sights at Innokenti. Her finger tightened on the trigger.

And a blast blew the bird out of the air.

Feathers flew. The eagle screamed in pain and rage.

Jackson Sonnet stepped out of the forest below, a .30-06 rifle against his shoulder. "Take that!" he shouted. "No one's going to hurt my goddamn daughter."

CHAPTER
THIRTY-TWO

Karen shot as Innokenti turned to wave his men at Jackson. The bullet blasted a divot in the side of Varinski's neck.

Innokenti fell, blood pumping from the wound.

The wolf pack charged Jackson.

"Daddy!" Karen screamed.

Jackson shot one, smacked another in the head with the butt of his gun, and as he fell beneath the onslaught, she saw his hunting knife flash.

The animals squealed, not dead — impossible, for Jackson might be an old son of a bitch, but he wasn't a demon. But he'd hurt them.

She was so proud of him.

Flinging herself flat on the floor of the cave, she crawled to the edge and positioned herself for the best angle. She shot a cougar as it turned toward Jackson, then shot another that pranced beneath Warlord's ropes, shaking them like a boy shook an apple tree. She shot one bullet after another, and did as Warlord had instructed — she made each one count. She emptied the pistol, and as she thrust more bullets into the clip she looked for Warlord.

He hung there like a target.

Blood covered his arm. Using one hand he descended a few feet, shot at the beasts below, descended again.

She *had* to give him the time to get to the ground. She *had* to keep the Varinskis at bay. Nothing she had ever done in her life was as important as that.

Her fingers shook, and she counted each bullet as she pressed it in place. Five, six, seven . . . She heard a roar from below, and glanced up.

Innokenti was on his feet, weaving back and forth. He looked around his battlefield.

His victory was slipping from his grasp.

Angry color flooded his face. He fixed his gaze on Warlord, grinned evilly, and strode toward the cliff to wait.

Karen didn't have time to load her weapon.

She refused to watch helplessly.

Grabbing the dangling rope, she kicked off, and from a height of twenty-five feet — more than a two-story building — she flung herself at Innokenti.

Maybe the Varinski blood in her made her stronger than ever in her life.

Maybe she was secretly a ninja warrior.

Maybe it was the strength of her love for Warlord.

She didn't know. She knew only that when she slammed onto Innokenti's shoulders, every bone in her body crunched, but the impact knocked him flat on his face. And she was still alive and fighting.

As he lifted his head, she smashed her gold-clad wrists against his ears. The bracelets clanged against his bolt earrings.

His head dropped again. He shook it like a dog shaking off water.

With a haste born of desperation, she wrapped the length of the rope around his neck and twisted.

Warlord was going to make it. He would be okay now.

But she . . . she was in trouble.

Beneath her, Innokenti's massive body bucked like a maddened bull. He choked. He gagged. He gasped for air.

But his Varinski blood was pure.

Inexorably he rose. He reached over his head. As she rode his shoulders, he grabbed her thighs, lifted her high, and flung her as hard as he could.